Out There

Iris Eliot

About the Author

Born in Croatia where Iris Eliot grew up during the war with books as her best friends. Very early on, Iris decided she'd become a writer so she could always get a happy ending. After earning her Masters in Literature, she decided to leave everything behind and move to the US to pursue her dream of becoming a published author.

She is an incorrigible binge watcher/reader, which tells you all you need to know about her character. Some might call it obsessive, but of course, she prefers intense and passionate.

She will only lose her composure if faced with a clothing tag. She cuts them out religiously, but they are a formidable adversary that finds a way to bite back.

Out There

Iris Eliot

BELLA
BOOKS
2024

Bella Books, Inc.
P.O. Box 10543
Tallahassee, FL 32302

Printed in the United States of America on acid-free paper.

First Edition - 2024

Editor: Heather Flournoy
Cover Designer: Heather Dickerman

ISBN: 978-1-64247-513-5

PUBLISHER'S NOTE

CHAPTER ONE

Country music wasn't punishment enough, so they sent in cymbals. And a parade. As Catherine Des Lauriers elbowed her way through pushy vendors, curious cowboys, and despicable enthusiasts who had laid claim to what used to be a sleepy little town, she could hardly think of anything other than, *I hate Jesse Morgan.*

Dying alone—that peaceful, inevitable future she counted on only a few days ago—suddenly seemed like the loveliest dream. All these individuals couldn't have been out purely to make her life *even* more miserable, but they were damn good at it.

Maple Springs Country Music Fest, also known as Jesse Morgan's homecoming, was part festival, part very successful nightmare. A picture-perfect main street had been flooded with people for three days straight. With only one singer performing, it was debatable if the event could even qualify as a festival, so the residents quickly threw in chili cook-offs, a Parade of Smiles, and an antique car show—which was just that: a display of a single antique car.

Stuck as a group of her beaming old neighbors marched down the street, Catherine couldn't avoid an overwhelming question. *What kind of loon leaves Paris for an out-there town with a median age of about one hundred?*

Resigned to the nasty, high-pitched ringing of the cymbals, she set eyes on a route behind the kettle corn booth, where ladies in pink hats and glitter boots performed line dances. If only she were into terrible music and riding invisible horses, she might have enjoyed this. Yet, all she wanted was that predictable old town where she could be far from people, far from her mistakes. Not that she would ever forget, hell no.

Catherine clenched her fists and pushed her way through the crowd, thinking about all the times that Chloe must have brought someone to their apartment, imagining all the women who drank from her mugs, went through her dresser drawers, came on her sheets.

It didn't kill me and it certainly didn't make me stronger, she observed dryly, enduring the hits of flying candy. *The next time they say life is blessed by the chances you take and the love you share, Catherine, please know they're lying.*

She hissed as she cleared her way through the joyous crowd until at last she found relief, spotting her grandfather's shop tucked away just off Main Street. When she grabbed the doorknob and finally left all the frenzy behind, her grandfather waited with his arms spread out.

"Finally! There you are." He let out a loud sigh. "I don't want to be late for the festival and I have to go pick up glazes."

So much for being worried she'd be trampled to death. God forbid someone missed the festival.

"All this for some ridiculous singer no one's ever heard of," she grumbled.

"You shouldn't be talking about Jesse like that."

Watching the man swooning over some washed-up country singer, Catherine longed for the moment when that pottery shop would again be the place where she could get away from the world and immerse herself in something that didn't include women and endless, agonizing pain.

"Jesse is the cutest creature in the whole wide world," Fletcher continued, his shoulders curling forward. "She is like ten little puppies, one on top of the other. Simply adorable."

"Hey!" Catherine glared at him, feebly attempting an irresistible smile. "Over here."

The old man grinned good-humoredly.

"You are adorable, just a slightly different type of adorable."

As if it wasn't enough that the whole town seemed possessed, her own grandfather couldn't get over Jesse Morgan.

"She put us on the map. The whole country heard of Maple Springs, Colorado, because of her. Imagine, one of the greatest stars of country music used to run these streets and climb these trees. The least we can do is throw her a party once in a while."

Catherine doubted anyone outside Maple Springs had ever heard of Jesse Morgan but decided not to break the old man's heart. She couldn't care less about the so-called hometown hero and the imagined attention she brought to her grandfather's tiny hamlet. If only all these people would leave while she was still somewhat sane. It was way too early for a parade.

Seeing her silent, Fletcher drew a deep breath and fidgeted, his gaze intently dwelling on Catherine like he sought encouragement.

"Catherine, have you thought about what we discussed yesterday?"

Oh, not again. He knew she was incapable of saying no to him, but of all the things, why did he need her to go with him to the meaningless festival?

"Marjorie will be there, and I need help starting a conversation. Please, just for a little while. You can slip out then."

"You've known the woman for twenty-five years. How can you still need help?" Catherine couldn't believe how coy and lost a seventy-five-year-old could be until she saw her grandfather around a quirky redhead and her ringing laugh. "Besides, if you're going to rely on my advice on women, you're not gonna get far."

"Please!" His look was imploring. "At least think about it. It's easier when you're not alone. Please. Besides, she only moved here permanently last year. In twenty-five years, I would have made a move, certainly."

Staring at his worried face, Catherine smiled without a word. At least now it was clear whom she took after in being so hopeless with women. She already knew what her answer would be.

Fletcher recognized her benevolent expression and hugged her with innocent delight.

"Thank you, Catherine! I better run to Mike's to pick up glazes now. Wouldn't wanna be late for the festival." He was again enthused, humming a lively tune. "I should hurry up, then. Could you please mind the shop till I get back, dear?"

Catherine had loved Fletcher's little store and its quiet corner at the back ever since she was a kid, never imagining that one day she would substitute Parisian lights with this little village in the middle of nowhere. Her father, an upright Frenchman, always had special plans for his only child. Piano lessons, sculpture courses, sewing classes. Her mother was even more practical. Ballet lessons, carpentry school, Chinese classes.

The tiny detail they forgot to incorporate into their plans was an arrogant, cheating photographer with a unique talent for misusing the word *love*.

I didn't even know I could love until I met you.
Loving you is the only good thing that has ever happened to me.
No one's ever gonna love you like I do.

Catherine certainly hoped not. *Fuck you, fuck you, Chloe!*

She'd rather stick needles in her eyes than face that despondent gaze of Chloe's, listen to her sickening excuses, or suffer kisses stolen from her hollow body. So, Catherine had escaped without a goodbye to the only place she could, where no one knew the person she had become, where no one cared. Here, for the first time, she didn't have to be anything except for what she felt.

Just as she picked up clay and was about to pull up a chair, imagining all the shapes and forms she could play with, the shop bell startled her. The unexpected sound caught her so unprepared that she dropped the whole bag of clay and the dust flew everywhere, mostly all over her.

"*Merde!*" she muttered and hastily wiped her hands on her already muddy pants.

"Fletcher?" a soft voice called from the other room.

Peeking into the shop, Catherine saw a blue-eyed woman peering curiously around the shop, long blond hair flowing from under a cap. She was so unexpectedly beautiful that Catherine forgot she was supposed to speak.

"Oh, I'm sorry, I thought Fletcher was here." The blue eyes widened in surprise.

"You just missed him. May I help you?" Catherine's brain finally managed to make a few words.

The silent, natural beauty of this woman caught her off guard, which could only mean one thing. God, she was about to say something dumb.

"I just wanted to say hi, never mind," the stranger replied politely.

"Well, I can take a message if you want."

Merde, merde, Catherine thought painfully in embarrassment, realizing only at that moment how she must have looked all dirtied with clay. Not that it mattered, but still, she didn't want to look like a gawky kid who knocked over every single dish in the room. Why now of all times?

"No, no, thank you, I'll just stop by later." A bright smile reached the woman's eyes. "I didn't know he had someone helping him with the shop. That's nice. You can tell the difference," she added as she looked around with interest.

Catherine figured that, if she somehow managed to grab the column in the middle of the room and hide herself behind it, this alarmingly pretty creature might not notice her grotesque appearance. Oh, why did she have to be such an idiot? The only thing she wanted from life, the only thing she craved at that moment, was to be a bit cooler, and the person in front of her couldn't care less. As if it mattered that she was covered in mud.

"These are amazing." The blond beauty was eyeing the exhibits when her gaze suddenly connected with Catherine, smiling. Catherine instantly forgot all her firm decisions and instinctively wrapped her arms around the column.

"Oh, oh. I'm Fletcher's granddaughter. I moved here from France a few months ago," she finally replied, silently cursing at herself. *No, Catherine, you're not awkward at all, hanging onto that column for dear life. Great job!*

"Oh, really? So how do you like Maple Springs?"

"Any other week I'd love it, but right now..." She waved her hand impatiently and rolled her eyes. "I can't wait for this insufferable Jesse Morgan to leave and give me my life back. Just leeeave already!" she said sharply, which amused the woman. "Why does everything have to revolve around this precious Jesse? Really, I just got back from the bakery, and they refused to sell me their banana bread as it was apparently the last loaf and they were saving it for her. 'They don't make these in Nashville.'" She waved her arms like the bakery Bertha. "It was right there in front of me! Myyyy banana bread! Imagine that."

"Noooo! Well, that's one really good banana bread." The woman laughed.

"Well, there."

Catherine didn't want this adorable creature to think she was some sort of small-town lunatic, but she'd had enough of this Jesse circus and no one else would listen to her frustration. So, yes, she had just made a fool of herself.

"I don't want you to think that I hate everything. As you can see, I genuinely love that banana bread."

The stranger flashed one of those smiles that makes you forget your name. Though, thankfully, Catherine did not forget hers, she did suddenly realize that the disarming beauty could be a Jesse fanatic and she might need to backtrack.

"How about you? Are you here for the festival?" she managed to utter.

"No, but I'll be there. I just came here to visit my family. I live out of state."

That was welcome news, and Catherine silently thanked God she wouldn't have to be near this woman ever again.

"Well, you probably should have picked another date," Catherine said with a wry smile. She couldn't figure out what to do with her arms, so she grabbed the column again. *Idiot!*

"And miss that car show?" the woman said cheerfully, shaking her head. "Never."

Catherine chuckled, then quickly attempted to school her features to a neutral expression. Knowing herself, she probably kept a stupid smile plastered all over her face the entire time. The stunning head-turner glanced around the shop once more, aware it was probably time to leave. Suddenly, those blue eyes settled on Catherine, and the corners of the woman's lips curled up again. "You know...you should give Jesse a chance. She's really not that bad."

"What's with you people and this, this so-called singer, who, honestly, no one has ever heard of? What are her songs about anyway? Selling her tractor for a bottle of gin, but then realizing she loves her little tractor and doesn't want to live this miserable life without it?"

The woman laughed.

"I'd say the part about being miserable is very, very true but...I hope I'll see you at the festival."

Catherine watched her turn and leave, still chortling. A few days ago, it would never have even crossed her mind to visit that ridiculous abomination of common sense. She wanted to go camping, far from everyone, and wake up when it was all over. But if this stunning creature was going to be there...

No, no. She'd been in this predicament before. Being around a woman this attractive was the last thing she needed now. Or ever, for that matter. She pulled herself out of that game. Still, no one should have such a disarming, melting, winsome, dreamy smile.

Fuck, Catherine.

* * *

As she left the workshop, Jesse finally breathed a sigh of relief. Safe at last! That dark-eyed knockout, though not the cleanest of people, had probably left a string of hearts weeping silently all over France at that very moment. It simply wasn't fair that someone could be that gorgeous.

Considering how hard she'd tried not to stare at her wild, long, curly hair and the well-defined muscles of her tanned arms and long legs, it was curious how she managed to recall every minute detail of her appearance. Her wrist tattoo with three little stars, all the different shades of her eyes barely crossed inward, the tiny scar on her forehead. All that after seeing her for approximately 3.2 seconds. *Well done, Jesse!*

She didn't even know why she was so convinced that Fletcher's granddaughter was into women, but every single sensation of her being came to life when she appeared from the back room. Not that it made any difference whatsoever, of course. The French potter would stay a thousand miles away, and Jesse should really find another source of inspiration for her pathetic songs other than the stubborn inclination to get infatuated with the women she couldn't have.

Yet, there was something vulnerable and untold in the woman's eyes, something Jesse wanted to tell. Something she could not forget. She had always loved the marks of life on human faces, each one telling a story, each one like a treasure map, each creating the raw beauty of a masterpiece. The entire world had faded into insipidity when that woman appeared. What was she doing in Maple Springs anyway? Oceans away from her home. How long was she staying? Jesse could still hear, in a tangible and profound sensation, the resounding melody of her delicate voice, her French accent incising her skin—oh, that accent! Was she lonely here? What would make her smile?

Upon realizing that she was sitting in a parked car in front of the shop, thinking about a complete stranger, Jesse lightly tapped her face.

"You should never be this happy to see someone you don't even know."

Before starting the car, she couldn't help trying to steal another glance. However, the woman was already gone. Probably for the best. She had to prepare for the evening anyway, but still, it would have been nice if she hadn't suddenly begun to worry about what she would wear.

"How did she get that little scar? Why did she leave France? Dammit, Jesse!"

CHAPTER TWO

It took three hours of preparation, one hour of nervous pacing up and down the room, and changing clothes seven times, and she still only came up with the same dress that looked like her mom's awful eighties' maternity wear, only somehow much worse. Catherine took another glance in the mirror and sighed. The only movement she should do in this dress was a short walk to the trash can.

She flopped down onto the bed and spread her arms. Some people were obviously beyond help. As much as she wanted to convince herself that she was only trying not to embarrass her grandfather, whenever she looked at herself in the mirror, she felt exposed in her vanity. Staring back was the uninterested blonde from the shop, running her eyes up and down Catherine's ridiculous Disney Princess outfit. She didn't dare ask Fletcher who she was, and now it shouldn't even matter. This was the day she'd get rid of that irritating Jesse Morgan, and as such, it should be celebrated.

She could already hear the music and the noise from the fair through the open window, so when she realized it was well past eight and her grandfather was probably waiting for her anxiously, she reluctantly rolled off the bed. No, she would not meet anyone, and she would certainly not talk to anyone. It was time to get it over with.

"Stupid festival," she grumbled before throwing on a shirt and shorts and storming out.

The walk down their abandoned street was pleasant, but as soon as she turned onto the next one, the craze was in full swing. How was she supposed to find her grandfather and Marjorie among all these people? Was there any limit to their folly? She had no idea how anyone could enjoy that music. Catherine jostled through the crowd, lazily hanging around the hot dog stands as the smell of beer permeated the air. She spun around in search of a familiar face, only to encounter fired-up cowboys singing and dancing.

This will finally put an end to Jesse Morgan. At last, I will be rid of that pest. She immediately felt a pleasant wave of gaiety tingling through her bloodstream.

As she left the booths behind, she could at last hear the dreaded music in its full and clear glory. With the stage in sight, curiosity got the better of her, so she raised her gaze in search of the very person responsible for her misery the last few days. In an instant, she forgot her grandfather, all the horrendous dresses of this world, the crowd around her, and every thought she'd ever had. Gaping, her heart stopped.

It couldn't be true.

No, no, it had to be some mistake.

The woman from the shop stood on the stage. With a guitar. With those perfect shining eyes. Singing with the crowd. Could that really be her?

She must have been staring with her mouth wide open for a while when she realized Jesse had spotted her. If only the earth could crack open beneath her. She caught Jesse's brief, fleeting smile.

"Lay naked with me," the crowd sang, as if it finally dawned on her.

"Lay naked with me," Jesse sang along with them.

Well, that was a bit too evocative. Her mind certainly didn't need any help undressing the woman in front of her.

"Lay!" Jesse slapped the guitar.

"Lay naked with me," hundreds of people sang.

If only they would all stop chanting, "Lay naked with me," she might have a chance at erasing the images of a nude Jesse from her imagination. Perhaps she had misjudged country music. Catherine turned around, despairing, as Jesse started a new song.

Thank God, Catherine thought, but still caught herself awaiting with interest what the next song would reveal about Jesse. Her idea of country music had always been very French, meaning, it was some music that belonged exclusively to Jesus Christ's America, where whiskey-soaked old dudes with gray beards sang depressing songs. This, now, was totally not fair. Catherine thrust her hands deeper into her pockets, glancing around the crowd but finding herself absolutely melting into Jesse's voice. Damn, she could sing. She was hitting soaring notes with ease, the sound of it masterful, almost casual.

Of course, Catherine wasn't even aware of how ridiculous she looked earlier. Jesse must have had a good chuckle when she finally left the madwoman's shop. Catherine firmly closed her eyes in a willful effort to suppress the thought of that moment and the fact it ever happened.

"Every other feeling rolls off me when you're near. They don't matter, baby," came the words from the stage.

They? Catherine jerked. Who are they? How many *they* were there?

Of course, the whole damn world had to be in love with Jesse Morgan, and she was probably taking advantage of it like any other woman would.

Why should Catherine care? She'd had enough of women addicted to attention, constantly craving everyone's adoration. The person on the stage was nothing to her, she reminded herself. If anything, Catherine was the one who'd been rude and should be embarrassed. Jesse could have all the people in the world, and she probably did. It had nothing to do with her. Thank God she didn't have to see her ever again.

"Catherine! There you are." She heard Fletcher behind her, and as she quickly turned, saw the tall, scrawny man and Marjorie, sprightly as ever, next to him.

"Hey, I was worried I wouldn't find you in this crowd," Catherine replied.

"Yes, it is pretty wild. Just the way we want it." Marjorie's astute eyes searched Fletcher's face for reaction, and the man inevitably blushed.

To avoid her playful gaze, Fletcher quickly turned to the stage and looked at Jesse with blatant adoration. "Isn't she something?"

Catherine cast a furtive glance at Jesse and found the energetic woman effortlessly entertaining the masses. What a fireball in such a fragile frame, she instantly thought. *Stupid festival!*

"Uh-huh," she muttered instead, forcing herself to focus. "Hey, Marjorie, do you have any plans for tomorrow?"

"Oh well, no, dear. Do you wanna take me out, perhaps? Girls' night out? *Coyote Ugly* style?"

"I was thinking of inviting you over for lunch and then seeing what happens."

Marjorie grinned, without blinking. "Of course, if that's okay with Fletcher."

"Oh, by all means," the man coyly agreed.

"I'm sure he doesn't mind spending time with his two favorite people."

"Oh, is that what we are, Fletcher?" Marjorie asked teasingly, and the old man only managed to crack a bashful smile and nod his head.

It couldn't have been more than ten minutes since she got there, and Catherine was already over the damn festival. Her grandfather seemed to be doing well enough without her as, thankfully, Marjorie took over. This might be her chance to slip away and get far from Jesse. Seeing that beaming face again and catching herself analyzing her words would just make her more upset with herself. She had no business wondering who was getting frisky at Four Roses Hotel, nor where the hell that was. Regardless of her charming smile, Jesse was a complete stranger, and Catherine expected more from herself.

If she only went home and left this day behind, tomorrow morning she would wake up and the very first thought after opening her eyes would again be about Chloe. That thought would set the mood for the rest of the day—meaning, hating everyone and mostly herself.

"It was nice seeing you, but I'm going to head home," Catherine said. "I just wanted to see what this was all about."

"Oh, Jesse is the most delightful girl you'll ever meet." Marjorie linked her arm affectionately through Catherine's, lovingly gazing at the stage.

Catherine sneered. "I'm sure she is."

"She likes women too, you know."

"I bet she does."

"Oh, you know what I meant."

Catherine reassuringly smiled and hugged Marjorie. "I know, don't worry, I'll see you tomorrow."

She couldn't wait to be alone again. As well-intentioned as people were, their every endeavor would only bring up memories of Chloe. She, too, was the most delightful person in the world; she was fun, she was generous. *It would be so nice to have her in my bed*, Catherine recalled fantasizing every day. Chloe was like a light cracking through her skin and illuminating something deep inside she didn't know existed. She was also a mistake that turned her into a person she despised.

Damn, she should have gone camping, that's what she should have done.

"I won't last another day," Jesse sang as Catherine finally bid farewell to Marjorie and Fletcher.

Perfect, Catherine thought. *Neither will I.*

* * *

Jesse noticed a faint light coming from the room upstairs. Fletcher was at the fair when she left, so Dirty Pants must have been awake. Jesse didn't even know why that notion gave her so much pleasure. She knocked hesitantly on the door. No answer. She knocked again.

In the quiet of the deserted street, Jesse knew Catherine would hear her through the open window. She cleared her throat.

"I know you're in there. I…I just brought you something." Still only silence. "Anyway…it's Jesse, and I believe this is your banana bread."

After a moment of silence, she could hear light footsteps coming down the creaky stairs. The door opened slightly and a dark eye appeared.

"Banana bread?" Catherine hid behind the door, managing to avoid looking directly at her.

Jesse offered her the bread, smiling. "Why are you hiding?"

"I am too embarrassed to look at you right now."

"Don't be silly."

"I am. I'm the worst. Your songs are actually not that terrible."

"Luckily, I've only got a few."

"No, you don't. Don't lie to me to make me feel better. You had a number-one hit with Brad Paisley."

"You've heard of Brad Paisley?"

"No, of course not." Catherine snickered.

Jesse's face lit up. "Fletcher told me you didn't go camping today to help him out. That was really nice."

"Well, this Jesse chick didn't turn out to be the disaster I had expected, so it was okay."

Oh, I'm a chick now. Jesse chuckled, unusually pleased and embarrassed at the same time.

"I saw you only briefly," Jesse began and instantly wriggled. Even that was too damn much. "Then I ran into Fletcher later on. He invited me for lunch tomorrow. I hope that's okay with you."

"As long as I don't have to cook, that's fine," Catherine replied, still hidden in the dark.

"You know, if we're having lunch together, you'll eventually have to look at me."

"Of course not!" Catherine said firmly, which made Jesse laugh.

"You're crazy." As she shook her head, Jesse could swear she glimpsed a smile teasing the corners of Catherine's lips, which somehow made her look even more annoyed. Or sexy. Why didn't she know all about this woman already? Catherine seemed so unmoored from hope, so tied up in desire, dangerously chasing her freedom, unworried about the objections of the world... Crap, she had to stop. What the hell was wrong with her? "Well, Catherine, I'm looking forward to that," she added, pleased to hear her voice remained steady, although her damn, feeble imagination had turned against her. "See you tomorrow, then. Have a good night." She snuck another glance and without any hesitation turned and quickly walked away.

CHAPTER THREE

The lunch didn't turn out to be a complete disaster after all. Fletcher had prepared ridiculous amounts of food, probably hoping to impress Marjorie when there had been no need for that since the genuine, playful postal service clerk had no intention of hiding that the interest was mutual. Catherine couldn't grasp how her grandfather managed to prepare the feast in only a few hours, but there were his famous poppyseed turkey sliders, savory bites of delicious goodness she remembered from her childhood, along with pimento cheese scalloped potatoes, crispy fried chicken, ribs, baked beans, zucchini panzanella salad, creamy mushroom soup, and traditional Southern tomato pie, full of flavor from two cheeses, fresh sun-ripened tomatoes, and a buttery pie crust. Of course, there was another Southern classic—probably for Jesse—Mississippi mud cake, incredibly appetizing with chocolate, marshmallows, and pecans.

Jesse, it seemed, enjoyed the interaction of the two burgeoning lovebirds and fit that picture certainly better than Catherine did with her exasperated expression of unhindered disdain toward anyone who dared to believe in love. "One would expect wisdom at this age," she mumbled, looking at Fletcher and Marjorie and trying hard not to roll her eyes, then glancing sideways at a positively radiant Jesse, who showed little interest in Catherine throughout the entire lunch.

Watching Jesse effortlessly capture the attention of those around her, Catherine felt both envy and melancholy. She imagined life was truly easy when you were Jesse Morgan and the entire world adored you. She probably had a girlfriend or two waiting for her to get back to Nashville. Young, slim bodies who worshipped her, undoubtedly all very fashionable, always in the mood, laughing at her jokes and saying the right things. Love was no torment for Jesse. Love hung around her estate in impossibly stringy bikinis, splashing around in her pool and serving cold drinks if needed. There were no heavy silences, infinite resentments, petty fights nor boredom. No, Jesse would take the best from people. She was not bothered, she was not afraid of being vulnerable. Her girlfriends would dance till dawn, topless on the rooftops, without a care in the world. Yet, what Catherine despised the most about Jesse was that in addition to all that, she actually was delightful. Her conversation with Fletcher and Marjorie was effortless as they reminisced about the old bridge, talked about Marjorie's cat and the new tax system—they even talked about detergent pods. No real star would know the first thing about those damn pods. She really hated Jesse Morgan.

Catherine realized with a sort of desolate relief that she had become redundant, so she took her glass of wine and stepped outside, finding an ideal shelter on the stairs overlooking the backyard. With her silence she played the role of a small-town lunatic to perfection, and now she could surrender to the lovely sound of birds and moving water in their yard.

The landscape around Fletcher's house had contours more reminiscent of a prairie than the mountains. However, he had managed to create a little oasis of pines and blue spruces in the backyard, and ever since Catherine added feeders and a birdbath, curious species had started flocking to investigate their thick branches and prickly needles, perhaps hoping they would provide a safe winter shelter. Catherine contemplated two inquisitive black-capped chickadees watching a white-winged crossbill separate the scales on the pine cone and extract the seeds. It was comforting to know that at least those two black-capped chickadees managed to stay monogamous and form long-term pair bonds. No wonder she wanted to be surrounded by birds. The only thing left to figure out was how to attract more cicadas to the yard. The lulling melody of lazy Provençal afternoons and hot summer days was what she missed the most about home.

She had only been sitting there for a few minutes when she heard the door opening and saw Jesse appear on the deck next to her.

"I figured I'd give them some space," Jesse said, sitting beside her.

Damn woman, Catherine thought to herself. Since when did a chat require this level of courage?

"So, what's the dirtbag's name?" Jesse asked resolutely, fixing her gaze on the limber pine in front of her.

"Whose name?" Catherine stared at her, perplexed.

"The name of whoever made you run to this godforsaken place after breaking your heart into a million little pieces."

"My heart was not broken!" Catherine flung up her defiant chin. She wasn't even thinking about Chloe. At least not directly, as she cunningly used birds as metaphors. Did her misery really have to be so evident to everyone? Especially to perfect Jesse Morgan, of all people!

Lying was certainly easier than facing her own failures.

"Can someone simply not enjoy nature?" she added calmly.

"You look everything but like you're enjoying yourself." Jesse chuckled. "Punishing yourself is the only reason I can come up with as to why anyone would want to live here."

"I like it here."

"So…I was kinda right?" Jesse's face lit up with a tenacious smile, and a sweet laugh finally escaped Catherine's lips.

Jesse was so insistent and so annoying. Yet gazing at her shrewd, vibrant eyes was a natural impulse for Catherine.

"Chloe, the name is Chloe, a deceiving woman of many charms and I profoundly despise every single one," she admitted at last.

For the first time, she had mentioned Chloe in the presence of a perfect stranger. For so long, every thought of Chloe would end by staring into a deep, hollow abyss she was about to fall into, and Catherine was astounded by the exceptional ease with which that dreaded name just slipped from her lips. Chloe. She was avoiding any mention of her ever since she moved to Maple Springs—including with her grandfather, who had never met Chloe nor pushed Catherine for an explanation for why she left Paris—and now her name just slid out. What was it about Jesse that seemed to bring down all her defenses?

"She sounds lovely. What did she do?" Jesse said, looking at her with interest.

"You mean who did she do?" Catherine scoffed. "Too many, I suppose. Until I caught her in bed with someone else." The words were flowing without any regard for caution. "Still, it's not her fault. I was a fool to think I could be enough."

"Your greatness does not depend on Chloe," Jesse said carefully. "Sure, you're a bit out there and somewhat on the grumpy side, but I'm sure some women would find that irresistible. Chloe does not define you, nor Ali nor Jen nor any other woman in the world. You're exactly who you need to be."

Tilting her head, Catherine locked her eyes with Jesse's sparkling blues.

"So, you can provide counseling, you can do taxes, is there anything you can't do, Jesse Morgan?"

The woman nodded thoughtfully.

"I can't sing."

Catherine burst into laughter. Damn you, Jesse, and your eternal smile!

Jesse was still eyeing her meditatively. "You don't believe in love, I don't believe in love, but let them." She motioned to the house. "They need hope," she added, "and Marjorie is not Chloe." Her face shone with force and curiosity.

Why wouldn't Jesse believe in love? Catherine wondered. The whole damn world was in love with her. She was so lovable that she almost had Catherine liking her. Sure, having fun was better than exposing yourself to—what had she sung? The "arrow of too many loves" or something.

Jesse even had dimples in her cheeks, for God's sake.

She should just stop being so damn cute. Catherine quickly scolded her frailty. She shouldn't spend any more time than necessary with this woman. She didn't want to like her. *Plus jamais, Catherine!*

"Hey, girls, did you enjoy your lunch?" Catherine could hear her grandfather behind them.

"Oh, Fletcher, it was delicious." Jesse instantly scooted over to make room for him.

The old man crossed his arms, stroked his neck for a moment, and finally sat between them.

You finally got the timing right. Catherine writhed. She had just started feeling the weight of Jesse's presence, of her scent, her voice, her intelligent eyes staring so earnestly at her. There was sweetness in them, overwhelming sweetness that she wanted to explore, that she couldn't escape.

She was so sunk. *You are so sunk, Catherine.*

"Hey, Catherine," Fletcher said, squinting his eyes against the sun. "Are you still going camping tomorrow?"

"Sure, why?"

"I invited Marjorie over for dinner."

"Nice, Fletcher!" Jesse instantly wrapped her arm around his shoulder.

Catherine also smiled and patted his knee. "I'm happy for you, *Pépé*."

"Oh, Catherine!" Fletcher's manner suddenly changed to bewildered elation. "You're not the only one who needs a break after the festival. Jesse does too. Why don't you take her camping with you?"

Catherine knew exactly what her grandfather was trying to do, and it was not going to work. The old man was not as naïve as he seemed, after all.

"I'm sure Jesse has better things to do."

Jesse shook her head innocently. "Not really."

Why did she have to do this to her, why? Catherine pierced her sullenly. This woman would drive her insane.

"Jesse is a local here," Fletcher said. "She went camping alone for the first time when she was nine. She's a pro. Plus, I'm sure Nashville can't compare to what we have here. Come on."

"I'd love to go camping with you, Catherine. Also, no more singing. I promise." Jesse looked at her innocently.

Catherine knew that the proximity of that woman could not be good for her, yet Jesse had brought her banana bread, and she didn't know how to turn down those vivacious eyes. She should have put aside her silly insecurities and finally showed some manners. There should be no reason to worry. After all, she was too old for vanity. Jesse just wanted to go camping. It had nothing to do with her.

"If you want to, fine." Catherine shrugged helplessly.

Merde!

To go camping with a woman who probably perceived herself as some big star who needed to be cosseted! Sure, she can seem nice, but people never fail to disappoint you.

"Wonderful!" Fletcher wrapped his arms around them. "You'll have so much fun together."

Merde!

CHAPTER FOUR

Just as Catherine's dusty Tacoma pulled up into the driveway, Jesse appeared in the doorway. Observing her, Catherine reluctantly agreed that the musician exuded sheer magnetism, even when she was just carelessly tossing her backpack in the truck bed, even when she was just walking toward the car, fixing her cap. The women in Nashville didn't stand a chance. Yup, God didn't miss a beat on this one.

"Miss Catherine!" Jesse shot her a cheerful glance as soon as she entered the truck, and Catherine found herself instantly embarrassed as if the woman had just stripped her to her very thoughts with only one look.

"Hello," she replied softly, gripping the steering wheel firmly to convince herself that she was in control and that her thoughts were still tucked away safely.

The attraction Catherine discovered for Jesse didn't perturb her too much, as she was well aware she would not make the mistake of falling for someone ever again. Not that Jesse would care, of course, but she finally didn't need anyone to love her, and that felt so liberating.

Not to mention, being the perfect girlfriend was exhausting as hell—reading *Vogue*, going running, pretending you know what you're talking about when she wants to discuss post-painterly abstraction. Even yoga unnerved her. The longest damn hour of the week! Chloe pushed her into joining her every Wednesday at four, and of course, she wanted to be the perfect girlfriend. What a fraud. She learned she would only ever be perfectly imperfect.

Sure, she may have wanted to drown under that shirt Jesse was wearing, perhaps disappear underneath it. No shame there. But she was not foolish enough to wish for anything more. Attraction was fine, as long as she knew it stopped there. She'd learned her lesson. One day, her mind would master that damn weakness as well.

As they were bouncing down the dirt road, Jesse seemed to be paying little heed to the trees and lakes around them, as if each had already marked her so deeply she didn't need reminding.

"So, how was the pottery business for you in Paris?"

"I only took up pottery when I moved here." Catherine chuckled.

"What were you doing in Paris then?"

"I was a choreographer." She noticed that Jesse wriggled but remained silent, so she added, "Last year I worked on the movie *Say Yes to Our Love*." Catherine glanced at Jesse like she must have heard of that timeless work of art. "It won the Cesar Award for Best Cinematography in March. Karin Viard was exceptional, totally robbed for not taking the Cesar for Best Actress."

"Wow, maybe I should hire you then," Jesse said, amused.

"You'd want to speak with your body more?"

"If you think you could teach me."

Catherine's imagination never needed any stimuli, and with this one, it already worked more than it should have.

"I'm sure I could teach you a thing or two. However, I'd need to know the stories behind your songs, like, 'Lay naked with me.'"

"Oh, of all the songs, that's the one you want to do?"

"Story intrigued me." Catherine glanced sideways at Jesse with a harmless grin.

The woman's blue eyes brightened, and she smiled widely for a second before her face suddenly scrunched up.

"Oh no!" Jesse muttered worriedly and spun around.

"What's wrong?" Catherine asked with a slightly apprehensive air as her heartbeat started accelerating.

"Oh, nothing." Yet, Jesse turned around again.

"What?" Catherine was now clearly uneasy.

"I think we are being followed by paparazzi."

"*Quoi?*" Catherine's eyes widened as she tried to look at the winding road in front as well as keep her eyes on the rearview mirror. "I don't see them. Where?"

"Try turning right here."

Catherine obeyed without question and stepped on the gas.

"Crap, they're still behind, okay, turn right again. Faster!"

Catherine had no desire to be photographed anywhere, and especially not with this woman. She refused to be the ridicule of the idle country fans and especially so in her camping outfit. Oh, these disasters always happened to her. Jesse's disquieted expression was certainly not helping.

"They cannot take a photo of me in these boots!" Catherine said, starting to panic. She had no idea where she was driving.

"Turn left here."

Catherine listened as she followed the dirt road in front of them. Before them lay a magnificent lake with the sun that was about to set, but Catherine was too distressed to notice any of that.

"Did we lose them? Did we?"

Jesse suddenly stopped turning and instead gave Catherine a long look until she finally burst out laughing. Catherine stopped the car.

"What? Where are they?"

"There was no one there," Jesse replied, and Catherine stared at her exuberant smile. "Just me messing with you."

"No paparazzi?"

"No! Good God, why would the paparazzi be after me? Are you crazy?" She waved away the idea. "I just wanted to see your face."

Still feeling foolish, Catherine finally gave a sigh of relief.

"I'm nobody special and actually, I just wanted to show you this little valley here."

"You could have just told me!"

"Your expressions wouldn't be as precious." Jesse started laughing again.

"We could have died."

"Well, this is one of my favorite places to get away from people, so I figured, after what I put you through the past few days, I could at least share it with you in case you need it again."

The sun was setting over the lake with trees reflecting in the water and Catherine felt uncomfortable breaking the perfect silence with her voice. It took her only five minutes to set up her tent, so when she turned to Jesse she paused in bewilderment, realizing the woman was still only accounting for all the components. Upon seeing what it was that Jesse was assembling, her face lit up. Little did she know a tent could have three rooms, large windows, and numerous entrances. When one of the sides crashed down on imperturbable Jesse, Catherine came to regret her moment of childish fun. Abashed, she gently asked, "Do you need help?"

"No, don't worry, I got it."

Still, Catherine grabbed the poles and helped Jesse raise the tent and stake it to the ground. It was more work than she expected.

"If this is your tent, what's your house like?"

Jesse disappeared inside for a moment while Catherine was still respectfully containing her laughter.

"Look, it even has a little porch! I never knew a tent could have that."

Her tone as sultry as ever, Jesse smiled and said, "I'm glad you like it."

Catherine couldn't discern what it was about that woman, but she could hardly remove herself from her gaze. She inspired a peculiar feeling of familiarity, and Catherine struggled to stay in command of herself.

"Well, thank you for not dismissing me as a kook when we met."

"You're too cute to be a kook. Could you hand me that fastener, please?"

Again! Jesse was melting her so effortlessly, with that air of easy confidence and charm, with that sensual perfume, and Catherine hardly recognized herself.

Putain! It was going to be a long weekend.

* * *

Jesse's tent seemed to cover the entire flat ground next to the lake, and Catherine's miniature tent resembled its lonely shed. Yet it was comforting to pick up the sound of waves in the evening breeze, far from everyone, Jesse thought.

Only a few minutes after Catherine had entered her own tent, Jesse let out a deep breath as she surveyed the campsite from her canopy chair. "I can't possibly leave you in that kiddie tent, Catherine. Come over here."

"This is not a kiddie tent, it's a tent for two."

Jesse got up and stuck her head into Catherine's relatively diminutive shelter. "How are two people supposed to sleep here?"

"One person sleeps here." Catherine motioned to the left. "And the other one like this."

Jesse wasn't convinced, but she shrugged. No way was she staying in that ridiculous tent mansion by herself, so she might as well prepare for the alternative. "Well, I guess we'll be sleeping here, then."

Catherine let out an ethereal laugh, and that new, earnest sound captured Jesse. She found that her gaze kept wandering back to the woman with an ease that startled her. God, she'd say anything to make those eyes smile like that again. Jesse couldn't recall the last time she felt this free with someone, free in her own being. Not only that, but she could be the worst version of herself. Catherine didn't have a single expectation, and she clearly thought that people were disappointments to begin with. Jesse wished she could prove her wrong, gain her trust, caress her face for no real reason, and stay close to her. Too bad she didn't know how to do any of those damn things. Even this moment, when she was lying next to her, would soon be lost among countless other missed opportunities. She was but a stereotype to Catherine, and she wasn't sure she could refute that.

The drive here was the first glimpse she'd gotten of Catherine's expression lacking any trace of frowning, annoyance, or impertinence. Even now, Catherine looked fresh, without any weight on her eyelids, as if ready to finally open her eyes to the woman next to her. God knows Jesse tried not to stare— she really did—but only with mediocre results. Not only was Catherine remarkably pretty, with classic facial features, well-defined arms, and a smile that made Jesse's knees weak, she was also enfolded in a scent of gentle ocean breeze, citrus, soap, home, and Jesse couldn't stop envisioning what it would be like to take a breath from her neck.

"Thank you for letting me into your tent."

Catherine's eyes looked amused. They'd just spent an hour assembling a lavish tent they wouldn't need.

"Of course," Catherine replied, and Jesse couldn't tell if there was a single inch of her mad body that didn't crave Catherine's touch, a single inch that didn't feel weakening tenderness. God, she expected more from herself.

"Sharing is joy." Catherine gave a rueful grin. "Except when you share your girlfriend."

Jesse laughed, adjusting the sleeping pads to give them more space for the preservation of sanity.

"It was not your fault, just so you know."

She appreciated Catherine for her candor, but this serene and genuine creature completely absorbed her. It wasn't like her to rely on others, it wasn't like her to hide. Catherine was revealing her vulnerabilities with effortless delicacy and the notion that she was this unreserved with her frightened Jesse as much as it provoked a desire to be even closer, to dare, to explore life, to touch her. Be free. Damn French people! She might just die in this cramped tent.

"Thank you," Catherine said. "I imagine you don't have to deal with that. You probably keep an eager girlfriend in every town you visit."

Jesse looked at her with a curious, thoughtful gaze.

"Is that what you would do?"

"At this point in my life, I can't say I wouldn't consider it." Catherine laughed.

"What else do you know about me?" Jesse watched quietly as Catherine sat down and crossed her legs.

"You often wake up next to a girl whose name you don't know, while she is dreaming of being the love of your life," Catherine said. "When you leave, they remain firmly convinced that you are going to call them, although they'll never see you again. They don't even resent you because they dismiss you as messed up. If someone gets too close, you find a way to sabotage it. And why not, since fucking is easier than loving?"

The candor Jesse expected, but she was pleasantly surprised to find herself entertained by the narrative. It was even endearing. "For someone who doesn't like country, you sure know a lot about me. Except you got one thing wrong." She spread her arms with a weary smile. "They do resent, every time."

It would be so easy to befriend Catherine, she thought, so easy to start caring for her, so easy to get used to her honesty. She saw her dancing over the dying embers of life, a bit unconventional, a bit impatient, all sincere words and open heart, and relying only on herself. It would be so easy to guard her, guard her from everyone, even if she waved away every concern, laughed it off, denied it all. To be on her side in every little obsession, injustice, poor decision—what would that be like? Skin removed, no armor, eyes wide open. On her side, instead of alone with everybody. Love her into loving herself, find understanding for all her weaknesses, insecurities, anxieties, and leave them all to love her more. Every day, every hour. Lose the form and find their own rhythm.

Yes. She'd be better off as a song.

Catherine was safer with a stereotype, and so was she. *That* she could control—and she would.

"As you say, dear Catherine, fucking is easier than loving. Why bother if you can just fuck your way to their heart, right?" She stared straight at Catherine.

Those harsh words had nothing to do with her true feelings, so she looked away, afraid her eyes might reveal her thoughts. "Do you want to go with me to feed Chuck?" she said instead.

"You don't have a bear, do you?"

Jesse chuckled.

"No, it's the fattest little chipmunk you'll ever see. Come on, it's getting dark."

Jesse briefly popped into her tent and emerged with two baggies of walnuts, almonds, and raisins, handing one to Catherine. She trod forward through the dense forest, showing no hesitation, which she hoped would reassure Catherine since darkness had started swallowing the path ahead. Out of the corner of her eye, Jesse noticed Catherine couldn't resist stealthily bringing one almond to her mouth. And then quite some more. The shameless woman was pilfering Chuck's food! Yet Jesse knew there was very little she wouldn't forgive her.

"How do you know which one is Chuck?" Catherine asked, catching up to her.

"He is the fattest of them all." Jesse smiled and felt an unexpected sorrow flicker over her grin. "When I was eight, he escaped from our yard. Years later, when I was camping here, of all the rascals in the world, I ran into fat Chuck. It's magic, isn't it?"

Catherine nodded softly, and Jesse felt a silent gratitude for that tender understanding.

When they encountered an overweight chipmunk at the foot of an old oak, Jesse felt her face light up again.

Of course she knew it wasn't really him—chipmunks don't normally live that long. But Chuck broke her heart by running away, and the guy who looked like him had been there every time she came back, so that was real magic. She beamed as she watched the fat creature chew contentedly. "I guess the worst thing that can happen to an artist is reciprocated love. Give me yearning, give me suffering, give me scars, and I'll turn you into art. Otherwise...I'll just make you miserable. Chuck knew me."

Jesse turned her gaze to the woman, and Catherine quickly reached out and wrapped her fingers around Jesse's hand. Jesse dropped her eyes back to the rodent and withdrew her hand, reaching toward the chipmunk. She'd be safer catching rabies. Perhaps that would be a less painful way out of this situation. This was definitely the last thing she expected when she came to the local village festival. *Damn.*

When they got back to the campsite, Jesse began building a campfire and the silence between them never lasted too long. As they sat around the warm, cozy flames for a bit, Jesse filled waffle cones with marshmallows and chocolate chips then wrapped them in foil and roasted them, while Catherine found peace in poking and adding wood.

"How does one get started in country music?" Catherine asked as she reached for a roasted waffle s'more.

"Oh, they are so desperate, they'll take anyone."

"Come on, I'm trying here."

"Country is personal, it's real, it's intimate. It's storytelling in music, and it always appealed to me. I started playing the fiddle when I was five and loved it. Learned trumpet, harmonica, accordion, banjo, mandolin, sitar, and guitar by the age of ten. Admittedly, I haven't learned a single thing in my life after that. But, I decided to go for what I wanted. Ten years ago I moved to Nashville, played in cafés at first, worked on my country twang, and then got this record company to sign me."

"Do you write your own songs?"

"I do, but mostly I write for others."

"So many girls deserving of a song?"

"We also like our Jesus, booze, mama, farm." Jesse smiled and looked at her with interest. "What keeps you happy?"

"Carbs, salt, and peanut butter."

Jesse grinned, adamant not to give in to fear no matter how fragile those indomitable, dark eyes made her feel.

"This certainly wasn't my dream growing up," Catherine continued, "but now I like it. I find it's easier being far from people, and I appreciate the silence. I wonder how I could have ever lived in a big city."

As the fire died out they sat stargazing for a while in silence, sinking into darkness and absorbing the vastness of the sky as the never-ending stars tirelessly flickered. Jesse found that silence around each other was as easy as it was rare. If Jesse wasn't asking questions she was constantly on the move, and even with the fire out, she didn't want the day to end. The mountain air was cold, but she was well acquainted with the lake and its tepid water. She craved a swim under the new moon, and although she was aware that she could come to regret such intimacy with Catherine's naked body, she decided it was not going to stop her. Besides, it was so dark that she could barely see the lake itself. God knows when she'd come back here again. The starry sky and dim, quiet atmosphere made it perfect for a splash. She didn't want to feel nervous around Catherine and secretly, she had to admit, curiosity was getting the better of her.

"Let's go for a swim. Water here is much warmer than the air."

* * *

Catherine was incredulous at first, but when she discerned that Jesse was undressing, the question she was about to pose became redundant. As much as warm water appealed to her senses, swimming naked next to Jesse would not be a smart decision—that was an easy guess.

"Come on!" Jesse seemed ready for a swim. "You're safe with me. I'm not interested in adding another girlfriend to my list."

"Thank you, you just made it less desirable," Catherine joked and removed her clothes without any hesitation. She knew she shouldn't worry about Jesse. This seemed to be a daily activity for her, and besides, she was old enough to trust herself. Still, the thought of Jesse's vigorous body only a few feet away sent shivers down her spine. Catherine could hear her swimming already, and with the mountain air increasingly chilly in the dark night she made haste toward the lake, following the faint sound of moving water. Suddenly, she fell into the lake with a huge splash, and she could clearly discern Jesse's chuckles.

"Glad you found me."

Her blushes remained hidden in the dark, but Catherine quickly found the lake was indeed as warm as Jesse had promised, and she abandoned herself to its pleasant caress. After a day spent under the fierce Colorado sun, this sure was a treat.

As much as she missed Paris, Catherine couldn't picture a moment more perfect than the one she was in now. Alone and free. As if that reminded her Jesse was still somewhere around her, Catherine jerked and narrowed her eyes in an attempt to find her, surprised to spot her only a few feet away. Two more strokes and their bodies would have collided. The thought of running into Jesse's naked body presented a raw yet thrilling peril, and required an immediate chiding.

Better swim in a different direction, Catherine. And fast.

She peeked once more, but the darkness decided it was for the best if her imagination continued to play with her, and Catherine didn't want to resist, not this time. In a way, she was glad Chloe hadn't killed that part of her. Of course, it was a dreadful nuisance, but if she was able to be attracted to someone, it meant Chloe didn't win. She would just never make the mistake of falling in love again. Yes, she would be fine. She should have thanked Chloe, for her life now was simpler and more peaceful than she could have ever imagined. Appeased, she smiled and, unworried by the surroundings, she surrendered all her senses to the gentle lull of water and the clear view of the starry sky.

CHAPTER FIVE

When she opened her eyes in the morning, Jesse found herself lying curled in the corner with her hands numb. Running away from Catherine's touch, her skin, the images of her naked body under the dim light of the stars, she almost crawled out of the tent. She couldn't tell if she simply convinced herself that she'd seen something, or if she really did.

Jesse lay listening for a bit, and when silence reassured her that she'd be safe, slowly turned. She immediately encountered dark eyes beaming at her.

"Good morning." Catherine's tenderness startled her, so Jesse attempted to casually stretch, but her legs got caught in the tent.

Crap. She should just remember the damn stereotype and she'd be safe. Give her what she thinks she knows.

Catherine appeared more relaxed as she gently continued, "Thank you for last night. I know this is not what you're accustomed to." She motioned her chin to the tent and found Jesse instantly amused, not avoiding her stare.

"Yes, waking up next to a woman with no resentments, that's quite nice. Now I only need to figure out how much longer till we make out."

Catherine smiled. "I wouldn't worry about that if I were you."

Still, Jesse felt pleased. "Well, mademoiselle," she said, "you know I do plan to seduce *you*. Eventually."

"I'd be offended if you didn't. Thank you."

Catherine's understanding was a rare gift, one Jesse was silently thankful for. Skeptical as Catherine was, she always had a way of putting Jesse at ease. Catherine didn't have a single expectation, and it infused her with a strange sense of possibility.

"Come on, let's grab a quick bite and head to Devil's Loop. I'd like us to reach the summit before it gets too hot," Jesse said and jumped to her feet.

Seemingly well rested and vivacious, Catherine readily joined her, and after grabbing a few eggs and crackers, they put on their backpacks and started following the shaded trail through the forest. Jesse strode ahead as someone well acquainted with every turn, every stone, every shrub, and Catherine was mostly in charge of casual chatter.

"I wonder how Fletcher's dinner went. Did you know he had a crush on Marjorie in middle school?"

"Those two will have us believing in true love. Certainly sounds like a strong feeling."

"People who believe that love is the strongest feeling obviously never hated anyone." Catherine smiled, suddenly stopping in the middle of the wildflowers and ferns, provoking Jesse's inquiring glance.

"Could you please wait for me here? I have to pee. Please."

"Again?" Jesse widened her eyes. "You peed twenty-five minutes ago."

"I'm unable to go on living if I don't pee right now. It will be the end of me."

"You seemed fine three seconds ago."

However, Catherine was already gone. Jesse shook her head and grinned. She seized the opportunity to rest on one of the fallen logs, determined not to create additional pressure on this sensitive matter with more words.

Jesse couldn't help but wonder what Catherine was like five years ago, ten years ago, when she was still able to trust, before her naïveté met with people. What had she been like with Chloe? In those lazy moments and in warm embraces. Jesse couldn't grasp why Catherine would agonize over one person when she obviously could have any. She was genuine and exceptionally straightforward, which Jesse found both amusing and admirable. Sudden silences, gloominess, skepticism. Was that true Catherine or new Catherine? Jesse shook her head again, sincerely sorry she'd be going back to Nashville and would never get to know this hot mess of a woman.

* * *

When she returned, Catherine picked up the conversation as if it had never been interrupted.

"When are you going back to Nashville?"

"It appears I'll have to go back sooner than I thought." Jesse carried on down the trail, an ever-present smile on her face. "Lola is experiencing separation anxiety. She is not used to not having me around, and she's becoming a handful, can't wait for me to be back, but not as nearly as much as Rachel." Jesse laughed.

Good God, this woman has a harem, Catherine thought to herself, not without a sharp pang of jealousy. Moreover, she wasn't even shy about it!

"Before you get any weird ideas, Lola is my six-month-old beagle, and she is ruining the life of my assistant, Rachel, who's watching her."

"Weird ideas?" Catherine ineptly pretended to be shocked. "I don't have any ideas." She waved her hand dismissively.

She was jealous of a stranger's dog. *Goddamn, Catherine!*

Jesse reached for her phone and after a few swipes handed it to Catherine.

"Meet Lola, my little troublemaker."

Yes, Catherine was supposed to swoon over that adorable puppy, but all she could stare at was the tall, voluptuous, blond assistant—undoubtedly a troublemaker as well. Huge, floppy ears and a bunch of cardboard boxes were pushed into the background.

Catherine couldn't imagine Jesse doing much around someone as gorgeous as that assistant. Well, at least not work, that is. She couldn't say she was surprised. After all, she pictured Jesse with someone like Rachel, someone young, someone carefree, someone who looked like she came from the pages of a magazine. Always at her service, no doubt prepared to drop everything after one call. She could even picture their bodies fitting well together, both very confident and not afraid of their desires.

"Luckily, Rach's husband, James, is a ranger, so he gets Lola to accompany him in the back country and get a good run on the trails outside designated wilderness. She would love it here."

Okay, damn! At times, she could have sworn that Jesse could read her mind. Perhaps she should consider simply asking before coming up with all sorts of scenarios regarding Jesse's sex life. So it wasn't Rachel, but surely there was someone else. Or several someones. Jesse was so serene and laid-back that even her brooding self liked being around her. Wasn't that what attracted her to Jesse? She was the joy Catherine lacked. It was hard to imagine other women weren't aware of it. She must have had them falling over her all the time. Even now, Jesse's damn gaze was literally inviting: *I'm the best mistake you'll ever make. Come on.*

Jesse stared at Catherine as if to figure out what she was contemplating. "Please don't tell me you have to pee again."

Catherine grinned at that imploring look.

"I could never here, we'd have to find a more suitable place. We're almost at the top, and the circumstances have to be right. You will learn on our way down."

Jesse grimaced helplessly, and since they only had a few more feet to Devil's Loop she stopped to take a sip of water before they traversed that last incline in silence.

The view from the cliff was breathtaking, and Catherine instantly returned to the present moment.

"Jesse, this is wonderful!" She turned around to soak in the canyon, the soothing creek winding through the lush green, the fresh air. "Thank you," she added, her gaze settling on Jesse's and a playful smile flickering on her face. "Your company is actually not that bad."

"I'm sure you can do better than that," Jesse teased.

"I have a reputation to maintain." She smirked and then paused on Jesse's eyes for so long she thought she had started melting all over the canyon from the heat.

Catherine hadn't thought of Chloe all day, and she couldn't remember the last time she'd been blessed with that liberty. She needed Jesse, of all people, to feel alive again, to feel both safe and free, to stop counting all her disappointments. There existed a tacit understanding between them, which Catherine could not deny, and the moment had arrived to acknowledge the person next to her. Even that fleeting attraction that was so out of her character had to stop. No more foolishly claiming Jesse and detesting every woman in her proximity. Jesse was just being nice to her, like she was to everyone else, and she had to start returning the favor.

"I had a lovely time."

There. That was candid. Now she sounded like a civilized human being, not a jealous nutcase.

"Wait till you try my famous turkey sandwich. It's known to have people wake up thinking of me."

"Too late for that, Jesse." Catherine grinned and playfully wrapped one arm around her. "But I'm still taking that." She laughed and swiftly seized the sandwich with her other hand. Thank God there was always food to distract her from her mistakes.

CHAPTER SIX

They had a pleasant ride back from their camping trip, sharing fun stories of childhood, family, and travels. Now, three days later in Maple Springs, Jesse realized she kept staring at her phone and hoping to see Catherine's name. Should she call her? No, the festival had ended, they ate lunch at Fletcher's, they went camping together, and there was no reason whatsoever to hang out with her again. She should just forget about Catherine. Go back to her life and enjoy what she had. Still, the thought irked her. Despondent, she flung herself on the bed when the phone buzzed.

She swiftly reached for the device.

"Hey, Jesse! Checking in on my fave to hear all about the next great hit."

As if someone had snatched her back from a rapturous dream and plunged her into vicious reality, she gave a sigh of dismay. How did she manage to forget her entire life in three days? She liked her agent, and she shouldn't be this disappointed to see her name on the screen.

"Hey, Annie. Don't worry, I'll be ready for our concert season."

"Did you work on the new material?"

"I found myself inspired, yes."

"Perhaps you should visit home more often," Annie said, as if she could read accurately the thoughts passing through Jesse's head. "How are your parents?"

Jesse always enjoyed touring, the fall season, the multitude of new places and faces that she would meet, the music she'd create along the way. Nevertheless, this time Annie's words left her peculiarly hollow. The standard elation she got when listening about all the places she'd visit simply wasn't there. Ottawa, Spring Valley, Seattle. She knew exactly what every single day for the rest of the year was going to look like. It was as if Catherine reminded her of everything she'd been pushing aside for years, all the fleeing and hiding behind the haze and loud music, all the vapid conversations with people who didn't care to know her or anything that didn't include fancy parties and mindless fun. They all loved Jesse Morgan, the friendly performer, the semblance of glamour, her famous acquaintances, her modern ranch just outside Nashville. A ranch that was fifty acres of sheer solitude.

Sure, it used to be appealing to a twenty-two-year-old. It was flattering that everyone wanted to be around her. Yet after ten years, she just wanted people to like her for herself and not the idea they had of her. Catherine couldn't care less about any of that. With her, Jesse could be that same person from ten years ago, before some other life took over and some other Jesse started mingling with people. She could not recall any other person outside her family who treated her just like her old self, with whom she could be so candid, so liberated. Not that she helped herself when she moved to Nashville and, mesmerized by the opportunities, surrounded herself almost exclusively with busy careerists who perceived her as one of their own, without any intention of getting to know her outside their fun times and barbecue hangouts. Apparently, a lot of money can buy you a lot of loneliness. Even her small town started viewing her more as a performer than the kid who used to live around the corner. Jesse never wanted any special favors, lavish festivals, or incessant whispers as she walked down the street. She craved being seen for her character, not her name, and the only person in the entire town of Maple Springs who appreciated her as a human being was a brooding French woman with a nervous smile.

Jesse rolled over and gave a sharp sigh.

Why did she need Catherine to remind her of all that? Could she come up with an excuse to see her again? She was a choreographer—perhaps she missed dancing. Jesse wasn't much of a dancer, but it could have been a valid excuse. Too bad there was not a single decent place to dance in a fifteen-mile radius.

Those two days she spent in the woods with Catherine infused her with freedom that was almost addictive. She could be vulnerable, she could be dirty, she could be real. Now Jesse wanted more.

Catherine had left everything behind in France, only to sit in a dusty pottery shop. What kind of freedom was required for that? Or kookiness. Jesse smiled. She had never experienced those feelings that made Catherine come here, and she'd never experienced such profound commitment. Had she even tasted life, then? How intense were the feelings Catherine had for Chloe, if her pain was this deep? How exceptional was her love, her loyalty, her devotion? For the first time, Jesse felt she was missing out and not on just anything, but rather her entire life. She'd penned so many love songs without ever having truly loved. Writing about longing, dark desires and loss, she surrounded herself with beautiful women to draw a house and doors and windows around her solitude. Jesse wanted to desire someone, to so profoundly yearn, that one day a single act would make all the difference between love and hate. Yes, she wanted a complete loss of control.

"Are you still there?" Annie's voice startled her.

"Yes, yes, I'll be back soon."

Damn French woman. It was about time to stop thinking about her. Her thirty-second birthday was a few weeks ago and the older she was getting, the more pensive those days made her. That had to be it. Jesse enjoyed her travels and her life. She should just return to Nashville without reflecting on the numbing sensation that she was missing out. Feelings were overrated anyway.

CHAPTER SEVEN

It was well past seven in the evening, but the temperature still lingered in the upper eighties. Catherine handed a cold drink to Fletcher and leaned back in her chair. There was not a cloud in the sky and only the faintest whiff of breeze, yet she had her silence again. A distant elk bugling was the only sound filling the air, and it evoked such a wonderful sense of tranquility that Catherine thought she could slumber for hours right there on that porch.

"Thank you, sweetie." Fletcher took a sip and cheerfully added, "Also, thank you for being so sneaky at the festival and inviting Marjorie over for lunch."

"It was obvious she likes your company, Pépé. I never doubted you." Catherine grinned, and his gaze settled on her with interest.

He was a tall, slender, distinguished-looking man with pale blue eyes and neatly combed silver hair. His pencil mustache and crisp, starched shirts evoked a proper gentleman from a different era, and Catherine wondered how it was possible that he looked exactly the same thirty years ago when he had read her bedtime stories.

"Uh-huh, but you do doubt love," he teased.

When she moved here four months ago, Chloe was the last thing Catherine wanted to discuss, and Fletcher understood enough not to bother her with questions.

"It just doesn't seem worth the struggle to find it, that's all," she remarked softly. "Perhaps it's not for everyone."

"I spent forty-two wonderful years with your grandma. Nothing compares to that feeling of belonging to someone for so many years. She was everything I ever wanted in a friend and companion. There is nothing in the world I'd wish for you more than to discover that feeling."

"Thank you, Pépé. *Mémé* Debbie did always understand dating better than anyone my age."

The man's wistful laugh brought a tender smile to her face.

"What we had together was worth every ache. You don't need to find millions. One person is all it takes."

"I just don't believe in that anymore, Pépé. Or at least not for me. There's seven billion people in the world. Not mathematically wise to believe someone will want to be with only one."

"Not everything's completely rational. For example, I can tell you like Jesse." He eyed her, amused.

"Jesse?" She was stunned.

"It doesn't have to be complicated, Catherine. She's a nice girl."

"Pépé, you know I love you and I understand your matchmaking skills are challenged by the lack of options in this town, but setting me up with someone who lives a thousand miles away and can't even name all her girlfriends is not the way to go about it."

"Cath, I love having you here. I understand that someone hurt you, and you don't want to talk about it, but you need to be aware of everything you're giving up on."

"Actually, I'm aware of everything I gave up to conform myself to someone else. I don't need anyone to feel good about myself."

"Of course not. Doesn't mean you can't have fun."

"So we're not talking about love anymore?" Her lips broke into a smile.

Fletcher shook his head and chuckled.

"You're rebellious, just like your mother. I swear, that woman is fifty-three and still out of control, equally defiant, stubborn, doing her thing and not minding the consequences."

"She's a sculptress living in Provence. I'd say she's got a good life."

"And having more fun than you," Fletcher joked, leaning forward. "Yet, I bet that's about to change," he whispered, looking over Catherine's shoulder with a smug expression.

Catherine stared at him in bewilderment.

"What do you mean?"

"Well, don't turn around, but I guess my matchmaking gods might actually be listening. Jesse's coming over, so be nice."

Catherine figured this was just Fletcher's way of teasing her, but she didn't dare move nonetheless. She could not come up with a single reason why Jesse would be visiting, and she wasn't the least bit prepared to see her, talk to her, or handle her attraction. After their camping trip, she just assumed that Jesse would disappear and go back to Nashville, or have fun with some of her local girlfriends. Yet, when she heard the creaking gate open and close, Catherine realized she'd have to turn around.

Fletcher was not teasing her, and Catherine got an instant confirmation that she was not prepared to handle the adorable smile of Jesse Morgan. She froze as Jesse's blue eyes settled on her. The singer was wearing a red-striped sailor shirt and quite possibly the sexiest pair of jeans ever, yet despite her confident manner, Catherine could sense the hesitation in her step.

"Hey, Jesse!" Fletcher jumped to his feet and embraced her.

"Hi, Fletcher, Catherine," Jesse replied, her eyes never leaving Catherine. "I wanted to see you before I left," she continued, stroking her hair. "Plus, Joe is having a disco night tomorrow, so I wanted to check if you might wanna come. I can't guarantee his choice of music will be that elegant, but it is a chance to dance." She made a barely perceptible pause. "I thought Catherine might miss that."

The fortress Catherine built around her pathetic frailty suddenly didn't seem so high. Jesse thought she might have missed dancing. She could feel her foolish heart melting.

"What a lovely idea!" Fletcher exclaimed, suddenly stoked. "We haven't had that here in years."

No, she couldn't possibly be contemplating *having fun* with Jesse. Of course, she could argue that there was no danger in having fun with someone who would soon leave and who didn't care to begin with. Wasn't this an ideal opportunity to *try out* the new Catherine? The one without illusions.

Could she trust herself that much? It was enough to catch a glimpse of Jesse's forearm, and her mind would swiftly denude every remaining inch of her skin. She would dissolve into desire so fierce it brought peace and oblivion. Jesse's one smile would take away the entire world. Could she stop before things went too far? Jesse looked at her unsuspecting, and if Catherine had any ego left, at times she could swear Jesse wanted the same.

Catherine tried to shake off her runaway thoughts.

"Are you going to dance?" she asked instead and finally locked eyes with Jesse. Even in front of Fletcher, that damn woman didn't shy away from holding a deep, intense gaze.

"If *you* ask me, I will." Jesse's laughter was effortless and Catherine felt her face flush hot. Jesse turned to Fletcher and casually asked, "Fletcher, are you joining us tomorrow?"

"I already made other plans." He cast down his eyes demurely. "But I'm certain you two are going to have a great time. Oh, no!" he suddenly shouted as if he forgot something. "Our dinner is burning." He put his hands on his head and ran inside the house.

Subtle, as always.

"So, just to warn you ahead of the village dance, Catherine, I only ever drink Sprite and I have a soft spot for Roy Orbison. Totally takes away my control."

"Your delicacy astounds me." Catherine grinned.

"Well, you saw me naked, so I figured I could share that as well."

"I did not see you naked!" she denied with a determined smile.

It was too goddamn dark.

"Sure, sure." Jesse sighed, and a wily, luscious raspiness in her voice was as vulnerable as seductive. "Oh, darling, what can I do, for you don't love me, and I'll always be crying over you." She paused, a stern expression on her face. "Crying over you."

Seeing those playful, warm eyes, Catherine couldn't help but laugh.

Jesse had an air of perpetual affability, with a genuine, serene smile indicating life was but a playground. The complete opposite of Catherine. Jesse was primal freshness to her arid soul. Nothing this woman said should be taken seriously.

"Left your baby behind on Blue Bayou?"

"I'm impressed, French, in a very dark, pathetic sort of way."

"Do you want to join us for dinner?" The question was out before Catherine could think better of it.

"Oh no, thank you, I'm on my way to Joe's. Just thought I'd stop by to see if you wanted to join me tomorrow."

"You know I love parties."

"You do. And you love people," Jesse stated with her airy disposition, and they both chuckled. "Want me to pick you up?" She gazed at her thoughtfully.

"Of course."

"Eight sounds good?"

"Sounds great."

"All right, well, I'm looking forward to tomorrow. Bye, Fletcher!" Jesse shouted in the direction of the man who just reappeared at the door holding a dishcloth.

"Hey, stay for dinner!"

"No, I gotta go, but I'll see you tomorrow."

Jesse only winked at Catherine and, maintaining her perfect poise, she turned and left.

This will not end well, Catherine thought, yet a broad, contented grin appeared on her face. *Damn.*

CHAPTER EIGHT

When Catherine showed up at the door in a seriously provocative red dress, Jesse's breath caught. How was she supposed to be wise around *this*? The red dress hugged the woman in all the right places, revealing her perfectly sculpted butt and long legs. With the flirty, ruffled hem, Catherine resembled a wild poppy, entrancing her and relieving her every pain. *What?*

Keep it together, Jesse.

With the slightest amount of makeup, smelling fresh, and seemingly in good spirits, Catherine let her dark hair fall down over her bare shoulders and her sultry, avid gaze settled on Jesse. Staring into those lively eyes was a temptation Jesse couldn't resist. She could easily let herself be seduced by the elegant and subtle games those eyes played with her, exploring the agility of her spirit and the confines of her imagination. That woman looked like damned Aphrodite, seashells and all, her stare still fixed on Jesse. Yes, Catherine was trying to kill her, and that might have been preferable to whatever feeling this was. If she started imagining things now, it was going to be a very long night.

They walked two quiet streets to Joe's and sneaked in unobserved. The boisterous crowd was packed around the bar, while the other part of the barnlike structure had been turned into the dance floor. Even with dim lighting, there was no doubt they were the only two people under fifty. Jesse found them a spot at the corner of the bar where they could have some privacy and watch the dance floor.

"So what would I need to do to get you to sip bourbon with me tonight?" Catherine placed her hand on the countertop and motioned to the bartender.

Jesse held her eyes with hers, a smile firmly in place.

"Alcohol suddenly looks tempting."

"Perfect, so I will get us shots now, and you figure out what you want from me later."

Lord have mercy. Okay, Catherine, no double entendre there. That damn tongue of hers came out as she smiled, and somehow every emotion Jesse ever had multiplied.

"What can I get you, ladies?" The bartender leaned across the countertop.

"We'll have two of your famous apple pie bourbon shots." Catherine held Jesse's gaze, tiny wrinkles appearing at the corners of her sparkling eyes.

"Even for Jesse? Thought your vocal cords don't appreciate alcohol," the man asked, gazing intently.

Jesse tilted her head and with a tender resignation motioned to bring it on. They both quickly downed their drinks, and the man quietly mixed two more in front of them.

"Since you're drinking, this is for your girls in Tennessee, Thelma and Louise," he added, serving their drinks and then swiftly turning to a high-spirited group of impatient ladies who had been waving their glasses for a while.

"Well, we gotta drink for your girls in Tennessee." Catherine chuckled, resting her dark eyes on Jesse, this time without any tension.

"Thank you. Thelma and Louise are my goats." She smiled and noticed Catherine choked on her drink. She should stop doing that to her. "Mo's father has a farm here, so I took two baby goats from them last year."

"I didn't know you had a farm."

Apparently, picturing her in dirty boots with mussed hair and surrounded by goats elicited the most delightful laugh she had ever heard. God, must be the heat from the shots kicking in.

"I'm a country girl, I have five goats, four llamas, and two horses," she replied, trying to regain her focus.

"Is Rachel taking care of them as well?"

"Uh-huh, I'm a one-assistant kinda person." She leaned forward, exploring intently the sensual features of Catherine's face.

There was something about Catherine that, as much as Jesse endeavored to maintain her own impression of insouciance and rationally downplay the woman's significance, she could not control.

"What kind of music do you like?" she asked briefly to stop her consuming thoughts.

Catherine paused, carefully weighing her words.

"I like J.Lo." She finally shrugged.

"No way I'd see you as a J.Lo fan." Jesse laughed.

"Her energy is spectacular, she's very talented." The fierceness with which Catherine stood up for her heroine both impressed and amused Jesse.

"I actually know J.Lo," she remarked.

"Really?"

"No, not really, but we won our Grammys the same year."

"You won a Grammy?"

"No, not really, but neither did your J.Lo." She pouted.

Catherine playfully shoved her.

"This is becoming too easy. I will have to try harder." Jesse smiled, realizing it was becoming more strenuous to separate Catherine from her gaze, from her thoughts, and she was certain those alert eyes would notice the trembling muscles beneath her skin, the pauses in her breathing. "But, come on," she added quickly to regain composure. "I've spent all of my life waiting for tonight, so…wanna dance?"

The bar blasted old-fashioned beats, but Catherine readily jumped to her feet and before Jesse had time to react, the woman was among the crowd, offering her body to the music and losing herself in passionate, wild movements.

As Jesse walked slowly through the dance floor, Catherine approached her, dancing with her arms behind her back, open and uninhibited, and Jesse quickly came to rue those shots because she could not help but merge the images of that dance with images of Catherine's naked body under the mountain sky. She had to remind herself to blink, as she could not force her eyes away from that body, endeavoring to follow her thousand moves in a second, so many movements at once, so much life, so much passion unleashed from her limbs, from a grumpy, muddy woman from the pottery shop. Jesse couldn't tell if it was five minutes or five days as she stood watching Catherine dance, enraptured, captivated by her moving body.

Who knew it was so easy to be happy? It took so little, almost nothing. One look, one spark. Her swift turns in the dark.

Undoubtedly, if this had been any other woman, she would have already had her pressed against the wall of some dark corner, but with Catherine, she wanted more, and her effort not to punish her with herself and her life was very conscious that entire time. While she was taking control of her hands, her mind was a different story. She could vividly anticipate every thrilling sensation, every move their bodies would make if she only leaned in, if they kissed, if Catherine slid her hands under her shirt…yes, there would be no more control.

Luckily, the sound of Catherine's voice stopped the surging thoughts.

"I think we need more shots," she exclaimed. Before Jesse could even react, Catherine had disappeared into the crowd.

Thank God she was lucky, because she certainly wasn't smart. Her treacherous mind just hit pause on Catherine's hands under her shirt and Jesse hoped this breather could help her block her brain from projecting Catherine's dance moves to under her sheets, because she could focus on little else.

When Catherine returned, she was carrying four more apple shots, but the real inebriation came a few songs later when

Jesse recognized the soft notes of her favorite singer. *Bold move, Catherine.* Nothing like Roy Orbison to make a girl second-guess her decision.

She took a deep breath. Her favorite singer, a dark room, a beautiful woman, and...feelings? *Just what I don't need.* Slow-dancing should have been number one on the list of things not to do with Catherine now. Okay, maybe not number one, but it was up there. Yet, she couldn't help herself. Locking her eyes with Catherine immediately, she stretched her hand toward her.

"Now we have to dance."

She should have made a run for it, that's what she should have done, yet it was utterly impossible to look away. Jesse felt distant, impervious, and indifferent to everything that wasn't Catherine's gaze, her touch. The woman took her hand and leaned in closer to her cheek. Both seemed acutely aware that after this moment they wouldn't be able to go back to indifference, both knew one was aware of the power held over the other, of intimacy binding them.

"Now." Catherine lowered her voice to a whisper and gently tucked a blond lock behind Jesse's ear. "I want you to lose control."

Jesse groaned. There wasn't a single part of her body that wasn't ruled by that soft accent, by the hand pressed at her lower back, by Catherine's beauty, by her clever, dark eyes. It would be so easy to hold her tightly against her body and discover her lips, their intensity, let them steal every inch of her naked body. The woman brought her cheek up even closer and leaned on hers, and Jesse barely restrained herself from letting out an audible moan. This would never happen with one of her flings, so what was Catherine then?

It used to be so easy with others that meant nothing to her. When she was younger, she was not ashamed to admit she was no saint. She could wake up next to a girl and move on to someone else the same day without a care in the world. Then somewhere along the way, every woman became like the one before. None would intrigue her, none was indispensable, none would inhabit her mind once they left the room. Most of the time, they wouldn't even have sex. She would send them home barely with so much as a kiss. After a while, every such encounter became predictable, futile. Jesse felt as if she had seen it all, and she gave up on the hope that she would ever feel the excitement of losing control of her mind. Feelings became a useless, dull weight.

She hadn't been on a real date for over two years and then, in only a few days, a morose French woman had managed to infuse her with a freedom she forgot she had. Somehow her life multiplied near Catherine—it was like living a million different lives, a new one in each nerve Catherine brushed, each in its own delirium.

Jesse had no idea which invisible strings were keeping her hands steady. Tangled in Catherine's hair, her only focus was the soft movement of their bodies and Catherine's hands, as if they could hurt even with a caress, even with a gift. The notion that Catherine wanted it as badly only made the whole ordeal more unbearable. With their cheeks being so close together, she could almost feel the corners of their lips brush, but she knew she couldn't afford to make such a mistake. She didn't want her only for tonight.

Goddamn, doing the right thing was difficult! How had she started to care about this woman in the first place?

She whispered quietly, as if talking to herself, "I don't even know your last name."

"I thought that was your standard. Why would you need my last name?"

"So I could go home and secretly stalk your Instagram, of course."

"You don't need my Instagram, you have me here."

Jesse whimpered. "Unfortunately, I can't have you here all the time."

Catherine beamed, holding an intense gaze, and Jesse never realized she had such firm control over herself. She fought with the force she was not used to, and she sure hoped it was alcohol. If this song went on for another second, she would have Catherine's tongue on hers, and any chance she ever had of convincing her she was not a sleazy womanizer would go down the drain. Catherine had to sense how much she wanted her, but she knew they wouldn't stop at a kiss. No one would ever understand how arduous it was to hold her body, her revealing dress pressed against her own, and then pull away.

"It's Des Lauriers," Catherine finally replied with such a strong French accent that Jesse only heard a light buzz.

"Thank you. That will narrow the search down to about three billion," she managed to utter. "I figured you'd be hard to find."

Their eyes held for a long moment before Catherine smiled. *Help!*

CHAPTER NINE

When Catherine had left to grab a few more apple pie shots moments earlier, the first person she encountered at the bar was the owner, Joe, himself—and boy, did he have news for her.

"I'm having such a great time, Joe. Great idea!" she said innocently.

The man grinned and immediately motioned to the dance floor with a bottle of bourbon.

"It was actually Jesse's idea. She said I should try something different on Fridays, and it looks like she knows business. I admit I needed some convincing, but she helped me set up the whole thing."

Luckily, she had no vanity left, otherwise Catherine would have melted right then and there.

"What are the chances we hear Roy Orbison tonight?" She gave Joe an imploring look, deftly grabbing the drinks with one hand, ready to return to the dance floor. "Please. Something like, 'She's a Mystery to Me'?"

The man's smile did not fail her, and when Jesse enfolded her in her arms for the slow dance, Catherine decided that for once she was going to have fun. Granted, she couldn't tell if Jesse would kiss her, if she wanted her to, and if yes, why. It was so complicated, but she couldn't deny that even without the kiss something happened between them, something changed. Jesse's cheek lingered close to hers, so close that Catherine was afraid to breathe, dismayed that one touch would release an implacable torrent of lust. Her every nerve seemed to live on Jesse's every move. Why was she so convinced that this would be something she could control? Just because Jesse would leave, because she would be a thousand miles away, because she was a womanizer? Yes. Oddly, Jesse's girlfriends reassured her. She knew she could never fall for someone like that again. If only she had realized that with damn Chloe, she never would have ended up here. However, she refused to lament her past choices. Instead of trying to be perfect, instead of trying to be enough, she only wanted to have Jesse's body underneath her, on top of her, in front of her. Considering she had done everything right her whole life and it never brought her any good, now she only wanted to do something wrong—and then forget Jesse ever existed. Catherine knew very well that she needed her only for tonight.

She sensed Jesse's leg in between hers, slowly swaying, their bodies moved together gracefully. How much did she have to drink? Only a few days ago, she was certain she would never be so weak as to act upon her attraction, and now she was negotiating with herself, arguing that tasting Jesse's lips wouldn't really mean anything. Just as she thought she could sense Jesse's breath close to her tongue, their warm kiss, an upbeat two-step blared through the bar.

Sonofabitch! Catherine never hated country more. Fate could not be this cruel to her. As if the first country songs of the night encouraged the crowd, they started approaching Jesse, asking for a dance or a few words. Jesse seemed particularly radiant and beaming as she took time to be cordial with everyone but remained close to Catherine, who cursed her luck, still vividly feeling Jesse's hands on her sensitive back. *C'est bien ma chance!*

The rest of the night passed in a cozy blur of lighthearted tunes, and she never got another chance to dance next to that silky cheek. However, Catherine seized the occasion to take over the dance floor, never forgetting the apple pie shots. She had no idea how many she drank, but she was feeling the daze, and she prayed it was from the alcohol and not Jesse's proximity.

One song was quickly turning into the other, and midnight caught them both by surprise. Catherine wished there was a longer way home, but they sauntered those two streets to Fletcher's house in a fearful anticipation of goodbye. The whole evening of longing looks and accidental brushes was not more difficult than that walk home. The entire street—hell, the entire damn town—bore Jesse's scent, and Catherine wanted her more than she wanted her next breath. Just when she gathered sufficient courage to start playing with the buttons of her blouse, Jesse abruptly embraced her, embraced her longer than usual, and then without any hesitation turned and hurried home. The damn woman couldn't get away fast enough.

CHAPTER TEN

The only sensation Catherine had was a throbbing headache. Unfortunately, that wasn't enough to forget her last night's failure. She pressed her eyes with her palms in an attempt to stop the pulsing and the surging thoughts of shame, humiliation, and guilt, but to no avail.

For once, she wanted to be spontaneous and disregard the consequences. Moreover, she was certain she felt something shift between them as they danced. She would catch Jesse staring when she thought no one was looking. How on Earth could she have been so wrong?

Catherine covered her face with a pillow, seeking to erase every bitter trace of recollection. Jesse could have had her last night, but she didn't make a single move. Even after Catherine showed her interest in every way imaginable, even after she was positive she spotted longing in those ocean eyes, Jesse did nothing. Nothing. Could she have possibly read the signs wrong? Catherine never imagined she'd feel so connected with someone again that she'd be ready to bare her body before them.

If Jesse had made a move, she wouldn't have heard no, and she had to be aware of that. Yet, this carefree womanizer decided to let her go as if she was not worth the effort.

She'd tried to use all the remnants of her charm, but that failed miserably. Jesse was simply bored to death in this drowsy village, and she'd taken pity on her. Meanwhile, Catherine got hooked worse than an impressionable teenager. Would she ever learn?

"*Mon Dieu*, what have I done?" she exclaimed out loud. She recalled playing with Jesse's hair and instantly buried her face deeper into the pillow, hoping it would erase the image. Was she out of her mind?

She knew love was difficult, but never knew flings were as well.

"*Alors*, this stops now."

Catherine despondently threw the pillow aside and spread her arms when she heard a light knock. Soon she saw her grandfather's head peeking through.

"Um…someone's here asking to see you."

Her eyes snapped open. Was it Jesse? She could blame it on the alcohol, but she couldn't deny that something between them changed, and it wasn't just drunken stupor.

"I'll make some coffee," he added and quickly withdrew from the room.

What was Jesse doing up this early? What was the time anyway? Only eight? The girl was insane. Why wouldn't Fletcher say it was Jesse? What was he up to? Catherine hurried to brush her teeth and stopped briefly in her closet, deciding what to put on. She didn't want Jesse to think she was getting ready for her, nor keep her waiting. Perhaps she just stopped by to say she was leaving. Slipping on a shirt, Catherine hurried down the stairs.

Yet what she saw in the middle of the room stopped her in her tracks. She didn't envision this in her worst nightmares.

"Bonjour, Catherine!"

With her hands in her pockets and a look of obvious disquietude, staring back at her was Chloe.

Just as she started forgetting and feeling traces of life again, why did she have to show up now? Fuck her luck! Catherine closed her eyes, hoping Chloe would no longer be there when she opened them, but instead she heard her timid voice.

"Your curls look so pretty. Did you finally give up straightening your hair?" Chloe asked.

I'm too hungover to deal with this now. Catherine hopelessly sighed and slowly opened her eyes, hating her life.

For a brief moment she hesitated, unsure if she should just return to her room, before realizing it was probably time to face that part of herself.

"I was hoping we could talk," Chloe continued.

So much anger and so much hatred, and now she didn't know if there was anything in the world she wanted to say to Chloe. It wouldn't change a damn thing anyway.

"Here's coffee for you girls." Fletcher placed the tray with coffee and cookies on the side table right next to Chloe and then with visible unease hurried toward the garden. Although he most certainly knew more than he let on, Catherine refused to bother him with her drama right now. She would have plenty to say to him later, in private, for pulling that not at all innocent I-don't-know-who's-at-the-door stunt.

"Thank you, Pépé. I'll be back in a few." She motioned Chloe outside, stopping only for a second to chug some coffee before setting it back down on the tray.

Her head was falling apart, and she reckoned death would have been easier than the conversation awaiting her. There was only one place that was open this early, and it would be mostly half empty for breakfast. Yet, walking five long minutes to Bertha's Bakery seemed too onerous, so attempting to shorten the time spent with Chloe, Catherine only sullenly jerked her chin to the black Tacoma.

"Just get in the truck. Don't worry, I won't kill you yet."

She drove those two blocks in absolute silence, ignoring Chloe's attempts at small talk. Not that she intended to punish her with silence, but her head was throbbing so insistently that her thoughts tumbled over each other.

Of all the days, the woman finds this morning to talk. She tried to quiet her thoughts as she pulled into a parking space in front of the diner.

The place was almost empty, so Catherine quickly settled at the counter, avoiding getting too comfortable and attempting to reduce the unpleasant conversation ahead as much as possible. She still couldn't bring herself to look at Chloe, frightened it might become real, so she started turning menu pages.

"I rented a lovely cabin up the road. I can't remember when I last heard silence like that." Chloe strived to keep the semblance of normal while Bertha was pouring them coffee. When she left, Catherine gave a heavy sigh and finally met Chloe's gaze.

The woman was observing her with somber, gray eyes but still smiling. Her dark hair fell to her shoulders, and Catherine could vividly recall all the times she woke up entangled in that fragrant hair, all the times those arms pulled her back to bed, the way her soft lips felt on her shoulders. Inevitably, she recalled their last encounter, unfamiliar laughter, unfamiliar arms around her, and all the ache, disappointment, and disgust came racing back.

"Listen, Catherine..." Chloe looked as though she was struggling to find the right words. "At first, I wanted to give you some time and then, of course, I started looking for you everywhere. I went to see Jacq in Angers, Edith in Toulon. It was like you disappeared off the face of the Earth. I visited your mother in Provence. What a lovely lady! I helped her get her garden ready for planting. It appears roses will be a hit this season." She cracked a tender smile. "She said she might come visit for Christmas, as she misses her home."

Listening to her persist with casual chatter, Catherine was fuming.

"Do you say these things just to infuriate me? Because you're really doing great."

"No, Catherine, I love you." Chloe captured her eyes with angst. "I can't give up on us. I'll move here if I have to."

"Nice. Tell me, is Gabrielle moving in with you? We could resume our bridge nights and talk about my mom's flowers!"

She hadn't meant to raise her voice, but now she felt she was yelling.

"Catherine." Chloe's gaze was imploring. "I'm sorry, I do want to talk about what happened. Please. I'll do all those odd things Americans do. I'll eat pumpkin for dessert, chew ice, and enthusiastically greet strangers. Finally discover the true meaning of baseball. I'll have a pill for everything." Chloe seemed genuinely dejected, which pacified Catherine's ire. She understood that even arguing was futile. It wouldn't change what happened. It was over.

"How is this a bakery if they serve sausages and bacon?" Chloe looked around.

"You really want to touch on every most insignificant subject in the universe?"

"It is most curious." Chloe was turning around with interest, and Catherine helplessly shook her head.

"When Bertha started this thirty-five years ago, it was a bakery. In the meantime, they decided to expand but keep the name because they became well-loved in this middle of nowhere."

Chloe nodded.

They sat silently for a minute or two as Catherine took a long sip of coffee, hoping to stop the throbbing. She just wanted this to end. Chloe's bubbly personality and attention deficit disorder had never bothered her. In fact, she considered them adorable up until that attention turned to the girl they met at the board games club. For so many years, Chloe's mind was a labyrinth where both would get lost. Still, one of the things she admired the most about the woman sitting next to her was how her emotions flew wild, out of proportion, and could not be contained. She would wake her up at four in the morning, anxious, because she remembered she hadn't told her she loved her that day, and then proceeded to talk about blueberry cupcakes. When she came across a story of elephant abuse, she refused to get out of bed for three days. She would get annoyed just waiting in a line for something. Fibers in fabric that most people wouldn't feel would itch her to tears. There were three TVs mounted on their living room wall, all three for Chloe. Even if she appeared absent, she remembered everything Catherine ever said. Her raw emotions and wandering mind that Catherine loved so much eventually turned to someone else. She couldn't blame Chloe for being who she was, she simply should have known better.

As they sat in silence, an older gentleman approached the counter to grab one of the magazines from the stack.

"Hi, how are you?" Chloe shouted enthusiastically, disconcerting the old man. He only gave a polite wave and bowed his head before returning to his table.

"Too much?" Chloe's eyes fixed on her again.

Catherine nodded, and a smile of despair flashed across her face. Just accepting the fact that it was over appeased the whirlwind of resentment, bitterness, and exasperation. As she stared at Chloe, she knew for certain: it was over. There was nothing she wanted to hear, nothing she wanted to say.

"I really screwed up this time, didn't I?" Chloe said, their eyes locking in a long gaze.

For as much as she longed to please her shattered ego, Catherine had to admit with a heavy heart that the burden of guilt didn't rest solely on Chloe. She loved the woman's amusing unpredictability, but she had realized a long time ago that their relationship was too much work, more than she could handle. If she'd only had the courage early on, perhaps she wouldn't have been punished with such an ending.

Chloe would constantly ignore the future and the consequences for the present. She couldn't even trust herself, and yet Catherine somehow thought she should. As it turned out, she wasted all those years chasing a lie. A lie she kept telling herself. It was her fault. There are some promises you should never believe.

"That you did. But sometimes you have to do what's wrong to know what's right. And we weren't right."

"No, Catherine, there is no one else like you. I know this is not what you want to hear, but Gabrielle is actually a nice person. But she's not you. No one is. I made the worst mistake I could have made, but nothing has changed for me. You're still the only person I could ever love. You're still my best friend."

"I wish your words held value now, but they don't." Catherine shrugged helplessly, startling herself by the calm of her voice. There was no quiver, no pause, no hesitation in admitting defeat. She'd loved this woman for five years, all the while sensing it would come to this.

"I've always liked that about you." Chloe smiled with a sigh. "I never had to guess what was on your mind because you always spoke your heart. Your heart has no brakes. You have no brakes. You always go heart first, and you are a complete opposite of everyone I've ever been with." She paused for a minute, her eyes fixed absently on the counter. "That day…I wanted to run after you, but I knew you'd kill me, and I didn't want you to spend the rest of your life in prison for my idiocy."

"Oh, I would have murdered you for sure."

"We're safe now, right?" Chloe dodged playfully.

"I don't know. Do you plan on talking about how wonderful Gabrielle is?"

A broad smile lit up Chloe's face.

"You're one of a kind, Catherine. It terrified me that you had all this power over me, and that I couldn't imagine my life without you. It's scary. It's scary not having control over your life, but I'm not here to look for excuses because what it comes down to is—you didn't deserve that. You've been an ideal partner to me for the past five years. You're such a sweetheart, you're supportive, you're funny, you're kind, you're considerate, and I'm sorry. Not having you near when I go to sleep is the worst kind of punishment. That, and knowing how much of a disappointment I am to you."

"My expectations disappointed me, not you, Chloe," Catherine replied in a soothing tone, hoping this conversation would end soon, once and for all. She didn't want to be reminded of that agonizing defeat anymore, and she imagined that just sitting here was an atrocity to Chloe. The woman had to be in constant motion, needing things to happen immediately, constantly playing with her phone, always on the lookout. "That's what people do, I get that. You don't have to apologize for the shortcomings of the world. I should have known better."

"Catherine, please don't say that. You did nothing wrong. I'll give you all the time in the world, and I'll win your trust back."

"You don't get it, Chloe. I don't trust myself anymore."

"It's not your fault, Catherine. How do I make you see that?" Chloe grasped her hand tenderly. "I miss my best friend."

Catherine sighed quietly and withdrew her hand.

Could this day just end?

CHAPTER ELEVEN

Her first thought after waking up was Catherine Demonier, or whatever her name was. A bright smile was fixed on Jesse's face as she stretched in bed lazily, reminiscing about every move, every word, every gaze from last evening, and every recollection broadened her grin. Resisting that woman was damn hard, and Jesse was proud of herself.

Admittedly, she probably slept the entire night with that ludicrous, silly smile on her face. Catherine liked her, she thought, letting out a contented sigh. Catherine didn't care about her name, she was not fascinated by her status, and she had no respect whatsoever for her career. Yes, she was perfect.

Jesse could not recall if she ever felt such attraction to someone, attraction that was not just physical. Catherine excited her mind. There was passion in her speech, in her gestures, in her hatred, in her whims, and Jesse couldn't imagine ever being bored next to her. Most women she'd gone out with were fun, but she would wake up in the morning to find complete strangers. She craved their conversations to be as intense as their sex, but instead she would find herself anxiously planning her escape.

With Catherine, she wanted every encounter to last longer. One moment, one look, one breath longer. Jesse couldn't just go back to Nashville and pretend like nothing had changed in her life. Catherine found parts of her she didn't know existed, and Jesse refused to give up on that. Yes, she'd visit Maple Springs more often. She'd ditch the world and Nashville to get to know this woman better. No more thinking. Jesse sensed that was the right thing to do. Catherine possessed a naïveté and innocence that Jesse longed to preserve, so different from the corruption she got used to in Nashville. Even if it ended in a disaster like everything else, it was worth a shot.

That fresh rapture incited other new sensations in her body, more precisely a devouring hunger. Jesse was not used to alcohol, and she was definitely not used to hangover hunger. Giving Catherine time to rest, Jesse decided she'd stop by later and see if she wanted to go horseback riding with her to Williams Landing, or for a swim. Catherine could have all the time she needed. She was not in any rush.

In a bid to avoid the probing of her prying family into hangover, hunger, and night out, Jesse concluded it would be wise to sneak out. It was well past eight and Bertha's Bakery seemed tempting as her only solution. She took a quick shower and, anticipating the taste of Bertha's scrumptious dishes, hurried to the diner. Jesse was so content that she planned on scarfing down the biggest burger without any guilt. Hell, she might even add onion rings or sweet potato fries with all the ranch she could get. Bertha must have had the worst hangover of her life when she came up with that Diablo Burger. Just the thought of pepper jack, Swiss, cheddar, and Asiago stuffed in that burger made her salivate.

Yet once Jesse opened the door of that diner, she quickly forgot the hangover, the hunger, and the onion rings. She stood transfixed by what she spotted in the left corner of that room. Was that Catherine sitting at the counter? She had her back turned to her, but that was undoubtedly her hair, those were the shoulders she could still feel under her fingertips. Jesse's gaze instantly wandered to the person sitting next to Catherine. The diner was half empty, and it didn't take long to realize the two were conversing in French.

Jesse's heart instantly sank. When did this happen? There was no doubt who the woman facing Catherine was. She was undeniably attractive, resembling Catherine even, with piercing eyes and wavy hair flowing over her shoulders. In all honesty, Jesse had to admit the woman was a smoke show. Tall, confident, wearing a stylish leather jacket, with a delicate jaw and a winsome smile that clearly possessed Catherine, she struck Jesse as one of those women who are tough to handle. A handful. But beautiful.

The sorrow that seized Jesse was a very active emotion, and in a matter of moments it hurt like hell. She couldn't grasp when this had happened. They got so close last night and she could have sworn Catherine felt the same. Though she couldn't understand a single word, it was apparent that the moment between the two women was very intimate.

Damn, it was not fair. Not fair. She really liked this one.

Jesse didn't know how long she stood there, petrified, but she needed to react fast or Catherine would notice her, and that was the last thing she wanted. She wasn't sure if she should just sit in the remotest corner or try to slip out. Conceding she couldn't bear watching Catherine with her girlfriend, she had taken two quiet steps back when Bertha spotted her and exclaimed, "Jesse!"

Instantly, Catherine turned around, stunned, the expression of incredulity lingering on her face as she stared at Jesse. Walking to the counter, at a safe distance from the couple, Jesse rigidly raised her hand in greeting. She could hardly think of a moment that inflicted more pungent disappointment.

"My sweet Jesse!" Bertha leaned over the counter and pinched her cheeks. "What can I get for you today?"

"I actually won't be eating in, I just wanted to grab a tuna sandwich." She smiled softly, attempting to hide herself behind a tall barstool as much as humanly possible. The first thing she would do when she got home would be to throw away these damn sweatpants and the washed cap. What the hell was she thinking wearing these? Chloe looked like an ethereal nymph, and she seemed like a forlorn teenager with no social life. Although she was utterly unprepared for the moment, Jesse knew she didn't want to show how affected she was or put Catherine in an uncomfortable situation, so when Bertha turned, she nonchalantly settled her gaze on Catherine, tipping the bill of her hat.

"Hi, Jesse." Catherine finally found her voice. "You're up early."

And your girlfriend couldn't possibly be any prettier, now, could she? Jesse forced herself to keep her eyes on the couple.

"Oh yeah, I have some important stuff to take care of down in Boulder."

"Buying more goats?"

"Oh no, I already have more than I can handle."

"Hey, doll, here's that tuna for you."

"Thank you, Bertha. I needed this. Well," Jesse muttered and turned her eyes back to Catherine and Chloe. Watching them together, at each other's side, she realized with despondent resignation it was only a matter of time when Catherine would return to Paris with Chloe. Surely, if Chloe was here and if they engaged in a civil dialogue, they were working on their relationship.

Jesse held Catherine's gaze for one long second, knowing she might never get to see her again, before gently adding, "It was certainly nice running into you, Catherine. If we don't see each other again, I hope life serves you salt, carbs, and peanut butter."

Chloe sat through the entire encounter with a courteous expression on her face, allowing them to chat, only slightly nodding as Jesse was leaving.

Once outside, Jesse tossed the bag in the back seat of her car and rested her head on the steering wheel. She had no appetite whatsoever. Perhaps the hangover could just kill her.

She needed to get out of this damn place yesterday.

* * *

Seeing Jesse so cool and undisturbed, Catherine wondered how much she must have drunk last night if she could have even for a moment imagined there was something between them. Jesse stumbled upon her and Chloe without so much as a flinch, with her charming smile, airy as ever.

Also, buying more goats? Where did that come from? She cursed her traitorous brain. The woman coldly rejected her last night, so she probably didn't care what Catherine said anyway.

"I never knew there would be such cuties in this town." Chloe smirked and interrupted her thoughts.

"Really?" Catherine looked at her with reproach.

"I'm sure you had the same thought at some point." Chloe chuckled. "Objectively speaking, she has regular features, memorable eyes, nice cheekbones, sumptuous lips, and is what you would define as pretty."

Chloe never wasted time when it came to observing people. Before she found her with Gabrielle, Catherine had to admit she never felt threatened or suspected any of those women interested Chloe. On the contrary, Chloe had made it a point to dissuade them, at least within Catherine's earshot.

"I'm a photographer, you know, I have an eye for detail." Chloe paused for a moment, waiting for Catherine to look up. When she finally did, with a teasing smirk, Chloe added lightly, "I think you like her."

"Oh, you don't get to say anything there."

"No, no." Chloe rapidly raised both arms. "I would never." She dropped her gaze for a second and then locked her eyes with Catherine again. "But you do have a little crush," she added and started laughing.

"Shut up!" Seeing her entertained, Catherine broke into a smile. "No, I do not like Jesse. You idiot."

"I am the world's worst girlfriend, but I can still read your face, Des Lauriers." Chloe nodded contentedly.

CHAPTER TWELVE

Catherine paced up and down nervously. The woman she loved for five years, her cheating ex, had managed to track her down to this lost town at the edge of the world. Furthermore, she was intent on proving she deserved another chance. She'd quit the job she adored and then charmed Marjorie into being her guide across the Colorado wilderness. By now, she'd probably made friends with the entire village and recounted every detail to everyone willing to listen—including, for some reason, Fletcher, who had inexplicably let her in without warning and still owed her an explanation. Yet, Catherine couldn't care less about what Chloe was doing. Why?

Because she was a moron, that's why. Once you don't see Jesse for seven days, you'll forget all about her, she kept trying to convince herself. Yet seven days had elapsed since their last encounter, and her temporary weakness was still all she could think about. Even now, she imagined, there was someone else next to Jesse. Catherine envisioned it without any affliction, almost as a punishment. She saw them laughing together, nimble fingers undressing Jesse. Her slightest sigh, her every nuanced expression would start a thousand torments.

Catherine stopped by the window and shut her eyes, striving to erase every recollection of the festival. Was she really that vain? Unable to forget because she'd been spurned? She walked over to her desk and sat down in front of her computer. What if...

A devious instinct took over.

So her heart was not made of stone. What if she just took a peek into the hell known as Instagram? Not even sure what she expected to find—certainly not a girlfriend, as she knew Jesse better. She was not the type to trivialize her feelings with sappy Instagram posts—no, she kept those to herself. Besides, it would be bad for business to let other girlfriends see the girlfriend. So, what did she want to find? If she was hoping for a brooding, dejected Jesse, well, no one ever showed that on Instagram. No, people there sat on the edge of a cliff and dwelled in the sunset. All lives were perfect and all relationships loving until you read they divorced and got a restraining order against each other.

What if she just wanted to glimpse her deep blue eyes or that mischievous smile? Indeed, was she prepared to see Jesse happy? Could a photo convince her that Jesse was not special, that she didn't have all that power over her, and that she was basically just a stranger? If only she uncovered something there that would make her despise the woman. Wouldn't it be nice to see Jesse mercilessly hunting baby fawns or lying in the bathtub full of one-dollar bills? It didn't really sound like Jesse, but a girl could hope. Yes, she wanted to despise her for something when rejection obviously wasn't enough.

After Catherine successfully assured herself that she would open Instagram for the sole and noble purpose of subsequently loathing the magnetic singer, she flung herself onto the bed and promptly grabbed her phone, entering those dreaded words into the search bar. *Jesse. Morgan.*

The first six photos that opened included one that showed her face up close with those big blues taking over. *She certainly is cute. Merde. Well, everyone's cute on Instagram.* Searching through all the likes was not an option, obviously, at almost 60,000. She would hardly manage to find the stunning jackpot girlfriend there. Also, a stiff competition, judging by the comments. Despite the sudden urge and destructive curiosity to devour as many images, as many stories as humanly possible, Catherine anxiously held her breath, careful not to leave any trace of her shameful presence. She rubbed her temples and sighed to release the tension.

Okay, should she start over or simply scan the latest posts? Unfortunately, there were no hunting photos and the bathtubs filled with cash were nowhere to be found, so that plan went down the drain, so to speak. No sign of Jesse's dark side unless you actually considered making country music dark side, and Catherine was sure she could make an argument there. Anyway, there was a picture with a woman she recognized as Dolly Parton—Catherine didn't actually live under a rock—a few photos of her performances; a few from the farm, including the last one from three days ago; a few with kids, most likely nephews; and a whole section dedicated to Lola, the beagle, and the mayhem she brought along as well.

Seeing her after seven days, distant and in good spirits, was thrilling and utter torture at the same time. Catherine succumbed to the mental agony and anxiety of scrolling quickly down and back up, dreading spotting her with someone else, even if it was three years ago, and discovering what it looked like when Jesse actually fancied someone. Oh, Jesse was really missing out on her. Jealousy, bitterness, vanity, and doubt. Catherine shuddered. She never expected it would be so difficult to put an end to something that never even started.

Jesse hadn't posted often, but in the last seven days she posted two very nice photos. One was taken in a place that resembled a tropical paradise, and the other showed two beaming llamas on what appeared to be a charming ranch. Tropical paradise seemed like a place where you would take someone special, so she focused her attention on that photo. Catherine observed every little detail in the background as if it was going to reveal some huge secret that everyone else missed. However, all her assessments and analyses of shadows, surroundings, palm trees, and reflections in sunglasses revealed nothing. She scrolled up and paused on the last post for a bit. Her gaze fell upon one of the grinning llamas. She zoomed in, attempting to discern…was that a hand? Someone was petting the animal, yes, and that was definitely a female hand! Finally, she had something. That was not Jesse's hand, no, and almost positively not Rachel's, as she was taller in stature. This hand was smaller, fingers paler, and no wedding band, so definitely not Rachel.

"I wouldn't let just anyone pet *my* llama," she determined quickly. "But also true, I'm crazy, and I stalk other people's llamas."

A sharp twinge of jealousy was not what she was hoping for. Why did it matter whose hand that was? Absolutely no difference. Still, what were the odds of Jesse posting old photos while in fact sitting on a couch eating Cheez-Its?

Catherine tossed the box aside and brushed the crumbs off her shirt. Why was she being crazy? She threw the phone onto the bed. So Jesse obviously went on with her life uninterrupted and had a female companion on the ranch. Good for her. She couldn't say that was not what she expected, but it was still a little disappointing how predictable Jesse was. It was foolish to seek any meaning in those few moments they spent with each other. Jesse was a performer, and a part of her job was deceiving and feigning feelings. Perhaps this was exactly what she needed. A confirmation that their everything—or rather, nothing—existed only in her head. She'd better figure out what to do with Chloe.

Exhaling deeply, Catherine buried her head in the pillow. How was she not wiser by now?

CHAPTER THIRTEEN

Jesse stared absently through her study window, out onto the gently rolling hills and the sun setting over a distant creek. With animals safely tucked in their barns, the old dirt road leading to the house made the whole lot seem abandoned, and Jesse only wished she could be left alone with her eroding misery.

Barely paying attention to what her ambitious agent was recounting, she was eagerly awaiting the moment she'd finally be alone. Not that she particularly enjoyed that solitude, no. It was mostly hell, consisting of incessant envisioning of Catherine and Chloe together, in every corner, at every opportunity. One moment they were sneaking around Maple Springs, another they were cuddling on a plane or in front of the TV, watching whatever Jesse was watching at that moment. She sighed softly and squeezed her eyes shut. Yet Catherine was still there.

She must have returned to France by now. Even if Jesse managed to overcome her feeble ego sometime in the future and watch Catherine happy with someone else, she was an ocean away. Why did they have to meet?

Three days spent in Key Largo with her sister dragged tediously, and Jesse couldn't wait to finally ensconce herself in the remotest part of her ranch, far from everyone. Her mind remained unaffected by the surrounding sounds, voices, and stimuli, and sensed only the burden of angst and desire to be somewhere else as her soul remained immobile, mute, and intangible to everything that wasn't Catherine.

Her intense longing was swiftly outlining the lovely contours of the sultry French woman, and her naked silhouette was firmly imprinted in Jesse's eyes. She was classy, confident, quiet, and unforgiving, effortlessly floating through Jesse's mind. Just when Catherine's naked figure emerged in front of her eyes again, Chloe's hands appeared on that delicate skin, and Jesse closed her eyes tight to chase away the images. *This has got to stop.* She couldn't fathom that such a common emotion like jealousy could provoke such a profound agony. Perhaps she should do what Catherine would expect her to do: invite a woman to stay over, occupy her mind and hands with someone else. However, as much as she wanted to come up with a name, she dismissed each one, irritated. No, it would just show her what she was missing. She needed to forget the damn French woman first.

"—but I'm pretty sure three days will be enough to get you over to the West Coast. Okay, you haven't heard a word I said." The agent put on her glasses and fixed her gaze on Jesse.

"No, I got it, in three days, I'll be ready. I can't wait, actually."

Annie paused and slumped into her chair, likely waiting for Jesse to notice the weight of silence between them. Jesse could be reticent but rarely without a smile, which she normally didn't have to use as cover for not paying attention. She spied Annie's brown eyes peeking over her glasses and finally decided to fully engage.

"What?" She grinned.

"Please don't keep me in the dark."

Jesse chuckled before absently shifting her gaze out the window again.

"Life could be beautiful. It's just the little things that never happen."

"Like what?"

"I met this girl."

"Oh my God, I never thought I'd live to hear that."

"It doesn't matter anyway. She's seeing someone else."

"You have to tell me everything and start from the beginning."

"She's irritable, distrustful, and has to pee every five minutes. Talking to her is effortless, natural. I don't even have to try to have a conversation with her, we just…talk. She's insufferable but cute, serious but vulnerable, and there is just something about her that's hard to forget."

"Did you tell her that?"

"I'm not crazy, am I?"

Annie sighed. "So you say she has a girlfriend?"

"Yeah. I completely misjudged the situation there. I was certain there was something going on between us, but she must have been buzzed. Now I'll never see her again and for some reason, that's too hard to accept."

"Why don't you call her?"

"What good would that be?"

"You obviously care about her. As a friend."

"It would just hurt more to listen about her girlfriend. I've never been the bigger person." She smiled broadly. "Also, I don't want to talk to Catherine, hoping her relationship fails and her heart ends up broken again. I'd like her to be fulfilled. Though I don't know how that could be with someone who cheated on her." She rose to her feet and walked over to the window.

"So your solution is to stare silently through the window?"

"Hey, I might write a song or two."

"Artists are allowed to be happy, you know?"

"I wish." Jesse huffed out a laugh and in her carefree manner came to sit next to Annie. "When will you be joining me?"

"I won't be with you until Charleston."

"Great, we'll go grab shrimp and grits together. I'll show you this place I discovered last time, looks like a submarine, you'll love it."

"So we're good with your schedule?" Annie worried her lip. "You'll have November and December completely empty to focus on your new album."

A reassuring smile played on Jesse's face, hoping to placate Annie's obvious fear that she hadn't heard anything she'd said.

"I can't wait, Annie."

"And don't you think you switched the conversation around! I want to know more about that woman."

"So do I, but it's not going to happen." She let out an amused laugh and wrapped her arm around Annie. "Come on, time we grabbed a drink."

CHAPTER FOURTEEN

Catherine placed a long, straight board across the pond and centered the level on it. After a few moments of deliberation, she shifted the board to a new position to make sure all the pond edges were level, then noticed the familiar figure of her ex-girlfriend leaning against a tree. Catherine quickly tucked her hair behind an ear with the back of her hand as her eyes fell to the ground. Her little trowel, plants, ropes, shovel, and rake were all scattered around her as she was on all fours digging her way through dirt. Chloe always knew how to pick the worst possible moment.

"I promise, I was going to offer help." Chloe finally spoke, locking her gaze with Catherine's. "But your back was so sexy arranging those rocks that I dared not interrupt the magic. It would have been so wrong."

With a sigh, Catherine shook her head, got up, and started sweeping dirt and debris from the liner that was cast aside, occasionally glancing at Chloe. And she thought the Festival was torture. *Bordel de merde.*

"You're still not helping, and the magic is long gone." She gestured to the other broom, trying to sound indifferent.

"That's debatable." Chloe grinned, and Catherine could feel those commanding eyes running up and down her sweaty frame. "You know, I remember you, five years ago, standing in the corner of that gallery in Le Marais. In a white summer dress, viewing a single painting for hours. I wondered, 'What kind of person could spend hours staring at the same painting?' until I realized I'd spent hours staring at you. You were a form of art I could not resist. I never thought I'd see the day you would be gardening, but there was something primal in this version of you that I didn't want to stop the spectacle."

This unwelcome conversation had definite potential to veer in the wrong direction.

"Chloe," Catherine finally uttered, pausing in her frank, playful eyes as if she could sense the woman's imagination going into overdrive. "In a way, I appreciate you coming over here because it is something that deserved a closure, and I wasn't brave enough to face it myself. But we are not getting back together. I just want you to know that."

"I don't expect anything." Chloe's carefree glow beamed back at her. "I adore hanging out with you," she explained, grabbing a large rock and lifting it, peeking over her shoulders, left and right.

"What are you doing?" Catherine sighed.

"Trying to establish if my shoulder blades look as sexy as yours under tension. I could totally get into this." She marveled with a contented smile, still glancing over her shoulder, lifting and lowering the rock to better track the muscle movement.

Catherine snickered and threw her head back in despair. She wouldn't get any work done next to Chloe. The woman's mind was an eclectic mess of tangled wires that kept connecting to a different switch. Just being around her made Catherine lack focus. She used to be so sure she would never live another love that wasn't Chloe. She adored her beyond reason, every single detail of her face, her silliness, her tousled hair every single morning.

Where did they go wrong? Contemplating her, she saw Chloe was still the same chaotic person she met five years ago. To a certain extent, she'd even missed that cheerful nonchalance over the past few months. Chloe had always been an animal of untamed, deep emotions that Catherine admired and loathed at the same time. Yet, it was all bound to vanish. Love was not built to last. It was a shiny jewelry window that we observed to distract ourselves from reality, knowing we'd never get what was inside. Just having something to fantasize about made life more bearable.

Catherine still couldn't look at Chloe without recalling that day in April and those unfamiliar arms around her. She used to love Chloe's frivolous vanities, her curiosity, her talents. Yet, perhaps it was time to stop believing in everything people told her. She should never make that mistake again.

"Why are we digging this hole?" Chloe asked. "It's far too nice to simply be my resting place. I imagine you could just throw me over into the river. This is too much work, really."

Catherine threw her hands up in despair, stifling a laugh.

"God, I wish you could just shut up."

Chloe looked at her mischievously and then in her best sensual voice said, "If I had a cent for every time you said that, Des Lauriers, I would buy you a damn hole, and we wouldn't have to dig."

Catherine whimpered in quiet despair, tossed aside the rake, and headed toward the porch, somewhat grateful that Chloe had always been a master of dissolving tension.

She leaned back in her chair, offering Chloe a glass of wine.

"Have you befriended the entire village already?"

"Almost. I only need to win you over. But I think I'm doing great."

Catherine grinned.

"You certainly haven't changed, Chloe. How is your painting coming along?"

"I feel very inspired. Marjorie is teaching me to release my fears and embrace my mistakes. I feel so American already. Did you know that she used to live in Sri Lanka? And she had an exhibition in Tokyo once? Her second husband was from Japan. She even drove me down to Boulder to purchase all the painting tools."

"I do have the second part of her fan club right here." Catherine beamed, gesturing at the house. "She is a lovely lady."

Chloe hesitated for a second before settling her eyes on Catherine again.

"I would truly appreciate if you could come over to my cabin to see the paintings I've been working on," she said and then quickly corrected herself. "Or if you prefer, I could bring them to you, of course, not a problem."

"Oh vanity! I don't mind being alone with you, Chloe. I could stop by tomorrow," she said lightly, astounding even herself. The sooner Chloe realized all this was futile, the sooner she'd leave. Anger was too intense an emotion and could often be mistaken for care. What Chloe needed to see was resigned indifference.

CHAPTER FIFTEEN

The first thing in the morning, just to cross it off her list, Catherine's Tacoma was speeding, leaving a pillar of dust down the mountain road to the right of Bedford Creek. The cabin Chloe rented was a ten-minute drive east of Notgrove Peak. It was the only property available for rent in Maple Springs, and Chloe had managed to negotiate a terrifying six-month lease. Catherine certainly prayed it wouldn't take that long. Not that Chloe bothered her, but she could not discern if she loathed discussing the past or the future more. Both felt like watching a movie with a horrible ending, and one *Titanic* was enough suffering, thank you very much. To rely on the reason of someone as unpredictable as Chloe wasn't much, but Catherine perceived today's encounter as another chance to assert her credence.

Two moose grazing and basking in the beauty of nature on the side of the road finally brightened up her face. In only under a month the whole side of this mountain would see the explosion of fall colors, and Catherine could vividly recall the last

September she experienced that spectacle. It was fifteen years ago, right before she headed to college, when Mémé Debbie was still alive. She steered her car deeper into the forest, crackling over pine needles and fallen branches, and soon spotted a log cabin with a yellow door a short distance up the slope.

Chloe waited, sitting at the front porch stairs, with a smile, dressed in an elegant green shirt and shorts, her hair pulled up into a sleek topknot, and she looked like she did so many mornings upon waking up—languid yet immediately in good spirits, something Catherine always admired. Perhaps she really was somewhat on the grumpy side, as Jesse put it, but Catherine never liked talking first thing in the morning.

The cabin had a solid log exterior and four bedrooms, significantly more than Chloe needed, but it offered a nice family atmosphere right from the door. A huge great room with tongue-and-groove ceiling had a full wall fireplace and overlooked a large country porch outside and the stunning Notgrove Peak.

Chloe being perennially restless, Catherine wasn't too surprised to learn about her newfound interest in painting. In the five years since they met, she saw Chloe's hobbies range from tattoo artist to calligraphy to basket weaving. She also displayed a particular enthusiasm for model planes, topiary, and web design. A small den that she turned into her atelier had a rooftop window, and Catherine could only imagine the sunlight gently caressing the canvas and initiating the dance of colors.

"I quit my job and I'm entirely dedicated to this art, so before judging, Catherine, please bear in mind that I'm a struggling artist now."

There were three easels in the middle of the room, which was to be expected. Of course Chloe was working on multiple paintings at once. As she approached the pieces, Catherine let out a resigned sigh. All three paintings depicted her.

"I think you could use more diverse subjects."

"Indeed, I was going to ask you to pose for me in front of the lake."

"No, Chloe, not me," she said quickly, shaking her head and forcing herself to look at the painting standing in front of her. "Why would anyone buy a painting of me?"

"Hmm, yes." Chloe observed the painting sternly, as if in deep contemplation. "Wives could get madly jealous, you are too gorgeous. Anyway, I'm still weighing whether I could even sell a painting of you."

Resigned, Catherine shook her head again. It was classic Chloe. Flippant, childish, and lost. Her gray eyes looked so alive and the spark in them would be like a wave carrying you to high seas, far from everyone, so Catherine toned down the exasperation.

She glanced at one of the paintings again. It wasn't even that terrible, apart from the fact that Catherine's ears appeared pointy.

"Could you fix my ears?"

"What about them?"

"Look, I'm Spock."

"If Spock were cute—"

"I don't have pointy ears!" she insisted, outraged.

"No, of course not." Chloe flashed her best irresistible smile. "My hand quivered."

"You couldn't draw vases like every other beginner?"

"I don't want to stare at a vase every night. I'd much rather look at you and hate myself."

Chloe took the painting off the easel. "Here, take one."

"Chloe, why would I want to stare at that every night?"

"Because it's a pretty sight. Tall, dark, unusual, reflections of a brilliant mind in those eyes. Girls dig Spock."

Catherine gave in to a laugh of despair. Chloe would spark a million dreams in a second, and a second was all it took to extinguish them. Their apartment at the foot of Sacré-Cœur was full of Catherine's photos which Chloe would carefully hang wherever she'd manage to find an inch of space, with some pinned to the closet door and bathroom walls. Catherine recalled how she despised coming home and opening doors to her own ghosts lurking from the walls, yet whenever she attempted to remove the photographs, sorrowful Chloe would glue herself to the wall and dissuade her, kissing each of those captured moments.

Viewing that painting of herself on the easel, she wondered if Chloe and Gabrielle found a special gratification in the fact that she was watching them from those walls. It was dirty lovemaking at the shrine. It must have made Gabrielle feel important, knowing that's where Catherine slept, knowing Chloe could see hundreds of Catherine's pictures around and still succumb to the impulses of the desire for her. When it mattered, Chloe didn't notice any of the photos. They didn't stop her. Moreover, it must have been a peculiar pleasure to get Catherine's silent approval from the bedroom walls.

Damn, she didn't miss that apartment one bit. She detested every single spoon, every glass, every piece of clothing, every chair, and every little detail Gabrielle had laid her eyes on. Including Chloe's body.

Evidently, she'd never forget. Catherine scoffed at herself, and her gaze rested on Chloe silently. She assumed Chloe felt truly remorseful now, as she never was good at considering consequences beforehand. But what about her? Catherine expected more from herself. She deemed their intricate course together to be profound, yet it was interrupted in an instant, with one mistake.

"What are you doing, Chloe?"

"What do you mean?"

"Why are you here? What do you want?"

Chloe paced the room nervously.

"I want you to forgive me," she said, practically stuttering. "I want things to be as they were. I want us to go back in time. I want a lot of things, apparently."

"That's not how it works."

"I know and I guess…I thought if you saw that I was still that same person you fell in love with back then, perhaps you'd want to be my friend and then, with time, because I'd give you all the time you need, I thought…I thought I could win your trust back."

For the first time, Catherine almost felt sorry for Chloe. It was only a bit easier than the hatred she felt so intensely a week ago.

Chloe continued, "We were good together. We laughed every single day. We supported each other in all our dumb ideas. We can still read each other's mind."

If anything, Catherine wished she had gotten out of that relationship sooner, before it came to all that. She was aware of her own limitations, and doubts and illusions had no place in her life anymore. Trust, loyalty, and togetherness, what was she thinking? It felt more like sitting in a hair salon, staring at herself in that dreadful mirror, discovering one hundred new ways of ugly while that little voice was screaming, *"You don't need a haircut, you don't need anything, it's all in vain anyway!"*

Chloe noticed Catherine was unresponsive, her look unfaltering, and she astutely seemed to realize she shouldn't push her luck.

"I'm sorry, I don't want to bother you. Can we resume talking about my paintings?"

Chloe never handled serious conversations well, or at least not for long. Her constant escape into verve could brighten the darkest of days, and that was something Catherine had loved dearly for years. If she were able to feel anything at that moment, she'd still be fond of that vivacity.

When Chloe turned to pick up a new canvas, Catherine finally spoke.

"We are not getting back together, Chloe. If you like Maple Springs, you can stay here for as long as you want, but don't do it for me. We are over."

Chloe nodded, remaining in silence for a few moments, as if only then she became aware of the weighty consequences of her actions.

"I'd like to help with your bird lake nonetheless," she said at last with a serene smile. "You must admit we did have the prettiest little bonsai, no thanks to you."

Catherine chuckled.

"Fine," she said. "Help if you want."

"Thank you, I'll paint you a vase." She winked and the familiar mischief played on her face.

More interactions, sooner ending. Catherine was convinced it wouldn't be long until she'd have her tedious old Maple Springs back.

CHAPTER SIXTEEN

You never think to look up a "Healthy Alternatives to Falling in Love" list until it's too late. Jesse's mind got stuck with the irritable French woman, at all times of day and night, so she could only pray the upcoming tour would provide some distraction.

Jesse and her band usually arrived at a hotel the night before the show, and she loved catching a new city under the dying flames of the summer sky. It was just after seven and Richmond glimmered with the freshness of late summer rain, immersed in the final rays of sun. She quickly recalled the four previous visits to the city, the Richmond she would discover alone—at dawn, green, luscious, somnolent. The little restaurant on the riverfront, the secluded bench hidden away deep in Maymont, the nutty aroma of freshly brewed coffee in Church Hill. But she also enjoyed the Richmond that Ashley had showed her— open, quirky, and exciting. Ashley was a thirty-something blonde working as a manager of the nice hotel where Jesse was staying. The first time she offered to show her around town, the second time she flirted with her, not in the least bit timid, and a few years ago they went a bit further in their flirting. Still, what used to be a harmless amusement now loomed as a source of discomfort, and it was all that fiery French woman's fault.

They pulled up to the hotel as a light breeze was dispersing the earthy scent of the wet soil, rain, and atmosphere, but all Jesse sensed was that she already missed her bed. As she got older, all the luxurious rooms, breathtaking architecture, and elegant decor could not replace her own mattress and sheets, and now, more so than ever, she longed for the solitude of her ranch and her thoughts. As torturous and French as they were.

If only she could casually flirt and joke around with women, without any ulterior motive, just for fun—enjoy their humor, wit, and grace. Instead, each attempt only reminded her of the futility of her existence and unmistakably pointed out what she was missing.

Last week, she asked her uncle to go buy a mug at Fletcher's shop and report back if Fletcher still had help there. The uncle reported being served by that cute French girl, which caused in Jesse an immediate overflow of euphoria. Surely that deserved self-reproach, not the will to jump for joy. Yet suddenly, everything around her was infused with life, enthusiasm, and color. She knew she shouldn't care, but the fact Catherine was still there, still in Maple Springs, offered an obscure hope. However, her uncle could also not understand the sudden interest the French had in their small town, as he reported seeing another French girl with Marjorie. Being reminded of Chloe certainly caused less enthusiasm.

So, both were still there. If Chloe was close to Marjorie, and if Marjorie was still seeing Catherine's grandfather, it could only mean the four spent a lot of time together. They probably double-dated three times a week. Why hadn't they returned to France yet? So many questions, and each sparked a new curiosity, each posed a new quandary. Perhaps Catherine had stayed a bit longer to help Fletcher with a sizable order and would be leaving in a few days. Perhaps it would be easier if she just freaking called her and asked.

Jesse sighed. This wasn't like her.

The last few days, she'd catch herself thinking about wanting to have Catherine in her life even if it meant listening about her stunner of a girlfriend making all her dreams come true. Her mind stubbornly refused to forget, and she just couldn't stay away. All that drivel that she wanted to lose control, feel, love, all of it was foolish self-deception. That auditorium tomorrow would be packed with people with whom she could explore her lustful biology, pleasures, punishment, pain. Yet, she wanted all that not with *a* woman, but rather *the* woman—and that woman stayed in Maple Springs with her hot girlfriend. This was probably not an appropriate thought to entertain right before a concert, yet Catherine somehow rendered every other woman insignificant. Furthermore, as Jesse revisited the list of songs she would be performing, she realized with horror that Catherine would fit each and every one. She recognized her in every verse, even the ones she wrote fifteen years ago for a guy named Brett she met briefly at a gas station.

Given her track record, Jesse probably wasn't the right person to render Catherine happy anyway, but why couldn't they be friends? Or why couldn't she just freaking forget?

As a friend she would be required to become an expert on Catherine's infatuations, dalliances, intense feelings for other women, her sex life, and her girlfriend's dazzling personality.

Yes, they could never be friends.

She might need to give advice that she felt was beneficial to Catherine, even if it broke her own heart. Did she have that level of selflessness? Jesse imagined the worst part wouldn't be listening to how ecstatic Catherine was next to Chloe, but rather how miserable she was, and wishing she had the power to change that, wishing Catherine's happiness depended on her. If only it were up to her. Was she prepared to feel so helpless? No, yet the alternative was to not have Catherine in her life at all—and that seemed inconceivable.

Jesse made a firm decision. *I'll give her a call tonight.*

Did she need a reason to call? What if Catherine happened to be with Chloe at that particular moment? She sighed, exasperated. Was she completely crazy? No, actually, *doomed* was the word.

She failed to notice they'd already reached the lobby and Ashley was waiting there, with open arms and a mysterious smile. If she could just forget the French woman for the next few months.

CHAPTER SEVENTEEN

It was a balmy Thursday evening and the sun was about to set behind Scarlet Peak when Catherine finally sat in her chaise to enjoy the view and the first sip of her cocktail. After a long day of work in the yard, it was a treat to lie back and let her gaze wander round the wondrous wilderness while savoring the soft feel of rum's enticing caramel fragrance on her tongue. Thank God her strong and healthy distrust of humankind pushed her closer to nature because this was spectacular. The drought brought fall foliage early this year as aspens coyly began to tinge the mountains with shades of gold, orange, and red, and Catherine took deep breaths, absorbing the view and the sweet vanilla scent of ponderosa pine. The tree came with the lot when Fletcher purchased it forty years ago, and on warm days it would unmistakably exude the delectable scent from the cracks between slabs of bark and pervade the stillness of their yard. She was almost sorry that in a matter of weeks all this beauty would vanish, stolen by the supple and nimble-fingered whiteness.

"We did well today, didn't we?" The old man appeared at the door with a glass of whiskey and ensconced himself in a rocker next to her.

Quietly pleased, they watched the pond gleaming in the September sun and the few oak leaves already floating on the water's surface. With a lot of care, Catherine arranged the plants that were to brave the harsh winter, and Fletcher was eagerly awaiting the colorful fish that would soon inhabit the pond.

"It was a lot of fun creating this with you." Catherine glanced at him with soft eyes. Welcoming and warmhearted, Fletcher simpered under his silver pencil mustache as his head rested on a cushion. Seeing him rocking in his chair, relaxed and with his eyes closed, Catherine had to wonder if she was becoming a nuisance. His relationship with Marjorie was coming along nicely, and maybe it was time she found her own plot of land and left him to his familiar tranquility. If she managed to find a lot of her own, it would promise to be a challenging project that would keep her mind occupied for a few months. By then, she might be ready to go back to France. Maple Springs had always been a temporary escape, and Catherine missed having a purpose, a career. That feeling when dance betrays your character and your restrained desires, when the body becomes an instrument for your most subtle moods, telling stories of sensuality and power just by where you keep your eyes or how you place your hand.

"Pépé, I really like it here. This place offered me a quietude I never believed existed. If I had faced Chloe in Paris, we would have ended up killing each other. Maple Springs calms me down. This street calms me down. This view bears away every unease."

"Well, except for the festival, of course. That was an infernal abyss, huh?" Fletcher giggled and Catherine readily returned a smile. Apart from her pathetic attempt at flirting and a perplexing desire for a night of debauchery, the festival hadn't been all that insufferable.

The recollection of that night made her squirm in her chair with embarrassment. Who knew she had it in her to fall for country singers? Thankfully, there weren't many witnesses to that misery. Maple Springs was a torpid little town in the Rockies with barely two thousand inhabitants, and Catherine found its secluded, immense, luscious natural beauty to be a generous companion. Its resilience and its kindness would whisk away every worry, every mistake, and every impatience. She felt safe in its green, fresh arms as they kindled her every cell with serenity. Yet, it may be time to give Fletcher his life back.

"I love hanging out with you here, but I thought perhaps I could find a place of my own and give you more privacy."

"What? Nonsense. I like having you here." Fletcher straightened in his chair at once, and his pale blue eyes pierced her as he briefly paused. "You don't want to go back to Paris?"

"Soon, definitely. But for now I prefer it here."

"Not giving Chloe another chance then?"

As Chloe had promised, she indeed arrived earlier that morning dressed for work and carrying two paintings. She kept her word and brought a painting of a vase, although the vase was embellished with Catherine's face. The other, for Fletcher, was the portrait of Catherine with pointy ears, except Chloe had added a raised hand with the palm forward and the fingers parted between the middle and ring fingers. Fletcher couldn't help but laugh whenever he looked at the picture, and it seemed Chloe's spirit and energy inevitably endeared her to everyone who met her. She spent the day navigating picks, shovels, and rakes with ease as she helped Fletcher install the aerator while Catherine kept her distance, engrossed in shrubs and rocks, leaving the duo to their chat. Catherine was occasionally annoyed seeing them goof around together but was resolute not to allow it to question her convictions.

"What good would that do?" Catherine replied calmly and took another sip, gazing at the distant mountain peaks.

"You are too young to give up on something as special as love." Catherine was quick to roll her eyes at the mention of that word. "No relationship is perfect. You learn to live with their flaws."

Fletcher spent over forty years married to a witty, skillful tailor in her Mémé Debbie and Catherine understood the emptiness he must have been feeling after her death. It might have been easier to pick up where she left off with Chloe and know exactly what she had and didn't have rather than chase illusions and relive uncertainties all over again with someone new at some point in the future. Yet Catherine couldn't bring herself to believe in that.

"I don't mind her flaws, Pépé. I accepted her clutter, her loquacity, her putting empty containers back in the fridge. I even accepted what she did with Gabrielle. Still, I don't want to live my life doubting everything she says, and that's what I would do. It would be hell for both of us. Even today, when she said she was going back to her cabin after ten hours of work in this middle of nowhere, I can't say I truly believed her. I don't want to be that person. I'm better off without her. I'm sure she means well most of the time, but she can hardly trust herself."

The old man was tenderly gazing at her, and as much as she wanted to argue she no longer cared for the concept of love if one afternoon was all it took to erase all the years together, his pure expression full of faith and candor dissuaded her from pursuing the matter further. So she continued, appeased. "Sure, Chloe is funny, intense, and creative, and obviously I wouldn't have spent five years with her if I hadn't loved her, but that's not something I believe in anymore."

"I just don't want you to punish yourself with solitude. I still haven't recovered from the grief of losing your grandmother—I never will. But I would not trade the years spent with Debbie even if it meant a lifetime of desolation without her. Love is worth every risk. You can't live fearing a mistake." Fletcher's eyes locked on her. "When Chloe showed up at the door that morning, it wasn't difficult to guess who she was. I didn't tell you because I wanted you to face it and move on. One way or another. The past is just a sketch. You can color it any way you want."

What would it take to fling her arms around Chloe's neck like she always did, take a breath off her skin, observe her in silence, leave everything behind?

Catherine exhaled deeply. It just didn't feel right anymore. If she were crazy enough to ever again engage in any sort of relationship, it would have to be an indomitable, combustible, arcane, animalistic thrill just like the one she would oddly experience every time she was around Jesse Morgan. She promptly reprimanded herself and smiled at Fletcher.

"Thank you, Pépé. I love you for that."

"I just don't want you to get stuck in this town, because there's no one your age here," he murmured apprehensively.

"Don't worry about me, Pépé." She cheerfully tapped him on the forearm. "I'll go back to Paris, but it won't be for a woman, I can assure you."

Catherine would never again allow anyone to determine her worth or her plans, even if an incredibly sexy country singer wreaked havoc on her mind.

"Fine, and no more nonsense that you're bothering me," Fletcher exclaimed jovially and jumped out of the chair. "Do you fancy some sweet potatoes with chickpeas and tahini?"

"I'll help you."

"No, no, please, stay. You know I love having that kitchen all to myself," he said with a broad smile and went back into the house.

Fletcher had a point. Maple Springs had never been a long-term solution, but for now, it suited her to be far from the world and its cruel sense of realism. Catherine's stare fixed on the pond shimmering under the evening lights and the timid birds gathering around the rocks.

Just as she was contemplating taking a nap, the perfect calm of the evening was interrupted by the buzzing phone. Catherine startled and glanced at the screen. The name that appeared flabbergasted her. Um, no, it couldn't be. *Pas question!* There must be some mistake. Should she pick it up? She narrowed her eyes and then forced them open again to make sure she wasn't imagining things. Still, the same name. The persistent ringing was breaking any illusion she might have had of dreaming. Her heart started pounding loudly, echoing with trepidation and indistinct, dark desires, and she dared not move. If she let the phone ring for a while more, perhaps the woman would realize she'd dialed the wrong number. What if she was calling because she'd left something behind? What would she say anyway? A thousand thoughts swarmed in her head as the phone kept ringing.

CHAPTER EIGHTEEN

The phone rang once, twice, three times. Yet, the only sound Jesse seemed to hear was the wild racing of her heart. With every ring and every beat, her breathing accelerated. Surely, calling the person you like for a friendly chat while she might be around an absolute goddess of a girlfriend had to be the right thing to do. How could that be wrong?

Jesse started sweating, yet it wasn't like her to spend an entire day thinking about someone, so when she finally reached her room and attained her solitude, she deliberated briefly and then grabbed the phone, determined to free her mind of the French burden. Crying herself to sleep was the sanest—and the only—backup plan she had at that point.

She could still sense that rare agony of watching Catherine closely, anticipating her dark gaze, delicate and raw, her senses hidden behind a vibrant slip dress, her blood pulsating through her body, the passion captivating her every move. Jesse recalled every precious detail of their last night together, the flame that arose to extreme vehemence, instilling the beauty of Catherine's face into a force of expression Jesse could not control.

The urge to feel her near, at least with that husky voice, was too fierce, and before she had any time to change her mind, Jesse quickly pressed the call button. If that meant listening about her bliss with that stunner girlfriend and raving about love, so be it. Jesse had no intention of losing such a pure sensation from her life, even if she lived across the ocean. She'd be honest when she'd say she'd like to be her friend. For the most part.

The entire room burned with desire and pulsated in angst, as the phone kept ringing. In hindsight, crying herself to sleep might have been a better idea. Oh well—too late now.

What if she'd left in the meantime? What if she was with Chloe? What if her phone was with Fletcher? Jesse could feel doubt crawling underneath her skin. What if the call went to voice mail? Still, it kept ringing.

Perhaps she should just end the call before it was too late.

Just as she thought the ringing would stop, she heard a hesitant voice on the other end.

"H-h-hello?"

It was Catherine. A sense of relief and sheer delight inundated Jesse's every cell, and she couldn't stifle her smile. Maybe doing dumbass things wasn't so bad after all. Sometimes that's exactly what you need.

"Hi, Catherine. It's Jesse, remember me?"

"Hi, Jesse! Do you honestly think I'll ever forget that horrendous festival?"

Jesse grinned, relieved.

"So you'll never forgive me for that?"

"Among other things, Jesse." Catherine's soothing voice was teasing and playful, and Jesse thought she'd disintegrate.

"Are you still in Maple Springs?"

"Where would I be?" Catherine chuckled softly, which confounded Jesse.

"Well, I thought you might go back to France."

"Why does everyone want me in France?" Catherine gave a hopeless little laugh. "I will go back, but I like it here for now."

Out of nowhere, a strange glimmer of hope emerged and Jesse's chest tightened. She hated hope. She should just ask.

"How does Chloe like it?" Jesse dared to mention the dreaded name and squeezed her eyes shut. Even if she sounded casual as ever, she could hear her own arteries beating in the distance as the entire world waited suspended for Catherine's words. This was the moment to demonstrate they could be friends.

"Chloe always lands on her feet. She's somewhere up in the mountains, having an art retreat with Marjorie. As long as she's staying away from me, I'm not complaining," Catherine replied, amusement in her tone.

"Oh!" An unexpected grin lit up Jesse's face. Could she have misinterpreted what she saw at Bertha's Bakery? Did they get into a fight in the meantime? She attempted to conceal the elation in her voice, promptly reprimanding herself for being such a miserable friend.

"So you didn't work it out?"

"Of course not, I don't believe in that anymore."

And just like that, the ludicrous idea of *friendship* went down the drain faster than it arose. Thank goodness! That never would have worked anyway. Jesse breathed a sigh of relief.

Determination in Catherine's tone was subduing Jesse's agitations, vanquishing her doubts, and awakening singular pride. Not only was this woman ravishing, but she was also damn smart.

"What?" Catherine asked, hearing Jesse chuckle.

"Oh, nothing, nothing, just thinking how Chloe is single now."

"Wouldn't that be a match made in heaven?"

Catherine's scoff made Jesse laugh. "No," she replied. "I'd never trade you for Chloe. You're somewhat temperamental, but I'm sticking with you."

Jesse trusted Catherine when she said her relationship with Chloe was behind her. She'd heard that poise, recalled her firm expression, and she was incapable of doubting her. Now the only thing left to do was to convince Catherine that she, the stereotypical promiscuous musician Jesse Morgan, could be trusted.

That would take time. Some patience. And, quite possibly, sorcery. She had no idea how she would accomplish it nor even how much time she had, but at the moment, she didn't care. Listening to Catherine was leading her to a distant world, at the break of dawn, far from everyone. Their every look, every accidental brushing of their hands, would reveal the bond neither of the two could deny. For Catherine, she'd figure it out.

* * *

Catherine squirmed in her chair. *Do I remember? Do I? Really, Jesse? "How do I forget?" is a much better question.*

She still had a hard time believing Jesse had, in fact, called, and at that very moment laughed on the other end, serenely asking about Chloe. Did Jesse actually want them to be... friends? Just her damn luck.

She regained her composure.

"Chloe was quite taken with you, so you might want to reconsider your last statement."

"Now you tell me, Catherine." Jesse's despair sounded playful.

As any other time when she caught that mischievous tone in Jesse's voice, Catherine's rebellious body trembled, yet she held back a smile, refusing to attach any importance to her words.

"Why is it so unusually quiet around you? Groupies asleep? Harem has a day off?"

"I just rolled into Richmond, Virginia. I'm performing here tomorrow."

"Oh, I bet their hot dog trucks are not as nice as ours and their grumpy French women are not as insolent."

"Nothing quite compares to that experience."

"Have you visited any other interesting places since I last saw you?"

Catherine cursed her possessive curiosity, but Jesse most certainly hadn't stayed alone in that tropical paradise. She considered asking directly. After all, she trusted friendly Jesse would gladly share, but in that case, she would have to admit she searched through her Instagram.

"This is my first concert, and before Nashville I only briefly visited my sister in the Keys."

Damnation, that woman had a perfectly sensible answer to everything.

"Oh, I didn't know you had a sister."

"I also have a younger brother who is playing in a band in Alaska. If you think my music is bad, you should hear his."

Catherine reluctantly had to admit that Jesse's music had her intense spirit, her charming personality, her dazzling smile, her tenderness, her lovable inclination to simple life.

She paused to collect herself. When the hell did she become an expert on Jesse's music?

"You are actually very talented," she remarked calmly.

"If I win you over, French, I don't need anyone else," Jesse said, then broke into captivating laughter, pulling Catherine in as well. "Anyway, Catherine, I want to know what you've been doing."

The truth that she was digging a pond and installing nest boxes for birds sounded everything but enthralling, but she had no reason to devise amusing lies. If she was serious about subduing the weird obsession for getting Jesse's admiration, then she had to recount every little detail about incorporating a few habitats around the pond to attract as many different types of birds as possible. So she talked about the work they did on the side of the pond with trees and shrubs, and the other one that would be more open with rocks and gravel. The following day she wanted to work on the shallow section of the pond all day, hoping to make that the hotspot for the songbirds.

"Did you already add the heater?"

"Fletcher installed the aerator and decided to wait for the heater, so we'll keep an eye out."

"You just made me miss my ranch."

"Where is Lola?" Catherine asked casually, secretly yearning to hear all about the dog sitter, of course.

"You've got to see this!"

After a few seconds, her screen lit up with a message from Jesse showing a video of a pup whose head was stuck in a cookie jar. There were probably some tasty crumbs in it, and Lola had to get every last bit of food. The puppy was still enthusiastically wagging her tail, sticking her head deeper into the jar, when suddenly Jesse walked into view of the security camera. Catherine was left breathless in an instant. Lord have mercy on her soul! Jesse wore nothing but an oversized white shirt as if she'd just rolled out of bed, and her rumpled blond hair was carelessly flowing about. Catherine almost forgot what kind of effect she had on her.

"There were almost fifty cookies in that jar!"

"That's adorable," Catherine replied absently, fixing her gaze on Jesse. Her long, tanned legs captivated her attention briefly, and then she looked up to encounter her bright smile. That really was adorable. Catherine played the video several times as Jesse spoke, barely able to focus. Their effortless chat lasted nearly an hour until Catherine heard Fletcher calling her for dinner.

"Dinner's ready!" he shouted from inside the kitchen.

"Fletcher doesn't want to waste all the food he prepared, so I better go."

"Oh, I envy you for his cooking," Jesse exclaimed and then paused. "Catherine, is it okay if I call you sometimes? I like talking to you."

Disconcerted, Catherine just stood speechless. *Merde*. What was it in that woman that prompted her to curse constantly?

"Of course," she finally stammered. "I promise to keep you updated on the nesting boxes."

As if pulling away from a deep embrace, they said goodbye, and Catherine's mind quickly wandered off to the video of half-naked Jesse. Holy smokes! Dim the lights and turn on Marvin Gaye. What was that woman doing to her?

Not fair, Jesse. Not fair at all.

CHAPTER NINETEEN

Rain was a rare occurrence in Maple Springs, so when she woke up to a torrential downpour on Friday, Catherine saw that as an opportunity to lazily lie around and then curl up with a book. When it finally stopped raining around noon, she talked herself into dressing and walking downstairs to the kitchen. Wearing a slouchy shirt and heavy socks, she descended the stairs quietly, but the house appeared empty.

"Pépé?"

Having received no response, she checked the basement and the shed, but Fletcher had already left for the pottery shop. Catherine leaned idly against the porch railing, absorbing the mountain placidity and freshness around her. If she missed one thing from France, it was surely dance. Raindrops from the porch roof were like distant drums, the melody of joy, reminding her of dance—a friend that had taught her how to listen, how to discover a story in each movement, how to embrace the flow. Dance was a cathartic experience from the first to the last moment. It had the power to dismantle her and create her anew.

Something she could use now. Yet, unlike that deplorable state of affairs called her love life, dance was something she missed.

She couldn't wait to go back to observing people, discovering their personalities, construing their lives around their movements. Catherine had tried every existing form of dance—ballet, jazz, burlesque, hip-hop, Latin—and they would all bring release. It was a complete escape, and she wanted it. Did that mean she was ready to go back? For the first time since she got to Maple Springs, Catherine paused thinking about her future. She was not ready to give up on herself.

Apart from that ultimate language of emotions, one other thing Catherine missed was the freedom of life without a car. On days like this one, she would walk down to Batignolles or grab a metro to Boulevard Saint-Michel and spend the day wandering the narrow, cobbled streets of the Latin Quarter until evening would surprise her and cozy bistros with *vin chaud* would beckon. It was comforting to know she at least missed something. The ease with which she had abandoned her past life both frightened and vexed her. Was the whole universe tangled with Chloe? How did she let that happen? Dance was her love long before Chloe, long before others.

Same with traveling. She'd climbed Mount Fuji, explored Istanbul, and walked the narrow paths of Jenolan Caves without ever feeling she needed someone next to her. When she met Chloe, suddenly she found herself coordinating the time off, avoiding planes, waiting for summer, and worst of all, photographing every step of the way from a million different angles instead of just seizing the moment. With a frown, she concluded she'd be damned if she ever again allowed her plans to depend upon someone else, especially a woman, and sneering at herself, she stormed back into the house.

In the last few months, she had stupefied not only her body, but her mind as well. She forgot how she longed to explore the world, explore herself, dare her own nature. As if everything stopped because someone decided to have sex one afternoon. Fuck it. She'd go to Mardi Gras in New Orleans, and savor chicken wings at Magic City in Atlanta. She'd explore every feeling, every impulse, every yearning and never pose any expectations to women other than fun. For a start, she'd pay a visit to Bertha's and get the biggest burger she could with all the cheese and veggies on the side. Inevitably, she recalled her last visit, the hat Jesse was wearing, her soft words. She spent the morning only occasionally thinking about Jesse because last night before sleep she firmly decided she was not going to attach any importance to her random call. Flirting came naturally to Jesse. She knew exactly what kind of effect she had on people, and she was not afraid to use it. Thankfully, hearing her on the other end of the phone was certainly easier than staring down those blue eyes. She could still sense that moment when Jesse danced enfolded in her arms, without heartbeat and without breath, and utterly surrendered to her touch. She was swaying to the rhythm of her voice, yielding to her scent. Ugh. Catherine scoffed. That woman was a thousand miles away and she needed her burger. Determined to ask Bertha if she knew of any parcels for sale in this area, Catherine hurried to get dressed. A quick run to the diner, lunch, and then she'd be off to help Fletcher at the shop.

Still, just as she entered the diner, a familiar call riveted her to the spot.

"Catherine!"

In a corner sat Chloe, relaxed, arms resting across the wooden back of the booth, her eyes shining.

"Weren't you supposed to go painting with Marjorie?"

"The rain was persistent, so we rescheduled. Back to painting you," she replied with that perpetual smile of hers.

Catherine had no desire to discuss her plans in front of Chloe, so she reluctantly concluded her conversation with Bertha would have to wait for better times. She ensconced herself opposite Chloe, absently staring at the menu.

Chloe sat silently for a few moments, observing her, before finally speaking without any hesitation. "Marjorie told me you went camping with that cutie Jesse we saw here."

"You and Marjorie are real besties," Catherine responded calmly, not taking her eyes off the menu.

"Did anything happen between you two? Of course, that's totally fine," Chloe quickly added. "You deserve happiness. I'm just dying of curiosity."

Her gray eyes shone with amusement, and Catherine couldn't say she was surprised. Chloe's instincts were infallible except, of course, when it came to cheating in the very apartment she shared with her girlfriend.

"Nothing happened," she confirmed, recalling their conversation last night and the joy each interaction with Jesse would bring. She could be fun, vulnerable, carefree with Jesse. "But I thought about it."

"So what stopped you?"

"She did." Catherine's laughter was ringing as she reminisced about her post-dance misery and the longest half-mile stroll in the history of the universe. Catherine understood exactly why everyone liked Jesse, and as much as she strived to convince herself that last night's call was just another courtesy of the perpetually cordial Jesse, her heart had a mind of its own. Even now, thinking about it, her senses were so acute they could penetrate the air. No one should have that effect on her. She was better than this, she affirmed bitterly. She would not attach any significance to that call. Nevertheless, Catherine had to admit, being prudent was an arduous task around Jesse. She remembered the short video in which she was supposed to swoon over Lola, but all she could stare at was Jesse. Again. Poor puppy.

She had to remind herself to snap out of those thoughts.

"Hey, doll, looking good." A stout woman in a blue polka-dot dress, with a shiny blond bouffant walked up to their table, the towel draped over her shoulder, and refilled Chloe's coffee cup. "Good to see you, Catherine. What can I get you today?"

"Hi, Bertha." Catherine politely smiled. "I'll have a smoky mountain burger and a strawberry milkshake."

"Coming right up, doll."

Chloe's gaze was still fixed on her, as if she wanted to pick up the conversation Catherine wished they had left off.

"You just missed your grandpa. He left with Marjorie five minutes ago," she finally said with a serene expression, and Catherine was silently grateful that Chloe sensed her reluctance. Chloe proceeded to chat about some friends in Paris and those forty-five minutes went by fairly quickly as, luckily, no cheating ex could ever ruin her appetite.

Catherine spent the rest of the day alone in the shop, seeking to finish up the orders that got neglected last week. Absorbed in the swirling potter's wheel, she barely noticed the darkness shrouding Maple Springs when the clock struck nine. It was a crisp evening, but Catherine appreciated the solitude and the quiet that finally reigned over the streets of sleepy Maple Springs. If she never saw another parade ever again, she wouldn't be sorry. The screeching hawks ruling the skies and the distant coyotes howling were the very sound of happiness. No human in sight on her stroll back home was a welcome change that made Catherine look forward to the colorful fall ahead.

Dinner was waiting in the oven, along with Fletcher's note saying he'd gone over to Marjorie's. The casserole was still warm, so Catherine hurried to the shower, hoping to be in time to savor the melted cheese. Ever since she'd moved to Maple Springs, she'd gone to bed at ten. At first to forget her pitiful existence, and later out of habit, so she firmly decided it was time to stay up at least one Friday night. Maple Springs may have boasted only one bar and one restaurant, but fortunately, it had Netflix.

Just as she crawled into her bed, ready to turn off the lights and immerse herself in the addictive dating show she was secretly watching, her phone rang. She glanced at the screen where Jesse's name stunned her. *Damn.* After the initial dismay, her expression softened and a smile broke across her lips. Her again.

"I thought you were performing in Virginia tonight."

"I did, it's past midnight here and everyone's asleep, but I hoped you might still be up. Wanted to see how your placing of the nesting boxes went."

Why would anyone choose to listen about her birds, especially after just playing a concert? So Jesse was a *country* singer, but surely she had better options.

"It rained, so we left it for another day." She hesitated.

"I hope I didn't wake you up."

"No, I was…" she muttered, "just about to watch this show."

"Oh, which one?"

Why did she have to be so inquisitive? Catherine cursed.

"It's called *Blast from the Past* and it reconnects old high school sweethearts."

"So they start dating again?"

"Oh, Jesse, don't get me going about this show. It's crack, it's bad."

She could feel a smile warming Jesse's voice.

"Come on, I love bad, tell me."

Jesse's unwavering support for her frivolous discourse was an exceptional form of intimacy, and it ignited Catherine's urge to hug her.

"So all these couples dated at some point, some five years ago, some fifty, and then life happened. Some moved away, some cheated, and some simply longed for a different experience. So now—" She took a sip of cocoa and put the mug back on the nightstand. Her intense spirit and her fervor could easily be sensed in her speech, which prompted Jesse to a laugh. She had no intention of dispelling that magic. "One of the two realizes they would like to get a second chance and writes a letter detailing their story, how they met, how cute they were, why they parted. The other can then decide to meet them or decline the invite. Of course, some are married now, some don't care, and some become irate just thinking about it. They are the fun ones. There was this girl Jordyn who didn't even want to touch the letter. As soon as she noticed the postman and the camera, she grabbed a fireplace poker and roasted that letter without ever reading it. That's my girl. Anyway, the person who sends the letter is waiting in the studio in front of a giant heart-shaped door and if it doesn't open, it means the person decided not to give them another chance. If the heart opens, they meet after all those years. Very trashy. Very compelling."

"So then they give it another try? Do we find out if it worked out?"

"Yes, we are introduced to them in the first few episodes, and then we get to see who was actually given that second chance. We are then shown their dates and their new life, new struggles. It's so good. You can tell that some of them won't make it. Again. So naïve."

"So who is your favorite couple?"

Catherine could not understand why Jesse cared to listen to this nonsense at one in the morning. After her concert, no less. Surely she could have found a far better amusement.

"There is this girl Jamie—"

"Oh, of course there is a girl," Jesse remarked with a chuckle. "Sorry, carry on, please."

"She grew up on a small farm in Ohio and then moved to New York after high school and broke her boyfriend Larson's heart. So, that was fifteen years ago. She works in New York as a corporate controller, and Larson moved to this beautiful ranch in Montana in the meantime. Larson is like a prince. Anyway, he agreed to try again, but is also very cautious. They are adorable." She finally caught her breath. "So there." Catherine briefly paused, striving to hold back her enthusiasm, and finally let Jesse get a word in edgewise. However, the woman remained quietly laughing, ultimately forcing Catherine to try to satisfy her curiosity. "Who was your high school sweetheart?"

"Oh don't worry, Catherine, I won't be receiving that letter, nor sending one, for sure."

Catherine grinned, instantly intrigued by the girl who could conquer Jesse's heart, make her lose her mind, her cool, her relentless optimism—the girl who could make her cry. She should have shut this conversation down, that's what she should have done, but she was not a sensible human being. Damn her insatiable curiosity.

"What did you do to a poor soul?" she asked avidly.

"Catherine!" Jesse instantly rebelled. "What makes you think that I did something?"

Um, you always say the right thing, and everyone falls in love with you. She bit her tongue.

"Actually, my high school sweetheart was this kind boy, Joshua, who loved horses and math. We played chess together. I was certain he'd never try anything. It was only toward the end of high school that I realized what I felt for women was attraction," Jesse added placidly, but was still quick to jump at the opportunity. "How about you, Catherine? Who was your first love?"

"My French teacher," she said, instantly blushing. "Anais Moreau, tall, stern-looking, profoundly disappointed in people. She was only ten years older than me and possessed wisdom, knowledge, eloquence, and green eyes that made the universe fade away. She quoted Paul Éluard, drove a Ducati, and smelled like palm trees."

"I'm falling for her too," Jesse said, the smirk evident in her voice.

Catherine grinned, thinking how exceptionally easy it was to talk to Jesse. As much as she tried, she couldn't envision Jesse as someone who'd be the center of attention, someone with important friends, someone surrounded by the decadent elite rolling in money. Jesse listened to her talk about her pathetic, uneventful life and made her feel good about herself. How did she do it? Why did she bother? Catherine was inquiring about Jesse's upcoming travels, her concerts, and plans, hoping Jesse would recognize their differences, but the singer never wavered.

"Listening to you," Catherine said, "I just realized, I want to visit Virginia."

"To see me, Catherine?" Jesse playfully laughed. "I didn't know you craved me so badly."

"No, it's your music I crave," she retorted and continued before Jesse could utter a word. "Seriously, I realized all my plans depended on someone else's, and now I can travel on a whim. I can go dirty dancing in that lake in Virginia or backpacking through Alaska or go to Atlanta and eat chicken wings in Magic City or blackened lobster in The Cheetah Lounge."

Jesse mumbled in amusement, "Does it have to be a strip club?"

"It's the sense of freedom. Don't you love that?"

"I sure do," Jesse replied simply after a pregnant pause, as if for the first time she realized the sense of freedom did not imply solitude. Or more likely, she just loved strip clubs. Catherine could only hope. She certainly wasn't the person to end Jesse's womanizing ways, even if the thought crept up more than it should have. *Ça suffit, Catherine!*

CHAPTER TWENTY

When Catherine came downstairs and walked out onto the porch just before seven, the sun was already creeping up over the horizon and Fletcher was waiting with the coffee. Catherine quickly zipped up her hoodie against the crisp morning and stretched in a lazy yawn. Saturday was the busiest day in the shop, so both made it a habit to have an early breakfast. Even in September, they could expect visitors to flock in, so Catherine silently cursed at herself for staying up late.

Two a.m. was for Hallmark movies and panic attacks. Not coquetting with ludicrously attractive, thoughtful, sweet, unattainable country singers.

"Who were you talking to last night? When I got home, I thought I heard you speaking English to someone," the old man finally asked as they were finishing up their breakfast.

"Oh, Jesse called."

"Uh-huh." He flashed an irreverent grin.

"What?"

"Oh nothing," he quickly added and began to laugh.

"Come on, Pépé, stop it, what?"

"Looks like Jesse grew on you, that's all." He threw his hands up, still amused. "Not that I can blame you. She's such a nice, lovable human being. With everything she achieved, she could have played the music star card instead of wasting her time on the old people who remained in this wilderness, but no, not Jesse. She's the same old respectful, charming girl she was fifteen years ago." Fletcher proceeded to light his pipe, and Catherine watched his silver mustache curl into a satisfied smile. *Great, Pépé, keep reminding me of what I'm missing.* "Every summer, instead of going to Miami or Hawaii, she visits Maple Springs and spends time with her parents, uncles, aunts, cousins, and old neighbors. Did you know that her family moved here from Connecticut in 1881, and they purchased over a hundred acres of land planning to quarry out the red sandstone, then helped build the roads, the first school, the church? That girl has a right set of values, and I knew you'd come around." He puffed away, his eyes never leaving Catherine, as if he was trying to penetrate something so hidden she didn't even know it existed.

"Well, I may have been quick to judge her, but we simply like conversing, that's all."

"You prefer talking to her over Chloe?"

"That's different. Chloe and I have a history together, one that left many scars behind, and Chloe knows that. I've been quite clear in what I said. She can stay here or wherever she wants for as long as she pleases, but we are not getting back together. With Jesse…we're just friends."

"Uh-huh," the old man murmured again, nodding his head and taking another relaxing puff.

Catherine had remembered him as a quiet man, absorbed in thought, while Mémé Debbie was always the chatty one. Yet, those rare utterances always bore a special meaning. His silence would echo. Although the last few months revealed Fletcher was not as taciturn, his words still had an astounding power to make her question her firmest convictions. On the one hand, she had a woman she loved for five years, and on the other hand, she had a simple phone call. Yet, there was no doubt which she enjoyed more. Damn, it should have been closer.

"Why do you think she's calling?" Fletcher said after a brief pause.

"Who?"

"Jesse, you fool."

"Oh. She's on tour, I guess she got bored."

"Sure. I've known Jesse since the day she was born. That girl has too many interests to ever wallow in boredom."

"Well, it was just a nice, friendly chat." Catherine refused to analyze it further, but if there was one thing she knew, it was that Jesse had no secret interest in her. It was still with shame that she recalled their stroll home after the dance.

"Oh, Catherine." Fletcher sighed as he rose to his feet. "Jesse is not Chloe, and she's not your other girls. I hope you remember that."

She watched Fletcher disappear into the house, pausing for a moment to think about Jesse and her reasons before concluding she better get ready too. Fletcher's was the only pottery shop within twenty miles, and Saturdays were always very busy with people visiting from the neighboring towns and curious tourists taking Route 36 from Boulder to Estes Park and deciding to take a little detour about halfway there.

Maple Springs had a gas station, a few stores, and an old lodge that operated only in winter and looked quite charming. Right next to that quaint old log cabin with a distinctive wraparound porch stood Fletcher's shop, another old house that resembled a cheery saloon from the Gold Rush era. A faded sign for Ol' Cass that Fletcher never wanted to paint over still adorned its side, and many visitors explored the shop with no intent of buying anything but simply wanted to experience the feel of history it gave them.

Catherine heard the story so many times. Back in the 1890s, Maple Springs had a telegraph office, a town hall, a church, three hotels, a number of saloons and dance halls, a newspaper office, and a schoolhouse, but when the mining industry started to decline and the railroad discontinued the service, the town's population more than halved. Luckily, the sandstone business had been revived in the 1930s, allowing the town to avoid the destiny of many other Colorado ghost towns, remaining active and rowdy. Catherine heard all about the Morgan family, so how was it possible she missed Jesse all those summers?

The building housing Fletcher's shop dated from that same era, the 1930s, when a mink farmer, John Cassidy, built his first shop there. The Cassidy family owned the mink fur coat shop for three generations until they sold the building to Fletcher in the early eighties. Once considered a luxury item, mink fur coats were curbed by high prices and animal rights activists, and the Cassidys decided to head north just when the Fitzgeralds—Fletcher, Debbie, and their eccentric daughter Pearl—decided to return to this sleepy small town.

Catherine knew her restless mother had always been somewhat of a wild spirit—the only child, artist, and activist. When Pearl turned eighteen, she left to travel the world and the following year gave birth to Catherine. Much of Catherine's early childhood was spent touring the remote islands of French Polynesia and Madagascar's tropical rainforest. Her dad was a stern, dedicated entomologist, much older than her mother, and he finally provided the family with some stability when he took a teaching position at the Sorbonne. After he passed away, her mom would ship Catherine to spend her summers with Fletcher and Debbie, while she'd go visit various tortoise colonies, rescue elephants in Kenya, or whales in Iceland. The last two years spent in Provence were sort of a record for Pearl, but learning to announce her visits was still a foreign concept to her, so she'd come and go as she pleased her entire life. Fletcher knew his restless daughter would never take over his business, so he found great satisfaction in teaching his reticent granddaughter how to turn clay into objects of beauty. Thirteen years ago, not long after Debbie's death, during one of those summers, Catherine helped him set up an online store that received orders from all over the US, sometimes a month ahead. Though his online business was thriving, Fletcher refused to close the brick-and-mortar shop. "I need a workshop anyway, so I might as well keep the Ol' Cass," he would say. Catherine remembered being around twelve or thirteen when she first started helping her grandfather. A lot of kids lived in Maple Springs back then, or so she thought. She recalled them running down dusty dirt roads and sneaking out to swim in the lake. Catherine wondered if one of those summers she had actually met Jesse. After all, Jesse was only two years younger, and Maple Springs pretty much had only two main streets where life was happening. Though she was a quiet kid, she remembered sprinkler runs with a certain Amanda from New Hampshire and playing Super Mario with nerdy Matty from Arizona. However, she had no recollection of Jesse. She imagined Jesse would have been a vivacious, outdoorsy blond kid building tree houses, playing baseball, or jumping on a trampoline, yet she couldn't recall anyone who'd fit that description.

Later that night, when Catherine returned home from the shop weary and spent, she flung herself onto the bed—both hoping and fearing Jesse would call again. As much as Catherine liked talking to her, she didn't completely trust herself, not when it came to Jesse and the uncanny closeness she felt around her. Being around Jesse seemed simple because she readily embraced any vulnerability and any discourse, but what scared Catherine was that she would often find herself thinking about her in the strangest moments of a day, when she was listening to a corny song or watching a sappy movie—even while Larson and Jamie were buying a foal for their ranch in Montana, goddammit. She knew she couldn't afford to be stupid again. She also knew she wanted to enjoy Jesse's friendship.

Just as she was getting ready for bed, the call inevitably arrived. The following day as well, and the day after that again. Over the next few weeks, Jesse continued to call every night. Never overstepping the boundaries and texting during the day, Jesse called regularly and devotedly every night, after a concert, from her ranch in Tennessee, from an airport. They would chat for hours, long into the night, and knowing that the phone call would arrive somehow became the best part of Catherine's day. She came to eagerly anticipate the moment she'd hear all about Jesse's tour and the cities she was visiting, her next destination, the moments when they talked about travel, music, and trashy TV shows, exploring every instinct, every weakness they had in common.

"Also, Julia and Martin are never going to make it. Larson, agreed, an ultimate prince."

"Seriously, you watched it?"

"Oh, it's good. I am on episode four, and please don't spoil anything for me. I wanna binge tomorrow and be surprised."

"I have yet to finish season one, don't worry." Catherine's eyes crinkled with merriment. "And totally, Martin will be thanking his lucky stars when Julia dumps him again. Even if she continues camping in front of his house. Also, did you see that Jeremy and Crystal pairing?"

They would spend hours on the phone talking, and every time the call came, Catherine inevitably wondered if that meant Jesse was spending the night alone.

"Don't you ever go out? Have fun?" she finally asked one day. "There's got to be something better than calling me every night."

"Not that I can think of, Catherine," Jesse replied calmly, pausing. "You're exactly what I need."

Catherine's breath caught. She didn't understand why Jesse wasted time on her when she could have had much better company, and more easily, but Catherine had to show respect for her patience and perseverance.

"Did it ever occur to you, Catherine, that I may just want to get to know you better?"

"Of course not," Catherine instantly denied, and both laughed.

"Think what you please, French, but I like you. Now I gotta go because in the morning, or more precisely in six hours, I have autograph signings, and if the ladies decide they want a photo, I would hate to disappoint them with my terrible up-all-night look."

"Perhaps no one will show up."

"Thank you. You really know how to console."

Catherine loved having Jesse send her off to sleep every night, perhaps too much. She knew that one evening the call would not come, and that would be fine. She didn't want to have any expectations ever again, and Jesse didn't owe her anything.

Undoubtedly, tours could get lonely, and perhaps Jesse only needed a friend. She could have been seeing her girlfriends in the morning or afternoon and that was none of Catherine's business. Jesse could do whatever she pleased.

Maybe she could get to know Jesse better without fantasizing about her kisses. Fuck, those were good kisses.

CHAPTER TWENTY-ONE

Catherine was sitting on the porch, legs kicked up on the railing, enjoying the view of the first snow of the season fluttering around. It was a quiet October morning and, wrapped in a blanket with a cup of hot coffee, she could sense the peace of that mountain vastness unfurling in her body. This was her first October in Colorado, but she came to learn long ago that its snowstorms were impetuous, unpredictable, and capricious shields from all noises. For those who took time to listen, the snowy display of silence was a magical experience. She closed her eyes and surrendered to the placidity of clear winter sounds. Wings flapping, trees expanding, contracting, and cracking, a rare animal sound in the distance would only highlight the wonderful mountain quietude. Snowy silence, cleansing and piercing as the cold itself, amplified the remarkable sensation of tranquility. Far from the clamor of the crowd, far from the grinds, groans, and creaks of machinery, the bustle of the metropolis, Catherine finally had time for nothing. She was looking forward to the winter, winds howling through swaying trees, sharp, pure sounds slicing through the air. Pulling her beanie down to her eyes, she adjusted the heat in the chair and slipped deeper under the blanket. She must have dozed off for a few minutes when she heard the squeaky sound of the gate opening and closing, followed by the crunch of footsteps in the snow. Peeking toward the fence, she saw Chloe approaching. Instantly, she pulled her beanie up and straightened in her chair.

Okay, count to five, Catherine. Keep going, goddamn.

"Hi, Catherine." Chloe stepped onto the porch, smiling at Catherine's plaid blanket and the red pom-pom of her beanie, swaying as her head kept turning. "Sorry if I woke you."

"No, I wasn't sleeping. Fletcher said he'd open the shop today, so I'll go later." She offered Chloe a chair, shoving her hands into her pockets.

In the last few weeks, she had seen Chloe only occasionally, at Bertha's or strolling down Main Street. She had politely turned down every invite to dinner or a hike, not only for her late-night calls, but because she'd come to a realization that there was nothing in the world she wanted to tell Chloe. Once the anger and bitterness subsided, she realized there was nothing else left.

A few months into their relationship, she sensed there was something that was just not right. Asked to envision her future with Chloe ten years out, all she could think about was hard work. Chloe was fun, generous, and well-mannered, but also equally insecure, restless, and impulsive. Catherine imagined that people talking about compatibility meant you needed compatible flaws, and theirs were anything but. Just learning to understand how to communicate with her took Catherine a year. Still, she abandoned herself to Chloe's whirlwind of emotions and let her charm and vivacity endear her to herself, forgetting that every little thing shouldn't be so darn hard. Considering that she never reached unstable five-year relationships with her previous girlfriends, she would persistently try to convince herself that long partnerships required concessions, ignoring the fact that those obstacles and differences were there from the very start. She felt she constantly needed to be someone else, to pretend, to compromise, and she simply didn't see any point in doing that anymore.

"Do you remember our first date?" Chloe kept her gaze fixed upon Catherine until she noticed her smile. "We were both waiting in 'La Mirandole,' thinking we got stood up. I waited two hours at the other end of the city."

"I couldn't imagine someone would suggest Aubervilliers for a first date." Catherine shook her head, incredulous as always when she'd recall just how miserable she had been waiting in Auteuil until she was politely asked to leave because they were closing.

"That bar is very cozy!" Chloe protested, and her face lit up. "Thank God I sent you that angry text."

"Nothing like being stood up, thrown out of the bar, sitting abandoned on a bridge over a cold river, and then being accused of insensitivity."

"You waiting on that bridge, half-frozen and your hair ruffled...It was the prettiest sight I ever saw. Ended up being a good night along the Seine."

They kept silent for a moment until Chloe spoke again in her usual spirited manner.

"Do you remember when we ended up at that swinger party because I got the address wrong? It took us fifteen minutes to realize why everyone was so welcoming."

They both burst out laughing, vividly recalling how they kept expecting their friends to show up as they sat huddled in the corner, watching everyone getting it on.

"I bought the ticket. I'm leaving tomorrow," Chloe uttered, forcing a smile. As much as Catherine was hoping to hear those words, she was still taken aback, aware that one part of her life was ending that day, on that porch. "You know I hate goodbyes and I don't want to view this as some fateful farewell," Chloe added promptly. "I would just like to know that if you ever need a friend, you'll think of me."

That was Chloe's quality that Catherine cherished the most—the remarkable ability to infuse nonchalance into her every action.

"Thank you, I'll keep that in mind."

"It wasn't all bad, right?"

"No." Catherine shook her head decisively. "We had some good times."

"One thing I won't miss is you stealing the clothes I was about to put on because you're too lazy to iron yours."

"You do have impeccable taste."

"And I can iron!" Chloe exclaimed playfully and then continued in a more serious vein. "I really believed in you and I, Catherine, and now I understand why you came here. It's so goddamn quiet that when I locked myself in that cabin every evening, I couldn't hear anything but my thoughts. After a while they start echoing, and you realize they are not as frightening as they seemed." Chloe sounded contrite yet serene. "I know you, somewhat distrustful and obstinate. You must be doubting everything now, thinking love is not worth the effort nor the time. People always disappoint you. But remember all the fun times you had. Like swinger parties." They both giggled. "Just find someone who's not as dumb as me, and you have no reason for concern."

"Thank you for making this easier than I ever could have imagined." Catherine's gaze expressed a silent appreciation.

"Of course. What I realized in this quiet is that I don't want to punish you with myself. You deserve much, much more. Don't give up. When you're given a moment with someone, make the most of it. Enjoy each other. Don't waste time thinking about all the mistakes someone else made. Be grateful while it lasts. You see, a few weeks in Maple Springs can make even me wise. The next time I'm dumb, I'm coming straight here." She paused to look to the mountains, seemingly absorbing their shape and sounds. "It's utterly breathtaking."

The swirling snow fluttered down and they could feel the cold approaching, so when Catherine offered a cup of coffee, they both entered the warm house.

"Do you think you'll ever return to France?" Chloe might have lacked prudence but never words, so Catherine grinned.

"I will, soon."

"Do you need me to send you anything from Paris? Our apartment is just as you left it. Well, of course, except Gabrielle. I assure you she's not there."

They both chuckled, and Catherine felt grateful they were able to laugh through their closure.

"I might give you a list with a few things. You can donate the rest."

Chloe cracked a smile, and they hugged each other one last time.

CHAPTER TWENTY-TWO

It had been three days since Chloe left, and Catherine felt unusually liberated—not only because she no longer had to fear stumbling upon Chloe on Main Street and be forced into futile discourses, but rather for the conclusion of the part of her life that had turned her into a distrustful, irritable, and insufferable creature. She no longer depended on someone else's mistakes, she didn't need anyone's approval, and she wasn't defined by anyone's expectations. It was a wonderful, liberating feeling. Hell, she was never once tempted to throw objects at Chloe. On the contrary, when the woman called yesterday to inform her that she had already sent her stuff to Maple Springs, they had quite a pleasant chat.

Jesse was still calling every night, and every night their conversation was a little longer. With every call, every intimate detail, their closeness, their bond seemed more sublime. Catherine thought she was lucky to have a friend, especially one like Jesse, who made her smile throughout the day. Do friends do that? Sure they do, she would confidently assure herself. So her friend happened to be a hot, irresistible, flirty, charming, passionate goddess. A goddess that she wanted to ferociously kiss and possibly press against the wall. Well, that was a long time ago. *We've evolved. I respect her personality. I'm not an animal. I'm not.*

After performing in Arizona, Jesse had a show in Fort Collins and two in Denver, and Catherine pondered whether she should attend one of those concerts to show support. Since they were getting so friendly and talking every single day, Catherine felt showing up might be the right thing to do. After all, it had been a month and a half since their last encounter. Upon successfully convincing herself that attending that concert would simply be a nice gesture, she quickly turned to the Internet and was astounded to find that both shows in Denver's Ogden Theater were already sold out. Not a single ticket left. She checked every online ticket vendor but wasn't able to find anything. *Merde!*

She stood immobile for a few moments, contemplating if that was a sign, but quickly shook her head and dismissed the thought. There were no signs in friendship. Again, she opened Ticketmaster, entered Fort Collins, and with utter delight found one ticket left. For that very night. Before someone else snatched it or before overthinking, Catherine swiftly moved to make the payment. The instant sensation of thrill gripped her entire being.

"I guess I'm seeing Jesse tonight." The thought made her chuckle. She imagined she'd be crammed with hundreds of clammy cowboys in a boot-scootin' hell, but a lot of questionable fashion, sunburns, sweat, and trucks couldn't subdue her exhilaration at the thought of seeing Jesse. The very sound of Jesse's seductive voice was a switch for her wild imagination. Friends, sure.

The only downside of her purchase was that the concert would start in under eight hours, and she had an hour's drive to Fort Collins. Catherine refused to dress up, unsure what to expect. Yet, it turned out a simple shower, makeup, taming of her hair, and picking a pair of jeans and silk blouse took four hours. She intended to text Jesse on her way there but never really expected to see her outside the stage. Well, maybe a little. She undid two more buttons of her blouse, grabbed her jacket, and hurried downstairs. It was Friday afternoon so she didn't think Fletcher would be at home, but an inquisitive stare waited for her at the door.

"Where are you headed all dressed up and pretty, smelling fresh like a mermaid emerging from the sea?"

Catherine tilted her head and swung her gaze to the mountains. Not that she intended to hide anything from Fletcher, but he could easily mistake this for something it was not. There was no reason to lie, and definitely nothing to hide. At the last moment, she stopped herself.

"I wanna go explore Fort Collins a bit."

"What's there to explore?" His skeptical brow furrowed.

"Oh, you know, just breweries, bars, drive-in movies." Remorseful, she thrust her hands into her pockets. God, she hated lying, but they were just friends, and even someone as well-meaning as Fletcher could have put on undue pressure. He wouldn't understand.

"You ain't hiking to Horsetooth Rock this late, are you?"

"No, don't worry, just a night out in town, maybe a gig."

"Sleep in tomorrow if needed. Hell, what am I saying? You don't have to come to the shop. We covered all our online requests and October Saturdays are usually the slowest with tourists. No more fall colors, and not a ski season yet." Whistling cheerfully, he walked outside and then suddenly stopped. "Do you wanna take my Outback?"

"Seriously?"

His mouth turned up at the corners as he tossed her the keys, and Catherine reciprocated with her Tacoma keys. She loved the man, and by God, she felt guilty for stretching the truth like that.

To shake off that sense of unease, she briefly paused at the door to assure herself that Jesse was just a friend and no one needed to understand that aside from the two of them. Damn, she shouldn't have lied. There was nothing to hide.

Route 287 didn't attract much traffic to Fort Collins, and her ride turned out to be smooth. Considering it would be remarkably rude to show up at the concert without knowing the songs, Catherine found Jesse's Radio on Spotify as soon as she was at a safe distance from Maple Springs. Gliding down the highway, leaving behind small towns and vast fields, she tapped her fingers on the steering wheel, humming and musing on the moment her eyes would land on Jesse. Truth be told, she may have started listening to Jesse's songs some time ago as she lay in the dark every night, awaiting her call, rushing to turn down the volume when her name lit up the screen.

What an arresting, sultry voice Jesse had! The first time she heard her at the festival, she was captivated by its power, its warmth, its expressive tone. It was raspy, dynamic, cool, and pure, all at once, and Catherine could almost imagine it whispering gently in her ear, pulling her closer with each breath. There was one song she particularly liked called "Wanna Take You Places." She could feel all that she loved about Jesse in that song. It had her acute sensibility, consideration for others, delicate beauty, audacity, wit, and Catherine would find herself passionately screaming, "I don't remember anything before you, and I can't imagine anything after. Anyyything."

I will never again scorn sweaty cowboys.

The playlist revealed many more wonderful songs about even more wonderful women, her family, recollections, relationships, failures—and for each, Catherine couldn't help but wonder about the circumstances that had brought forth such art. What inspired Jesse to sit down and write something so beautiful? How much of her did it take? She imagined Jesse was asked that a lot, but listening to her music, a dark desire emerged to get to know the people behind her lyrics. Who was Claire trapped in an unsatisfying marriage? Was it someone who realized how unhappy her marriage was when she found Jesse's bed? Was it one of her unrequited loves? She wanted to know all about Jesse. What spurred her, what excited her, what anguished her. Jesse once told her she'd been involved with a woman who left her because she entered the witness protection program. Or so she said. Couldn't get out fast enough.

Who were those people lurking in Jesse's verses? Catherine remembered their hike when she came up with all sorts of scenarios about Lola and Rachel only to have Jesse change the narrative in the next instant. Imagining the ease with which Jesse would do the same now, she smiled and turned up the volume.

Just as Catherine rolled into Fort Collins, Jesse was singing about staying in bed with someone all day. Catherine could feel both heat and excitement kick in at the same time. Soon she'd see her. While surprised by such weakness, Catherine still couldn't restrain the thrill of staring down those intense, blue eyes and whatever they might bring. *Reste calme, Catherine.*

As she pulled up into the parking lot near the venue, the sun was still high. Catherine decided she had some time to explore the town just like she told Fletcher she would. She glanced in the rearview mirror and quickly grabbed her jacket and her purse. It was a pleasant afternoon, so she leaned against her car for a few moments, contemplating the message she was about to send to Jesse. The sooner she gathered the courage to do it, the better. She imagined Jesse was busy preparing, rehearsing, warming up her voice or whatever routine she had, and probably wouldn't even see the message.

At first, the two only had late-night calls but when Catherine informed her that Chloe was leaving, Jesse started texting her in the middle of the day to ask how she was doing, so Catherine felt more comfortable hitting that send. Relieved to finally have carried that out, she decided to stretch her legs a bit. She had to go channel her inner cowgirl and get ready for the boot stomping.

* * *

When she received that text, Jesse rubbed her eyes in disbelief. Sure, they had been talking every single day for over a month, but the sheer thought of Catherine now being a few feet away fueled both unexpected panic and savage thrill through her body. She was here. Jesse had to steady herself against the wall, contemplating, aware she wouldn't manage to hide her idiotic smile once she had her near. Catherine was here to see her. She grinned at herself and shook her head, refusing to waste any time. After quickly tapping out a reply text with explicit instructions, she rushed to the back door of the venue to wait.

Not more than five minutes later—faster than she'd dared hope—Jesse saw her approaching with soft, nimble steps, a teasing expression, and dark eyes piercing right through her soul. God, she was even more gorgeous than she remembered. To be completely honest, Jesse would occasionally look at the photo she had playfully taken when they went camping together, yet standing in front of her now was a different, sweeter form of torture. Catherine was right there, offering herself to her imagination, and all Jesse could think was that she'd wasted so much time. A month and a half, what was she thinking? She'd never make that mistake again. Catherine had eyes that were turning dreams into reality—immense eyes, a mysterious masterpiece—and the proud poise of the head as if she were a queen. For as much as she wanted to break the misconceptions Catherine harbored about her, and for as much as she wanted to appear nonchalant, it was with exceptional ease that Jesse got lost in thoughts of Catherine's lithe body, the gracious tilts of her neck, her wavy hair flowing over her firm shoulders, her outstretched arms waiting for her to lean in. She could already anticipate Catherine's soft touch on her tense skin, the press of her body against hers.

God, this was one of those moments she'd seen countless times in movies, when time slows down and the lustrous sound of violins start filling the air, some weirdo passersby begin twirling like Cossacks, and a fickle white mist appears out of nowhere. A full musical number was not out of the question, and Jesse realized that she didn't give a whit what soundtrack was playing as long as Catherine kept walking toward her with that look in her eyes.

Catherine's whole weightless figure held her captive, and Jesse kept reminding herself to move her eyelids.

"I can't believe you're here," she managed to utter brightly, finally locking her arms around Catherine, and every fiber of her being came alive with ease.

"When you finally decide to hire me, I better come prepared." She heard Catherine's muffled voice and sensed her breath burning her neck and running down her spine.

In moments like these, Jesse thought, life seemed so simple. She didn't worry about overpopulation, ozone layer depletion, and acid rain. There were no wars, nor insoluble problems. To be happy, her life needed only that person to be close. Could it be that simple?

They held each other long, much longer than appropriate, enjoying the intimacy of their entwined bodies a bit too much. Jesse endeavored to find something safe to say.

"We just ran through the sound check." Reluctantly, she somehow managed to pull away from their embrace. "Such a welcome, unexpected sight."

"Is that your concert outfit?" Catherine's eyes were moving over her body, baring her with their intensity, making her skin burn, and Jesse could think of little else than exploring Catherine's naked body for hours, for days, her lips imprinted on her back, her ribs, her thighs. There was no other person in the world that she wanted to feel under her fingers. A month and a half was definitely too long for her imagination.

"It is. Not what you expected?" Jesse glanced down. The light purple strapless top and leather skinnies complemented with feminine ankle boots were quite different from those horrendous sweats she was wearing the last time she saw her.

"Not quite. I imagined you would be something like Doris Day in *Calamity Jane*."

"If I had known you were coming, I would have fulfilled your fantasy." Jesse's mischievous grin could not conceal how much she fancied the woman in front of her.

Catherine's fast-moving eyes never left hers as they entered the room where four men sat with their instruments. Seeing them, Catherine stopped so quickly she nearly fell forward.

"I didn't mean to interrupt you, I'm so sorry. I only came for Jesse's performance, so sorry to disturb your routine." She halted at the door.

"Nonsense, I'm glad you're here." Jesse pulled her into the room.

"We are a well-coordinated team," the man closest to Catherine added and extended his hand. "I'm Jackson."

The man had a scruffy white beard and robust long, white hair. Slightly scaled cut, with the tuft brought a little upward, and a disordered line as if he just passed the fingers through his hair, he came close to what many people pictured a country musician should look like, and so did the other three men. Randy was probably in his forties with thick, ginger hair tied back with a black bandana. Logan wore a black hat curved up on the sides and a bolo tie, and Brent was the definition of a rugged yet refined fifty-something man, tenderly clutching his fiddle.

Jesse regarded the embarrassment forming on Catherine's face as she introduced them. Her blushing as she attempted to make small talk with them only intensified Jesse's consuming urge to kiss her. Finally taking pity, she gently grasped Catherine's forearm and led her to the corner of the room where they had more privacy. As soon as she sat next to her, Jesse sensed Catherine's perfume exciting each fiber of her being and stealing away her thoughts.

"I'm kind of disappointed, Jesse. I envisioned your backstage area would feature an endless parade of racy girls, only to find four manly men."

"I sent the girls home when I heard you were here," Jesse retorted helplessly. When would she stop perceiving her as some relentless seductress? Jesse always found she was the happiest on her own. If she had never met Catherine, she could have been perfectly content alone on her ranch. But whenever she was next to this woman, she always longed for more. Just one moment more.

Jesse found something safer to say. "I'll get you a place right next to the stage."

"No, no, I want to mingle with your audience, get the real feel of your concert. Don't worry, I want you to enjoy your show and forget I'm here."

"Well, I will enjoy the show."

Jesse let her eyes settle on Catherine's for a while. Goddamn, why couldn't they just stop pretending? Longing looks and eager bodies made of desire for each other—didn't Catherine want this as much as she did? There was no denying the tension suspended in the air, the attraction they couldn't control. Jesse wanted to know how she tasted, how her kiss felt. She wanted to sit in a chair and watch her sleep. Yes, she wanted all those creepy things. Damn French woman.

Randy was warming up his fingers playing the guitar, and Jesse noticed Catherine startled.

"Oh, I know this song!" It was the one about Claire, freed from her unhappy marriage.

"Heard it on the radio?" Jesse chuckled and Catherine cast down her eyes, a delicate blush gracing her cheeks.

"I heard it on Spotify, which I intently played in my car." Catherine's expression was so genuine, leaving nothing but bliss in each of Jesse's capillaries, in her every bone, every suspended breath. "I was curious…Who is Claire? From the song. She sounds like a strong, badass woman."

"Oh, that's Nicole Kidman," Jesse said easily. "I had a crush on her when I was a kid. I was devastated when she and Tom divorced."

"Not the answer I expected," Catherine said and laughed.

"Most of those songs are fiction." Jesse shrugged, musing over her reluctance to admit she had never really loved anyone. "Anyway, we used to be neighbors. She's a lovely lady. I also wrote songs about Clint Eastwood, SpongeBob, and a slice of pizza, before you start thinking I'm some sort of woeful romantic."

Logan, sitting closest to them, grinned and shook his head, and soon a smothered laughter rippled around the room.

"Rascals." Jesse turned to her band.

"I know you have to get ready, so I'll get going," Catherine said with a soft smile. "I really didn't mean to be a bother, but I am glad I got to see you."

"Why don't you come back after the show? We'll have more time then. I can text you when we wrap it up here."

With a slight nod, Catherine bid a cordial farewell to the band and then stopped and turned once more, wrapping Jesse in another tight embrace.

CHAPTER TWENTY-THREE

The first thing Catherine did was go to the bar. What was it about Jesse that she couldn't control? She didn't have to clutch her like she was a *Titanic* lifesaver, goddamn it. She took a sip of her rum and let out a long exhale. The crowd had already started gathering, and Catherine was soon taken aback by the diversity of visitors swarming the entrance. There was a family with kids, all four wearing cowboy hats, a few old ladies persistent in their two-step, a few middle-aged moms wearing T-shirts with Jesse's printed picture. Well, it was a pretty face, she had to admit that. A few couples couldn't keep their hands off each other, and there were plenty of women—plenty. Good for Jesse. Perhaps it was time to admit that Jesse Morgan was known outside Maple Springs. If only that could affect Catherine's obviously blind desire for self-destruction. The ardor kept building up in her muscles, and her whole being had been weakened by that secret pleasure roaring inside her. Just being close to Jesse for those few brief moments was enough thrill to last for days. Entering the venue, she felt awkwardly self-conscious, as though every single person in that room could tell the shameful reason for her visit, as though they could read her dirty mind, so she cast down her bashful gaze and found a safe spot in the corner.

What seemed like an intimate room for under one thousand people soon transformed into a vibrant place of jubilation and good times. Catherine reluctantly admitted the crowd was actually civil, and their cordial smiles helped her break the tension of her impending encounter with Jesse.

When Jesse finally appeared on the stage, Catherine caught her breath, unable to scream like the rest of the crowd. Jesse still sported the same outfit, though she'd added a dark-brown cowboy hat to the ensemble. Catherine could hardly focus on the music, on the roaring, elated bunch dancing around her. Even Jesse's words receded into the distance, and the universe faded away into the mist of her human frailty. It seemed as if that hat had transformed Jesse's whole body language. A boho-chic statement ring and a necklace complemented her girly outfit and suddenly presented an audacious bandit, a wild spirit, a fearless outlaw that Catherine wanted to fight. She wanted to fight her until she possessed every single inch of her body. Already feeling Jesse's warm breath on her skin, fierce kisses conquering her neck, Catherine wanted to snatch her off that stage and plunge her fingers into all her imperfections, relish in all her weaknesses. How could someone's neat outfit make her picture them naked so vividly?

Oh yeah! Jesse Morgan, douze points!

Heat possessed her, yet shame not so much. She could hardly focus on anything but Jesse's sensual moves, her poised manner, picturing her all over herself with astounding ease.

"Damn cowboy hat. Merde. Jesus." She should probably stop calling for Jesus because he would hardly approve what her imagination was conceiving. Catherine kept reminding herself, "Jesse is a nice person, Jesse is a nice person." However, it did little to dissipate her desires. The woman on the stage sent that audience straight to heaven, and Catherine was leading the way.

Mercifully, after two songs Jesse tossed the hat into the crowd and the next two hours Catherine spent admiring her passion, vigor, and exuberance. Her energy fueled the atmosphere, and the audience spiritedly sang along to her hits.

As the concert went on, Catherine realized with some surprise that she recognized most of the tunes, but what she noticed for the first time was that the majority of Jesse's songs were in direct address. While it made her songs more intimate, Catherine wondered if she used that point of view to avoid revealing they were written to another woman. Jesse was lighthearted, she liked having fun, and it appeared she wasn't overly concerned about what other people might think, so she must have done it to reach a wider audience. Still, Catherine couldn't help but wonder if there was something that could hurt perpetually cool Jesse Morgan.

Catherine didn't have to wait long for Jesse's message after the concert. As the crowd began dispersing, Jesse invited her back, only this time, the band members were gone and Jesse waited alone. Catherine didn't know if she should feel relieved or mortified. Jesse stood there with her adorable smile and slightly wet hair, bashfully tucking her blond strands behind her ears. Her fresh, sensual, mysterious scent was haunting Catherine's senses and making her weak. How was her mind still resisting?

"The guys went for dinner and drinks before we head back to Denver," Jesse said.

"Oh, too bad. I was really looking forward to chatting with them."

They both chuckled, and Jesse held her dark gaze, spreading her arms inquisitively.

"So, what are your first impressions?"

My panties get all wet just from looking at you, but I can at least pretend to be normal.

"Congratulations, you were amazing," Catherine said instead, still unable to tear her eyes away from Jesse. "I should do this more often."

"You know, Catherine, you don't have to buy concert tickets to see me." Jesse grinned, and Catherine became acutely aware that staring into those alert eyes was a temptation that was not going to end well. "You are one person I'll always have time for."

Jesse spoke with confident serenity, her hands safely tucked in her pockets, and Catherine wondered how that woman managed to uproot her every belief with such utmost ease.

Next to Jesse she never worried about labels, failures, opinions, time, or space—none of it mattered. She wanted what was best for Jesse, but perhaps she also wanted her sweaty, sinewy body in what some might define as animalistic sex. What was that called again?

* * *

While she talked about any safe topic she could think of, Jesse kept feeling an almost compulsive need to touch Catherine, and for as much as she fought it—and she did, God knows she did—she would find her hand casually brushing Catherine's knee or forearm, and then Catherine's light graze thrilling her skin. As Jesse stared into those dark eyes, she could anticipate her raw kiss, her taste, her own hands on Catherine's ribs, on her breasts, as if they had already been there, her scent, her gaze so recognizable and gratifying.

When Brent and Ryan appeared at the door, Jesse silently cursed herself for instructing them to give her only forty-five minutes because she didn't trust herself more with Catherine. Damn. She should have found another form of painful, medieval self-torture rather than falling for this French woman. Jesse could feel their burning kiss suspended in the air the entire time, her face so close to Catherine's, obscure agitation of continuous impulses clouding her vision. Tonight she was so close to crossing the line, surrendering to the attraction pulling them together. To make matters worse, she could sense Catherine yielding to the impetus of desire as well. Jesse had no idea if she was any closer to gaining Catherine's trust, if they would ever connect emotionally, or if she'd just be some torrid affair Catherine would forget come summer. However, she wouldn't bear just being her rebound. She'd do this the right way.

"Do you still want your call tonight?" she asked with a soft smile, cool as ever, without any trace of tension.

"Of course, I need to hear all about the girls in your backstage," Catherine replied, never avoiding her gaze. Despite Jesse's compelling need to feel her lips, Catherine went for the cheek. She leaned in and imprinted a teasing kiss near the corner of her lips.

"Don't miss me too much."

"You shouldn't leave then." Jesse smirked.

"Oh, damn you, Jesse."

"You really need to stop cursing me," she replied playfully. "Have a safe trip back to the mountains. I'll call you."

CHAPTER TWENTY-FOUR

Well done, Jesse, you virtuous warrior against stereotypes, you valiant moralist! Too bad you have no idea what you're doing.

Wretchedly resting her head on her palm and nursing a mild headache, Jesse listened to her friends argue.

"Sorry, sweetie, this has friend-zoning written all over it. Not gonna happen."

"I think it's commendable that Jesse's giving her time. The woman just got out of a long relationship."

"You should have been honest, Jesse. You should have told her by now."

"Angry sex is the best sex."

"You don't want to be a rebound listening about her ex's firm ass all day long."

"Angry, angry sex."

"Give her an unflattering nickname and focus on her flaws."

"Oh, that's a good one. She's nothing but a hypocritical egomaniac anyway. With ugly feet—you can't go wrong there—

and if you ever wonder what she is doing, picture her strutting in a velour tracksuit and sandals, kicking every puppy that comes her way with her hideous feet."

This was worse than listening to her subconscious. Asking friends for help wouldn't yield any fruitful results—she needed to fix this mess herself. It was three days after her concert in Fort Collins and Jesse could still feel Catherine's scent all over her body. Fresh, alluring aroma on her hands, in her hair, on her hotel pillow. The places Catherine had never been to. Sadly. What made things even more difficult was that she *knew* their attraction was mutual. It would be so easy to dart her tongue between those soft, warm lips, drive her fingers into Catherine's hair as their breasts pressed against one another. Break their long, ravenous kiss only to slide her tongue across Catherine's neck, feel her hard nipples under her lips, her wet yearning through the pants. Listen to Catherine's gasps as Jesse's tongue and lips played around her thighs before they finally hit her wet center and closed around it. She could feel Catherine's hands imprinting on her shoulders, grinding against her mouth. She could vividly anticipate sliding in, the wet sound of fuck erasing everything around. Meeting the woman's hungry eyes and relishing her scent permeating the air, with each thrust, with every flick of her tongue, until she felt her hips rising to keenly meet her, followed by the clenching around her fingers. That she knew how to do. Courting, listening, being a damn friend, perhaps she was the wrong person for that. Even when they were talking over the phone, all she could think about was Catherine's kiss traveling over her neck, her supple fingers roughly pulling her clothes off. Catherine's one hand would deftly seize her wrists, forcing her arms above her head, forcing her surrender, as the other hand slid down to rub over her soaking wet panties.

Afraid her friends might notice the heat spreading over her entire being, Jesse closed her eyes and gulped down a glass of water.

She never played these games because she simply never cared enough to try to manipulate the outcome. Now she finally liked someone and wanted to earn her trust. It wasn't supposed to become a conundrum. Yet, staying cool around steamy hot Catherine Des Lauriers proved to be more demanding than she had imagined. Even if Catherine was miles away, her damn scent was trailing Jesse everywhere, determined to drive her mad. At bars, backstage at her concert, even at Trader Joe's, she could swear Catherine was somehow always there but just out of sight. She had been turning around, hoping to find her, for three days straight like she was a psychotic maniac, and she couldn't tell if she was about to die from a brain tumor or really see Catherine and get an instant ride to bliss.

Their phone conversations reached a point where Catherine's voice was like a breath down the neck that preceded a kiss. Every word, every pause was becoming an endless anticipation of pleasure. After their last encounter, it was as if her primal instincts took over and she could no longer hold the eruption of desire her skin had tried to restrain for so long. For as much as she enjoyed them, their late-night chats started to weigh on her. Every joke, every smile had an outline of a lie, and Jesse knew she could no longer contain herself in Catherine's presence. This was turning into a chess match, and she had no intention of playing games, not now, not with Catherine. She had to be honest with her.

Three days spent in Denver after that concert in Fort Collins dragged on like a rare agony. Jesse welcomed the opportunity to have brunch with her childhood friends as a much-needed distraction, but as it turned out, she might have been a bit too naïve to do so.

"She'll think you're a womanizer."

"She'll think you're weak."

"She'll think you're not into her."

Instead of distracting her with their own lives, they readily turned to hers. Yet, for as much as she wanted to listen, her mind kept betraying her. It was just Catherine. No one in the world was as easy to talk to. So why was she afraid of the truth? She had six days till her concert in Seattle, and although she had no idea what she was going to say or achieve, she just knew she had to drive up to Maple Springs tonight and kiss Catherine

Des Lauriers. Even if it ruined everything, even if it was the last thing she did.

She refused to contemplate the consequences, she refused to contemplate the expectations, the labels, the future, anything that wasn't Catherine's lips on her own. Sure, most likely it was not the right thing to do, but it seemed the most natural thing in the world, and she'd be damned if she wasted any more time. She spent their last encounter trapped in an inertia of what she assumed she had to do, while her every single instinct screamed the very opposite. Yes, she could be patient for Catherine—but first she'd kiss her and *then* be patient.

CHAPTER TWENTY-FIVE

In spite of the unfamiliar eagerness sweeping over her, Jesse managed to finish the concert with a clear focus. As if the crowd could sense her excitement, they reacted with electrifying encouragement, and Jesse decided to convince herself they were cheering for her wise resolution. It was time.

While her band went back to Tennessee, she impatiently jumped into a rental car and raced to Maple Springs. It was Monday night, just before midnight, and the road was almost deserted. Forty-five miles of suspense did their best to make her waver, but she remained steadfast. For a brief moment she considered calling Catherine, but she quickly dismissed the idea. She knew she'd blurt everything out over the phone, and you don't blather on about certain things, you enjoy them. No, they'd talked enough, and she was done dancing around with conversation. She could only hope Catherine was still awake. Please God. If she had to wait another day, she would die a very ignoble death. It had to be tonight.

It was a typical October in Colorado. Low forties and brisk winds had whisked away traces of gold and red from the landscape, so Jesse lowered the window, hoping the cold air would keep her from overthinking. As she was nearing Maple Springs, she decided it was finally time to briefly text Catherine, and all her hopes and all her weighty trepidation were reduced to seeing that name pop up on her screen.

Good riddance, sanity.

* * *

Catherine stepped out onto the porch, her breath hitching in her throat at the sight of Jesse walking toward her. Well, luckily, a ridiculously sexy leather jacket and a sinful smile didn't work on her. *Merde.* It appeared the whole world paused waiting for that first sound to crack, air suspended, their eyes locked. Then a firm, poised voice broke the silence.

"I like you, Catherine. This is not about me and *some* woman. It's about me liking one particular person. You. I spend my days thinking how you would feel against my lips, how my hand would slide through your thighs. I don't want anyone else. I wasn't looking for anything when we met, I was happy being on my own. Too bad you had to be so annoyingly lovely," she said and inched closer to her, so close Catherine could sense time fade away, all her feeble righteousness receding, while there remained only one reality, governed by Jesse's soft yet confident gaze. "You are enough for me, and I can feel you want it as much as I do. It's that simple."

Sensing her so close, Catherine could hardly breathe. There was nothing she wanted more than to explore the source of this maddening lust, of this incessant fever. Everything did seem so simple with the two of them standing alone on that porch in the middle of the night, one short breath away. She knew she would soon feel Jesse's hands on her back, her hot tongue on her own. It would be so easy to believe her. Jesse was a libertine, she was a friend, and it would mean nothing.

She had to collect herself. Quickly. Not wanting to risk Fletcher overhearing, Catherine grasped Jesse's arm and dragged her across the yard to a dark corner near the shed.

"Nice, straight to the point." Jesse grinned as she trotted by her side. "You don't have to be so charming to get what you want, Catherine."

Their eyes met again. Seeing Jesse look so amused, Catherine couldn't stifle her laugh. She pummeled Jesse's chest lightly with her fists. "I don't want to like you, Jesse. You are bad for me. You are nothing that I want. You're a person, for a start. I don't think I'll ever be ready for another person again. You are driving me crazy, you are charming, you are sweet, you're all over the place, you have a lifestyle I'll never fit into. You have a head full of songs for other women and I could never trust you—and I need to stop liking you," Catherine murmured, annoyed that even now there was nothing in the world she wanted more than the woman in front of her. She briefly paused in Jesse's calm, deep blue eyes, then grabbed the collar of her jacket and shook her gently. The want only intensified. "I have to focus on real life and work instead of thinking of undressing you all the time. I don't want to like you."

Jesse's breathing deepened.

"What happens then?" She paused. "When you undress me."

For a long second, neither moved. Then, just as Jesse made a step toward her, Catherine reacted faster and backed her into the wall, bringing her mouth down on hers. At the first brush of Jesse's lips, Catherine's mind was erased. She was consumed, wanting to possess her lips, devour their taste. Her arms hurriedly wrapped around Jesse's neck, her fingers sinking into her soft locks before tugging her blond hair sharply to bring her closer. Jesse arched her body against hers as though in response to a rush of lust. With Jesse's breasts pressing into hers, the feel of her lips, her fresh scent, her knee pushing in between her legs, Catherine drew a deep, helpless breath, locking her leg around Jesse's, craving her even closer, reveling in the wondrous bliss of their firmly pressed bodies.

When Jesse's tongue slid past her lips, Catherine opened for her with a gasp. Instinctively, her hands slipped under Jesse's shirt, her fingers running along her firm abdomen, across her ribs to her willing breasts still pressed tightly against her chest. A satisfied sound reached from deep in Jesse's throat as she tightened her grip. Her kiss was ardent, her tongue audacious, and her teeth lightly pulled her lower lip, catching Catherine in a mindless torrent of pleasure. The way this woman kissed was a fucking delight.

"Finally," Jesse managed to whisper against Catherine's mouth, finding her hungry, intent gaze just a moment before her lips slid to Jesse's neck and her skillful tongue elicited groans with exceptional ease. Sure as hell, Jesse hastily pulled Catherine's shirt over her head, and when another one was revealed underneath, she yanked it up too.

"God, how many shirts do you have?" she whimpered desperately when she faced the third one. "Did you do this to drive me crazy?"

Catherine smiled through their kisses as her hands intrepidly traveled down Jesse's waist to her hips, pausing on the corners of her inner thighs. She brought her pelvis to Jesse's, and the feel of her wet jeans against hers urged her to touch her. Jesse hooked her leg around Catherine's like they were dancing, and in one gliding, flowing motion turned her and pressed her against the wall. Her fingers that were teasing around Catherine's ribs and breasts finally caught the last shirt, and as she was pulling it up and off she held Catherine's arms above her head.

The move thrilled Catherine, and she leaned into her, capturing her mouth with fervor.

"I hate you," she murmured against Jesse's lips, freeing her arms and sliding her hand straight between Jesse's legs. Even through the fabric of her jeans, she could feel how ready Jesse was already. As if they were competing over who would drive the other insane first, Jesse weakened from her touch, releasing a deep moan and lowering her head, pressing her open mouth to Catherine's nipple.

Catherine could not form a single thought that didn't have those lips on her. Jesse pulled her closer as she tugged at her nipples with her lips and teeth, gently caressing her exposed ribs and dragging her confident tongue up to the arch of her neck.

"Oh, I'd hate me too." Jesse grinned, surrendering to their voracious kiss.

They weren't heeding the fact that they were leaning against the exterior wall of a shed, finally immersed in the well of lust pacing through their bodies, but Catherine pulled them inside with only a few steps. The arc lamp from the other side of the street was offering just enough light to further their desires.

When Jesse finally slid her hand into Catherine's pants, firmly planting her fingers on her butt—never interrupting their kisses—bolts of pleasure streaked through Catherine's body. Jesse's touch and kisses were consuming her with a raging need in her hot, wet center. Jesse's jacket and shirt were lost somewhere around the door, so Catherine didn't hesitate to hastily pull Jesse's jeans and panties down her legs. She stood and gazed at the marvel of Jesse's naked body, her fiery eyes showing abandon, adoration, and the urge for more.

Jesse gently took Catherine's chin and settled her mouth upon hers, robbing her of breath and again gathering her into her snug embrace. Damn, Catherine couldn't wait to feel the scent of their fuck all over the room. Jesse pulled Catherine's pants down, stepped onto them, and threw them aside, then with the same determined dedication removed her panties. Now they were both naked, no barriers between the fiery touches of their bare bodies. Their curious hands were roaming across their bodies, learning each other's forms, ardor, pulsations. Jesse was a force of nature and this bare, strong, passionate side of her, focused entirely on Catherine, catching her every tremble, kissing her every weakness, sent Catherine's body into sheer bliss.

"You, Jesse, got me to the point where I just wanted to fuck you, again and again and again."

"Oh, yeah?" Jesse's voice was the very sound of temptation. "Then you're not leaving here until I have that cum all over me."

Jesse's hand was slowly drawing up Catherine's inner thigh and as she neared her hot, wet clit, all her thoughts about how terrible of an idea this was disappeared without a trace.

* * *

When Catherine responded with genuine gasps, Jesse thought she might perish from the pleasure created by those soft sounds. Up until this moment, she'd never realized just how profoundly she desired Catherine. As their naked bodies stumbled through the shed, knocking over nameless objects, all she longed for was to feel her more, savor her more, make her moan even more.

"You're fucking gorgeous," Jesse said, holding her fierce eyes captive.

"*J'ai besoin de te sentir en moi.*"

Between the sensual sound of those mysterious words and her intense kisses, her fingers tangled in her hair urging her on, Jesse could feel Catherine inside like the life running through her bloodstream. Catherine's leg was locked around hers, imploring her touch. Before moving her hand, Jesse softly pressed her lips back to Catherine's. She wanted to look into her eyes, to capture her sighs of desire when she touched her for the first time. Catherine clasped her, arching lustfully against Jesse's hand, the heat between her thighs taking control over her existence.

"I can't wait for you to finally fuck me," Catherine whispered.

Jesse couldn't wait anymore. She eased her hand down and slid gently over her wet folds. "God, yes," she said as delight unwound within her and Catherine's wetness gladly surrendered to Jesse's fingertips slipping in between. Their unyielding lips covered their sighs, and their gazes gathered wondrous rapture when they locked into each other's eyes. As Jesse parted Catherine with two fingers and rubbed her clit in small circles, she could feel the air fill with her fragrance. Catherine moaned against her lips and Jesse could feel her own pussy starting to drip with want. That woman's kisses, her compelling lips, the feel of her skin so tightly pressed against her own, her incredibly profuse fluids—all this was driving her absolutely insane. There was nothing else in the universe right then but Catherine's gloriously naked body, the rhythm of her breathing.

"*Chaque fois que je te vois, chaque fois que j'entends ta voix, je veux me masturber sauvagement.*"

Jesse surrendered to the susurration of that voice and her hand moved down. "Look into my eyes."

A loud moan escaped from within Catherine as a natural response to Jesse's fingers sinking right in and Catherine answered by running her tongue along Jesse's warm lips, tasting her as Jesse delved deeper, stroking more firmly. Catherine was now breathing heavier, which only intensified the urgency within Jesse. With each thrust she would swallow Catherine's throaty sigh, and with each move of her slick hand over Catherine's clit she would feel pulsating around her fingers, avid and rhythmic, squeezing her.

Catherine continued teasing Jesse with her lips, teeth, and tongue, and her hand lowered as though curious to feel the reaction of Jesse's pussy at that very moment. Catherine's heavy breathing, her sensual and almost muscular lips, her keen, dark eyes following Jesse's every move, every desire—the way she kissed her like she'd never let go—consumed Jesse's senses. Catherine's nails dug into Jesse's back, and the pressure built in Jesse as well. Seeing the savage look in Catherine's eyes, listening to her suggestive murmurs against her lips, neck, and ears, feeling her wet, hot pussy so close to her own, she knew she was close. As Catherine gasped her name, Jesse's wet fingers continued pressing her pulsating clit with determination, and a moment later orgasm shuddered Catherine's body. She threw her head back, helplessly exposing her neck to more of Jesse's kisses. Their sweaty bodies were still glued together as Jesse's hand relished the shudders of pleasure coming from deep inside. With her hand full of Catherine's warm, exquisite wetness, Jesse slowly brought it up and with a smile spread it over her own arms, ribs, and neck.

"I wanna wake up tomorrow and smell you on every inch of me."

As if that electrifying ecstasy and Jesse's low whispers had energized her, Catherine gripped Jesse even harder. Her breathing heavy, a whole new craving seemed to arise as her eyes flashed and she directed Jesse to the old desk in the corner, never parting from her lips.

"I wanna feel your pussy around my tongue."

Jesse's breath shortened, her skin burned, and as Catherine's lips touched her burning folds, with the smell of her cum so close on her neck, she knew she was moments away from curling her toes.

"Not so fast, Jesse. We are just getting started."

To Jesse's ears, this was the sweet sound of torture.

CHAPTER TWENTY-SIX

When Jesse finally roused from sleep, the sun had already crossed Oak Valley and was headed to Scarlet Peak, which meant it was well after two in the afternoon. She stretched out in her bed, readily acknowledging that she was excessively euphoric. Surely the world wasn't this weirdly wonderful and all the clouds hadn't become smiling rainbows in a matter of a day. So perhaps she was a bit too cheerful, but still, life suddenly seemed so damn easy. All it took was one chaotic, neurotic French woman. Her thoughts drifted off to Catherine's body breaking under her kisses, her confident gaze following her every move, herself coming all over her with safe ease. Catherine was daring, fearless, and gorgeous, and Jesse could feel the heat building up in her panties again. Damn.

She could hear the clatter of plates reaching from downstairs of her family home, and she just wanted to hide in bed and think about last night all day. Make it last longer, feel Catherine's intensity under her hands, put her tongue between her legs. For those few hours she had been completely hers—yesterday and tomorrow didn't matter, only their bodies together. They didn't sleep a single second, and she lost count of how many times she came. She only knew it felt like minutes, and she wanted more.

Anticipation was slowly building in her body, picturing Catherine's gaze when they met again. Would she get to feel those lips on her own one more time, that firm thigh moving against her? She didn't seem repentant at all this morning when they finally parted, and Jesse could still vividly feel the shape of Catherine's smile under her lips.

She had aroused her imagination from the start, but now that she'd experienced Catherine's lust, her body, her horizons, her own force, she didn't know how she could stay away from her. It felt as if her fingers had never touched anything so alive. Jesse recalled the first moment when there had been nothing between their bodies but their sweat, and the thought instantly made her sink deeper into her reverie. If she ever wanted anything serious, for some reason, it was now and with this crazy French woman.

Catherine's raw scent was still fresh on her skin, which made her remember all the ways Catherine had fucked her the night before, and her folds began pulsating again. Damn, she couldn't go through her day like this. The astounding ease and confidence they had with each other's bodies generated a kind of pleasure and intimacy Jesse had never experienced before. She wanted Catherine in her arms, pressed against her body. Craving her long, inebriating kisses on her neck, she could no longer ignore the need to slip her hand in her own wet panties. Jesse closed her eyes, feeling the throbbing clit under her fingers, as she vividly imagined pulling Catherine into her arms from behind, caressing her waist, tracing her shoulders with kisses, one hand softly traveling to her nipple as the other traveled down, rubbing through her panties. She could picture Catherine's arm instinctively reaching for her and wrapping around Jesse's neck as her butt started pressing harder into her, as she began to curl around her.

Breathing a little faster, Jesse hastily yanked the shirt up over her head, wanting to be naked thinking about Catherine's hands on her skin, her ear right next to Catherine's lips, capturing her hungry moans.

Catherine's heavy breathing… God, no one could ever resist that sound. Jesse whimpered at the sensation of Catherine's breath on her skin, sending a shiver of anticipation through her. She was sexy, she was fierce, and the way she was inviting her touch and smiling greedily in lust made Jesse want to fuck her for days.

To watch her sleep, to wake up with her kisses. Fuck. That was too much. Pressing her fingers into her clit, Jesse moaned and bit into her bottom lip. She could feel the wetness soaking through her panties and the insides of her thighs, and she knew she was close. Damn this woman. As she pictured Catherine's slick fingers sliding into her at that very moment, a rush washed over her body and she exploded in rhythmical contractions, her hips thrusting wildly, her hand grasping the bed.

God, she was in so much trouble. She refused to question herself, but she had undoubtedly fallen hard for someone who was nowhere near ready. Wasn't it silly that she who never experienced love was now in a position to depend on someone else's feelings? She saw how those illusions ended, yet she was so naïve as to believe there actually might be "the one." *The one?* Was she out of her damn mind? This wasn't like her, yet everything with Catherine felt so easy, so right, so obvious.

Jesse pulled the covers over her head and heaved a deep sigh.

Craving Catherine's presence, her experiences, she'd researched the history of dance. To feel closer to her, she bought a French dictionary even though Catherine was perfectly fluent in English. *Tu es stupide, Jesse.* She rolled over to her side.

Catherine had the purity Jesse no longer saw in other people, and that was something that would be hard to forget. Even her lovemaking was uninhibited, raw, fierce. In her arms, Jesse could surrender to her own true self, and for the first time she was afraid to lose something. Staring into Catherine's eyes, she could see a completely different reality, some other life…an excitement, like there was still hope for this world.

Well, there was no hope for her. Fuck.

She didn't want to call it by its proper name yet, but if she did, she would have to admit she'd fallen in love with Catherine Des Lauriers. However, more than anything she wanted Catherine to feel safe, so she'd keep her happy mouth shut and stay cool. She picked up her guitar from the corner of the room and, with Cath's scent still on her fingers, started picking the strings in an attempt to give her hands and lips something else to think about.

"All this honesty between us, aren't we perfectly matched? Aren't we perfectly matched for pain?"

Yet, her body refused to listen, and her entire being surrendered at the thought of Catherine's touch. This dopamine thing was a heavy drug.

Jesse played for about half an hour when she realized that she was running the risk of becoming seriously pathetic unless she quickly reclaimed her pitiful common sense. She definitely needed a shower before facing her family, so one last time she inhaled the familiar scent her skin still bore and hopped in the shower.

Jesse had intimated to her family a few days ago that she might swing over, so after she snuck in this morning at seven and left a note, no one was overly surprised. They'd never been too formal, and their house had seemed like a county fair ever since she was a child, so when she came downstairs and found only her mother ensconced on the sofa with her reading glasses, engrossed in her phone, she was instantly relieved. She had no idea how she would have explained her sudden visit to her eighteen cousins.

"I heard you play. New material?" Her mother patted the sofa next to her and Jesse swiftly perched beside her, grabbing a shrimp egg roll off the plate.

"Uh-huh. The album is mostly ready." She nodded affirmatively. "I'm considering squeezing in another song or two."

"Oh? What are they about?"

Jesse had never been secretive, especially not around her parents, but she had no intention of speaking about the first song, not today. As far as the other was concerned, well, she couldn't stop thinking about that one all day, even if she didn't know what to make of the intense attraction between Catherine and her.

"About this woman I like."

Jesse's mother took off her glasses and dropped the phone on the coffee table.

"Honey! You better tell me all before I read about it on *Taste of Country*."

"Are you still hooked on that?" Jesse chuckled.

"If they come up with something mean about my little girl, I better find out right away. Then I can warn you."

Jesse settled next to her and hugged her tight.

"You won't find anything on me there. But you can always share what you *do* discover." She winked, but her mother had no intention of letting go.

"So tell me about this lady. Is she from Nashville? How did you two meet?"

"Well..." Jesse paused. She couldn't wait to say her name, but as much as she wanted to talk about her and as much as she longed to bring up Catherine in random conversations, Jesse recognized that the two of them were far from anything defined.

Catherine, Catherine, Catherine.

"It's Fletcher's granddaughter."

"The French girl?" Her mother gaped, flabbergasted.

Jesse trusted her mother with sensitive information, but a feeling of unease came over her all the same. "Please don't mention anything to Fletcher. Or Marjorie. I'm not sure Catherine would want anyone to know."

"Oh my God, so there's something to know? Oh, Jesse Emerson Morgan, you better start talking."

Lisa Morgan, a retired teacher whose passions included jazzercize and Garth Brooks, was used to her middle child's particular candor. Ever since she was a kid, Jesse had readily admitted to any mischief, any naughtiness, any trouble she provoked—and that meant confessing to a lot. Because of that honesty, Lisa knew that of all her kids, Jesse would require kindness the most. One would hardly guess how an outgoing, lively, cheerful, friendly kid could be so vulnerable, but Jesse had always been very cautious with her feelings. When she finally came out as a teenager, Lisa encouraged Jesse to yield to her emotional self, but instead Jesse harnessed her vulnerability, her unbreakable spirit, and her sincerity, and turned them into art—and, subsequently, art turned into her indestructible shield.

Jesse knew her mother rarely worried over the lack of scruples and the relentless nature of the world she'd chosen as her home because she trusted Jesse's maturity, but Lisa was also aware that her daughter had closed herself off in her own small, secure universe. Jesse could only imagine how silly her beaming face must have looked now.

"Catherine just got out of a long relationship and she's not ready for any sort of commitment. I don't think she quite believes I'd ever be into that to begin with. And I...I simply like being around her. She's pure and honest. She can make me happy with just a look."

"Is that why you popped in this morning?"

"Mostly. You're here too." Jesse wrapped her arm tighter around her mother. "We hadn't seen each other in over a month before she came to Fort Collins for my concert. Seeing her there made me realize I don't want to waste so much time ever again."

"Oh, Jesse, first thing tomorrow I'm going to Fletcher's to buy some plates."

Jesse darted an admonishing gaze at her before breaking into laughter and serenely adding, "I don't know what will come of it."

Catherine infused her with a strange calm, even when she was a thousand miles away, and never once did Jesse doubt what she wanted. She would only occasionally feel exposed by the effortlessness with which she was prepared to move her boundaries for Catherine, intent on leaving her enough space while maintaining her own.

"I'm not in a hurry," Jesse said. She shrugged and quickly grabbed another roll off the table. God, she was hungry. Catherine had robbed her of the final atom of her strength last night, but she could hardly think of a more breathtaking spectacle than Catherine's naked, sweaty body on her own. There was a volcano under her hands, an unpredictable, raw power devouring the darkness and ruling her senses. Her mind quickly wandered to the way Catherine first slipped her hand in between her legs, as if she was reaching for her soul.

"But whatever comes of it, I don't want to miss a moment," she briefly added.

"I've seen her around. She is gorgeous," Lisa added.

"I swear that's not all. I promise," Jesse replied quickly with a solemn expression.

Lisa laughed. "So, what's the song about?"

"Wanna hear it?"

"Do I? Of course!"

Jesse ran upstairs to get her guitar and just as she perched on the edge of the sofa ready to play, her father appeared at the door.

"I see I've arrived just in time. What are we singing?"

"A song Jesse wrote for her new girlfriend," her mother replied.

"Oh, please, play it for us. If you tell me all I need to know through your lyrics, it's a hit."

While it wasn't entirely helpful with afflictions like love, her ability to bare her soul had made Jesse a thriving artist soon after she moved away from Maple Springs. Her breakthrough came only a year after she left for Nashville. Even though her debut album was released to critical acclaim, it was only a few months later that its sales skyrocketed. Jesse's song detailing the transience of love and passion, and a human pursuit of something timeless was recognized by BMW and featured in their commercial that aired during the Super Bowl. Her hypnotic voice paired with dramatic music and indignation over the waning emotions was apparently all the auto giant needed. As the black SUV sped down the burned highways and collapsing bridges powered by "Timeless," the song's sales increased by almost 400 percent, and it had sold over 600,000 copies to date. All the heartaches, broken promises, vain desires, forlorn memories that she'd poured into that song were finally and officially declared insignificant. Under those shiny wheels none of her feelings were timeless, but that car sure seemed like it, and that was all it took to present her singular talent to the world.

"I'm in so much trouble," she murmured as her fingers finally touched the strings.

CHAPTER TWENTY-SEVEN

Catherine spent the day in the shop, trying to entertain her mind with something that was not Jesse's body and her tantalizing touch, while her mind industriously kept downplaying the significance of what had occurred last night. She was still free, and as long as she was free, she'd be fine—but, damn, that woman could kiss. Just when she wised up and decided not to have a love life for the next thirty years, the last thing she needed was to enjoy someone's company, sense of humor, and now sex.

It was just that, sex. Everyone does it, Catherine. The fact that it took you thirty-four years to be casual with it doesn't mean it should be different.

Oh, Jesse better be the womanizer she appeared to be. Catherine's entire wisdom depended on it. Yes, it would be so much easier to forget the curious feeling of being safe with Jesse's body if she knew that eager, sinewy, addictive body was there for others too.

Fletcher had a big order for Halloween, and Catherine worked on the custom carvings all day, trying to suppress the thought of Jesse's lips covering her entire body with hungry kisses. Those lips were all kinds of erotic, as they were sliding down her body, making her desperate to touch her, dispersing her thoughts into stardust. Catherine decided to abandon the carvings for a bit and go to the wheel, but she could hardly focus on the clay in front of her. As her hands glided over its smoothness, she could almost sense Jesse under her fingertips. Her sighs, her shivers, her tense muscles, her firm hold, how she responded to Catherine's touch as her hands continued to trail down her back. Crazy, absolutely crazy, that's what she was.

This is how civilizations collapse, Catherine.

After a few hours of feeling Jesse under her fingers, Catherine decided she needed a break if she was going to get through the day. She washed her hands and sat to check for any incoming orders when the shop bell startled her.

Just like the first time, there stood Jesse. Again surprising her, again curiously turning around the shop, again leaving her speechless. That woman…could she possibly be any sexier? She stood in the exact same place where everything had started, and with the same hat, now that their relationship was at the beginning of its end. Why was it so hard to resist her? Catherine responded with a smile, cursing her frailties.

"I figured you'd be here," Jesse said.

"Fletcher got an online order for Halloween, so we're trying to finish up by Saturday."

Their eyes instantly resumed the duel, the undressing, the relentless pursuit of lust.

"Does that mean you can't take tomorrow off? I was going to ask you to join me for whitewater rafting."

"In October?"

Jesse's intent stare was driving her wild with desire. It was as if she could touch her naked body with every gaze.

"That's when it's exciting. Come on, I'll keep an eye on you."

Catherine promptly envisioned Jesse's intense, ardent kisses on her neck, and her attention slipped to her half-unbuttoned shirt. She pictured Jesse's well-defined, wet arms glistening in the sun, the familiar fingers trailing down her spine, the swift current carrying them over the rapids, their drenched bodies passionately locked together in the raft, fighting the river and the invading torrents. Jesse's arms had a strange power to reveal her every weakness, overturn her every certainty, and tempt her very soul, yet her caresses were always tender and confident. When Jesse's hands would slide around her waist, Catherine would surely take a moment to gaze at her, admiring and memorizing every detail of her naked, wet beauty. Her breasts would sway in front of her as she leaned forward to taste the river from them, leaving Jesse shivering at her touch while Catherine's fingertips slid in between her legs. Already feeling Jesse's heavy breathing against her chest, Catherine could hardly say no.

She took a few steps closer to Jesse. Fletcher had left early, and it was up to her to close. Her skin recollected Jesse's scent, her kisses, her caresses, and she longed for more. Here and now.

"I just wondered what it would be like to have sex with you in that raft," Catherine whispered.

She pressed a soft, teasing kiss at the corner of Jesse's mouth, and the woman whimpered.

"Surprisingly, I'm not after sex. I just want to get to know you better," Jesse said, apparently to resist the temptation with the noblest intentions.

"Shame," Catherine said. "That was really good sex."

The moment of deliberation was brief. Jesse cradled Catherine's face and took her mouth in a fervent kiss. "Thank you very much, Catherine. Rafting will never be good enough again."

In their passionate embrace Catherine pushed her against the counter, knocking over the vase standing next to the register.

"Fuck, Catherine, and I really wanted to show you that I was not what you thought I was."

"What? Sexy, fun, great time?" Catherine had no intention of stopping anytime soon. She wanted to pick up exactly where they had left off that morning. Ravished by Jesse's kisses, Catherine lifted her on the counter, overturning a chair this time, hastily untucking and unbuttoning her shirt.

"I genuinely like you, Catherine." Somewhere deep among her frailties, Jesse seemed to have stumbled upon a grain of sense.

"Oh, that's a bummer." Catherine's fingers stopped, leaving the unbuttoned shirt to outline Jesse's perfect breasts. She could still see the waves of her fast breathing, so she took a step back.

Catherine could not allow this to become something more, and she cared for Jesse enough to be sincere.

"Listen, Jesse. I like you too. You're not a rebound. Even when Chloe was here, all I could think about was you. I like you, it's okay. It's just that I don't believe in commitments anymore. I love spending time with you, but it ends there." Jesse deserved the honesty, and Catherine gave her all the truth she had. There was no place for any complications or resentments in her life anymore, and though Jesse didn't ask for anything, Catherine wanted to make it clear, to make Jesse aware of her void. It was only fair. She liked the woman and wanted them to be honest with each other. Strangely, she trusted her enough for that.

* * *

"I get that." Jesse didn't flinch, and her voice was calm as ever.

Of course Catherine needed time. Jesse wouldn't want it any other way. Catherine wasn't one of those people who could substitute one emotion with another in a matter of weeks. Rather than taking Chloe's place, Jesse wanted her own. Sure, this was probably how every single heartbreak in the history of the universe started, but she treasured Catherine's devotion, honesty, and dedication. Catherine was not giving her heart easily, and that made it even more valuable to Jesse. It made her like the woman even more. If that was at all possible at that point. Probably not.

This may never work out, but she'd be damned if she didn't try. She'd play by Catherine's rules and give her time. She enjoyed what she had so far—Catherine's vulnerability, her sincerity, and obviously her masterful touch. Moreover, Jesse had formed a quiet impression that no way someone could make love to you like that, tune into your body and mind with such ease, and then say it was just physical. That would hardly be fair.

"So, Catherine." Jesse gently took her chin and pulled her closer again. "Back to the important bit. I'm sexy, huh? I think it's got to be my shoulder blades. That's my whole game."

Catherine smiled gratefully, as though she needed Jesse to be promiscuous and let her experience their attraction without too many questions.

"I really don't wanna wait till that raft to have you again, you paragon of virtue," Catherine whispered.

"Definitely shoulder blades. The sexiest part of *your* body—"

Catherine's mouth crushed down on hers before Jesse had a chance to finish the sentence. Grasping Jesse's waist with both hands and scooping her up in her arms, Catherine urged her legs around her hips. She carried her in a savage kiss across the shop, quickly bolting the door and turning the closed sign, and proceeding to the back room. It was as if they'd waited too long for the first time and were unstoppable now that they finally tasted the bliss. They hadn't lasted last five minutes after Jesse showed up in the shop.

Jesse's hands slid around the back of her neck, and with her legs locked firmly around her waist, Catherine apparently wanted closer contact with her butt as she slipped her hands inside the pants, looking for her burning skin. Jesse could feel her pleased smile between their kisses.

"No panties, Jesse? Now, that's just wrong." She gasped, never ceasing to kiss her, and Jesse could not look away.

"You're so fucking beautiful when you come."

At the sound of her words, Catherine's body responded, arching her hips up toward Jesse's pelvis, anchoring her, squeezing her butt, pressing so close to her that she could feel the heat. She didn't think they'd make it to take off their clothes this time. Their movements were delirious and impatient as they stumbled over the edge of the couch, unzipping each other's pants. Jesse quickly found herself under Catherine's body, stretching her arms over her head.

At the first touch of Catherine's hand on her pulsating folds, she instinctively closed her eyes and groaned. The way Catherine was teasing her was so fucking lovely. She could feel the tempting touch of her breath on her bare neck, and she readily surrendered under the strength of her kiss. Tender yet confident, Catherine's fingers explored her entrance before her hand slipped to her inner thigh and just like that, she could sense Catherine's clit rubbing against hers. Was this how she died? Under the body of this gorgeous, implacable force of a woman?

Catherine slid her tongue along Jesse's neck and then ran her lips across her jawline to her earlobe, lightly nibbling them. The softness of their two bodies against one another was so fulfilling that Jesse couldn't bear it anymore and went looking for her tongue.

Only two undone buttons of her shirt, her dark, unruly hair teasing her neck, her confident hand parting her legs, her relentless stare... Jesse could feel herself dissolving in a wave of heat rushing through her body. Gripping the curve of Catherine's butt, she began to thrust in a consistent, intense pace. God, she loved the look of Catherine on top of her, next to her, inside of her. She was so graceful yet strong, her lines well-defined, displaying a relaxed confidence and comfort being naked that was so fucking irresistible. Her body was curious and fearless, her eyes determined. As if Jesse never lived outside her touch, Catherine controlled Jesse's every breath, her every impulse, her every desire—and this woman's sharp yet calm focus on her was sending Jesse over the edge.

As Catherine pushed harder into her wetness, Jesse's thoughts were dispersed into thin air. With their bodies together, still half-dressed, their gazes primal and undisturbed, Jesse responded with a fast, pounding pace that left Catherine searching for air. She could recognize every single delight, every sweet torture, every impulse in her eyes that held her captive. The ferocious way in which Catherine's arms held her close, the lust in her raw stare, were devouring her from the inside out. Jesse's entire universe was reduced to the body pressed so tightly against hers, the sound of Catherine's wet skin rubbing against hers, her breath on her neck.

Catherine's fingers danced upon Jesse's skin, creating her anew, free and restless. They couldn't get enough of her, pausing to adore her aroused nipples, her insatiable thighs, her burning lips, still swollen from last night, and Jesse turned into one infinite sensation. Their sweaty legs slid rhythmically, incessantly, permeating the air with their scent and heat.

There were no restraints in their starved gazes, nothing but their bare, hungry need for each other. Weakened by the waves of bliss coursing through her, Jesse was close to closing her eyes, but she held on, never leaving those dark, unrelenting eyes that entranced her so. Moments away from absolute abandon, Jesse gripped her butt stronger and relished in the firm movements, in the power of their wet friction. When she met wild, fiery lust in Catherine's stare, all her muscles contracting, she could no longer hold it and she surrendered to the explosion of pleasure from deep within. Her hips pressed into Catherine's and she bit into her shoulder as a torrent of joy invaded her nerve endings. Utter gratification erased the reality around her and rendered her distant to anything that wasn't the wet feel of that warm skin on hers. How could such calm, such a firm sense of right, coexist with such chaos of feelings? Damn French woman.

Catherine's final push only prolonged Jesse's search for air, and a moment later Catherine's hips undulated, her gaze intensified, as she joined her in that intense excitement. Their bodies remained immobile, their minds blank, their clits still pressed against one another. Breathing heavily, they were unable to take control of their limbs, their balance, all of space and time, yet Catherine's dark stare still attentively followed her. Jesse couldn't recall anyone ever looking at her the way this woman did now, as if she were a work of art in some rare exhibition. God, she would drive her insane. Jesse knew it was only a matter of moments before they started over.

CHAPTER TWENTY-EIGHT

When they pulled over on the side of the gravel road that Jesse knew so well, the air was rich with a sweet, resinous fragrance of cottonwoods that lined that stretch of the picturesque Arkansas River. The tall, proud trees were turning gold against a bright blue Colorado sky, inviting them to slow down. The light breeze teased the heart-shaped leaves, creating a pleasant rustle overhead that accompanied them as the red canyon walls loomed in the distance.

Ever since she was a child, Jesse had been visiting this magnificent, lonely canyon to enjoy the snowcapped peaks and crystal-clear immensity as the river sculpted its way through the valleys. The women quickly grabbed the inflatable raft with life jackets and helmets from the outfitter and began their float down the river. Unlike Jesse, Catherine had never been rafting, which was obvious from the very first moment she showed up that morning, unworried, dressed in skinny jeans and a red cotton shirt with rolled-up sleeves. Even now, stealing glances at her as she was completely immersed in the placid, warm, colorful scenery around them, Jesse couldn't help but chuckle, yet Catherine quickly shrugged aside the suggestion that she change her clothes.

"You'll come to admire my resilience, Jesse."

"I just know that things can go so wrong so fast."

"I go so wrong so fast all the time."

Jesse laughed, shaking her head and taking a moment to observe Catherine in her silent beauty. She could not think of a pursuit more worthy than to make that woman smile every single day. Catherine was never interested in being perfect, gladly poking fun at herself, embracing her weaknesses and wrong choices, and she always gazed at Jesse as if she saw something no one else could, as if she could reach the darkest abyss of her desire with only a look and take complete command of it. It was so easy to imagine the spray and mist of the river cooling their ardent bodies, feeling the breeze as they struggled for air, the smell of wild nature and each other teasing their senses, nothing between them but the crashing waves. Damn woman just had to share that fantasy with her, didn't she? To prevent her imagination from going into overdrive, Jesse briefly shifted her gaze to the scenic river. They were crossing lower-class rapids that allowed Catherine to practice her strokes and gave Jesse time to watch her as she navigated them through the canyon.

"This was my favorite place to go as a child," Jesse said softly, looking around. "You move and the river follows." White noise of the wild and scenic river trailed through the ruddy colors as Jesse continued, "The water flow is perfect. You've got rugged mountains in the backdrop, marmots staring at you curiously from their rocks, trees towering above, and birds soaring over. Just as you start thinking the sun is too intense, water sends you barreling over the rushing waves."

"Who brought you here?"

"My aunt, while she was alive. She would take me up to Pine Falls to jump off the waterfall. She would always tell me, 'Live your own adventure, otherwise you'll end up telling other people's stories all your life.'"

Somehow, she'd ended up doing just that, hadn't she? Now next to Catherine, for the first time she felt like the most riveting adventure was what that woman made her feel inside. Something with a life of its own, beyond her control, savage and unpredictable.

"She died when I was fifteen, in a car accident."

"I'm sorry."

"After that, I've been mostly coming here alone. My besties, Chelsea and Kelly, preferred sitting at Bertha's waiting for the boys to show up—and they never did, of course. So when we turned seventeen, we'd go down to Boulder and hang out with kids from our high school. And it paid off. They met their husbands and I met Catherine Williams."

"Oh, why don't I already know all about Catherine Williams?"

"I wrote a billion songs for her in those two months. None of them good. No wonder she dumped me."

"I'm sorry." Catherine chuckled.

Jesse shrugged and gave a sharp sigh.

"Good name, bad girl. I should have paid more attention to our French tourists. I would have had more fun there with *this* Catherine." She leaned in, smiling and cupping Catherine's chin, and then kissed her long. Deep and long. After a searing kiss, Jesse pulled back a little and paused in her eyes, tucking a rogue curl behind Catherine's ear. Catherine pulled her closer and with her face inches from her, Jesse could feel the sun reflecting its warmth, her lips inviting another kiss. Where did she find this woman? Damn, her heart could be loud.

They maneuvered the inflatable raft around rocks and dropped through narrow chutes before hitting the quiet patch. The river felt equally thrilling whether it brought rolling water and huge drops or the peace and solitude of the quiet alpine scenery. The sensation of floating seemed to release all worries and anxieties.

Jesse interrupted the silence, her blue eyes earnest in their exploration. "What do you miss most about being a kid?"

Catherine beamed, wrinkling her nose. "Falling asleep somewhere and still somehow waking up in my bed every morning?"

"Oh, now you tell me." Jesse laughed.

"My dad studied insects in what I thought were jungles, so I didn't have many friends growing up. My mom would try to compensate." She paused and sighed as soon as she thought of her restless mother. "She created four friends for me and then played all four. They had their distinct outfits, so whenever I would see a purple dress and a wide-brimmed fedora I knew Rochana Saeli—nicknamed Fon—was visiting. She was from Thailand, loved elephants, and was my bitter rival for the affection of the only actual person I knew, Max. Together we learned how to do hair and makeup, and we used to read *OK Magazine* religiously. Fon wasn't fluent in English, so I had to explain to her what happened between J.Lo and Ojani. We were both heartbroken there.

"My mom played all four rather convincingly. Omar was a blind Boy Scout who wanted us to climb trees, and in the end somehow he would always keep me from falling. His sister Irene would send him letters from Argentina that I would then read to him. He loved stealing oranges and gorging on candies, so whenever I would get a chocolate, Omar would show up next to me to share. Eva Arnarsdóttir was from Iceland. Always wearing ski jackets and pom-pom beanies, she traveled around the world and had a little kitten, Trjegul. We'd hold each other's hands, but then she would leave for Timbuktu and send me homemade postcards. Farai Tshuma from Zimbabwe was smart—a know-it-all but also timid. With glasses and a red silk bandana around his neck, he knew all about dinosaurs, the universe, and *Star Wars*. Sometimes I would want to chat with Eva, but then Farai would show up, and I'd get stuck talking about apple oxidation."

"That is definitely better than Catherine Williams." Jesse laughed.

"My mom is definitely not your average parent. Even now, she tells me she ran into Fon."

"Is Fon still wearing the same hat? Did she get Max in the end? I want to know."

* * *

They laughed and talked until they approached the biggest rapid and decided they should get out on the pebble-strewn shore to scout it out. Catherine was already soaking wet but valiantly suffered in silence while Jesse was lifting the boat out of the water and tying it down. The flows didn't appear to be that high, but since they were close to Pine Falls, Jesse suggested leaving the boat for a moment to hike the banks a bit higher up.

"You could leave your clothes here to dry," Jesse added and pulled a towel, a change of dry clothes, and dry shoes out of her backpack. Catherine tenderly smiled at her, unable to stop her eyes from moving over Jesse's body.

"Do I get to undress you as well then?"

"It would only seem fair." Jesse smirked and then walked up to Catherine, feeling the wet shirt around her forearms. She slid her hands up and placed them on Catherine's face before claiming her lips in a long kiss. Catherine quickly responded, brushing her fingers through her hair, tasting the moment with utter delight. There was no way she could ever regret something that delicious, was there? No, this was perfectly acceptable, her body agreed. Jesse's tongue was still ruling her when the woman reached for something and placed it between them.

"Your clothes," Jesse whispered against her lips.

Oh, come on!

"You downright enjoy doing this to me, don't you?" Catherine smiled, capitulating and grabbing the clothes.

God, that smelled just like Jesse. Damn woman. She unbuttoned her shirt languidly, and Jesse's amused gaze turned into wriggling when she started taking off her pants. Dry clothes felt good, though. Perhaps now they could pick up where they left off.

"Let's go, we have another good hour here," Jesse said, and as if she could read Catherine's wicked mind, she turned airily and set out for the trailhead.

"How long does it take to walk up there?"

"Is it time to pee?" Jesse asked.

"Perhaps."

"Come on." Jesse encouraged her with a waggish grin. "It's half a mile, and when we come back you can have the entire banana bread to yourself."

"You brought banana bread?" Her eyes widened.

"Of course. They don't make these in Nashville."

Catherine beamed. Jesse really had thought of everything, and there it was again, the sound of her stupid heart melting. She followed her obediently, only occasionally burying her face against Jesse's shirt she was wearing in search of that calming scent.

After a ten-minute hike, they reached the top of the waterfall just as the evening sun created a perfect reflection. Cascading water gleamed brilliant yellow, orange, and red like it had been set ablaze, and the loud sound of its crashing, its roaring, its rage created profound awe. A simple droplet of water in that glittering mist resembled a furious volcano. Catherine drew nearer to the edge, and the yearning to be part of that breathtaking beauty overtook her every sense. She admired the waterfall's display of vivid colors, the hues of cliffs that were distant and intact, the imposing sound of its pounding into water, and a gentle tranquility descended upon her and made it clear she was going to jump.

The waterfall wasn't too high, and she needed to feel its life, its colors on her.

"Jesse, this is beautiful. We could be one with it." Catherine grasped her hand and led her to the cliff above the waterfall. With a calm expression, she readily divested herself of clothes.

Jesse was staring at her, incredulous.

"Let's live our own adventure," Catherine's silky voice added.

One smile was all it took, and Jesse promptly started taking off her clothes, her eyes never leaving Catherine.

Jesse's hand waited outstretched, the hand that could tell a story of everything that woman had ever done, that could comfort, caress, hold, and drag her into death, apparently.

Catherine gripped Jesse's hand and, sharing nothing but a reassuring look, they leaped off together.

The water was not as cold as she expected, and as soon as they emerged they passionately reached for each other's lips. Yet, that kiss was different from every one they'd shared in the past two days. It was softer, as if they were discovering something new, something more profound in their intimacy. The waterfall towering above them suddenly turned into a quiet observer and there was a moment of stillness right after they kissed, a perfect calm except for something arcane, something mysterious, moving between them.

Gazing at the droplets shimmering on her eyelashes, Catherine was lost in Jesse's loveliness.

Why was this wrong, again? Jesse's kisses were intoxicating her senses. She was forgetting the love she no longer believed in, forgetting all her worldly duties, all the insecurities and apprehensions, all except the desire to possess the secrets of Jesse's body. Catherine didn't question Jesse's affection, and the woman had a way of showing it. Sure, it was more than a simple attraction, but Catherine never doubted that Jesse's fascinations didn't last. She was an artist. Feelings inebriated her and feelings bored her. Catherine harbored no illusions. But damn, did her body create an addiction! If they just had sex again, then she could legitimately argue a case that this indeed was all about sex and decidedly not about her unbearable infatuation and need to hear more about Jesse, explore her more, wrap her arms around her, hold her close, know her better. It would be about their mind-blowing sex. Not about how comfortable she was sharing things with Jesse, finding unwavering support for her every whim, patience for her every doubt.

It's totally just sex. You're basically made out of stone, Catherine.

They shared a few more kisses before they hiked up to get their clothes. The sun was lazily setting over the distant peaks, so they carried the boat on the bank past the raging rapids, then launched it back into the river once they reached calm water. As they paddled back, they saw a black bear meandering in the distance, snacking on berries and insects, and getting ready to savor a salmon dinner. It was time to go.

CHAPTER TWENTY-NINE

The entire week seemed like a dark marathon of desire and lust, and when Friday finally arrived, Catherine was secretly relieved. She knew very well she wouldn't be able to part from Jesse's beguiling body on her own, and to spend more time with her was perilous for her newfound dignity.

No wonder people listened to country music, though. The woman was sexy beyond belief, yet Catherine was not going to be anyone's toy, she was sure of that. Now that Jesse got what she wanted, she could return to her life as a country star and leave Catherine to her sweet oblivion. Jesse had no reason to pursue her anymore. The intensity of her desire was so powerful that Catherine feared she didn't have control over it, and not having the source of such temptation around should certainly help her regain her sanity. Jesse turned her into a sex maniac who could hardly keep her hands to herself. They had sex in the shed, in the shop, in the shower at the bank of the river, even in the Tacoma's bed. When she woke up on Thursday morning, after a day spent rafting, a fleeting, dangerous thought passed through Catherine's mind, and it was simply too much. Being a sex maniac she could handle, but envisioning Jesse asleep, that was off-limits.

Catherine knew Jesse's flight out of Denver was around four in the afternoon, so when noon had passed, she hoped Jesse would simply skip the goodbye. She didn't owe her anything, of course, and it would be ideal if they could just leave it at sex. Still, a few minutes after twelve, she heard a car pulling up, and noticed a black rental Audi in front of the house. Closing her eyes, Catherine muttered a curse. Jesse was walking toward her wearing that goddamn sexy brown leather jacket, and her roguish grin quickly thrust Catherine into a whirlwind of lust. *Okay, Jesse, you don't have to be so sexy every single time, now, do you?*

"I bet you thought I wouldn't come to say goodbye."

"I didn't think, period," she uttered softly.

"Liar."

Jesse took a step forward, stroked her cheek and then cupped her face, imprinting a brief kiss. Catherine was about to protest, but Jesse kissed her again, bearing away time and space.

One more kiss couldn't kill anyone, I suppose. Jesse's tongue was playfully exploring her, teasing, weakening her knees. As her mouth slid down to Catherine's neck, it made her wriggle. Good God, how could something so wrong feel so right? Every single time, Jesse managed to pull Catherine into this savage yet intimate tempest she had no control over. These, these... instincts she had were most inconvenient. She could really do without these now. Jesse's lips would start a fury of senses, the fury to possess her, and she couldn't tell if it was something so deep inside her or something completely beyond her powers, a feeling or a primal instinct?

She finally collected herself and pulled away, breathing hard. Jesse seemed to be looking for a breath as well.

"I know I'll be thinking about that for a long time." Jesse finally took a breath and adjusted her hat.

"It's time for you to focus on the tour and finishing your new album," Catherine said calmly, her eyes never leaving Jesse's.

"Come on, you can't kiss me like that and tell me to focus on something else. Please," Jesse begged, then smiled, reflecting Catherine's cool. "Fine, I can focus on more things."

"You are wonderful, Jesse, but the timing is just not right. If we had met five years ago or in five years, it might have been different. At this point in my life, I cannot commit to anything. I like you and I respect you enough to let you go. You don't owe me anything."

"I stopped listening after 'You're wonderful, Jesse.'" She grinned, and after briefly pausing in her eyes, she spoke with reassuring poise. "Listen, Catherine, I don't care what you call it. It's been ages since I wanted to be around someone, since I wanted to get to know someone as much. That's all I want," she said easily.

That's all Catherine wanted too, so why was that so bad? *Because that's how it starts, you idiot.*

"Fine," Catherine said, "but know that you can do whatever you please. You don't owe me anything."

"I know, but I don't want anyone else. Not because I owe it to you, but because I don't feel it."

"Well, should you feel it, go for it."

"Thanks. I won't, but thank you, babe." She beamed and gently enclosed her chin as if she was about to pull her in for a kiss.

Catherine gave a hearty laugh, almost choking.

"Babe?" The woman did her best to drive her crazy.

"You're the biggest babe I know," Jesse said.

"God, you're stubborn."

"Not more than you, Catherine. I can't prove that I'm not a womanizer except with time, and that's fine. I genuinely care about you and I don't think about other women. It's all right if you don't want anything to do with me, but that doesn't mean I'll want someone else. I feel good about where I am right now."

"Fine, as long as you know I can't go any further. It was just sex," she said, more to herself than Jesse. She didn't want to hurt Jesse, but gazing at that resolute expression, she realized she already loved so many things about the woman in front of her, and being harsh was all she could come up with to break the spell. Why did Jesse always have to say the right thing? Even now, she was unperturbed, firm, and Catherine was captivated by her tenacity, her serenity, her ease, her infectious enthusiasm. Even their intimacy was more profound than Catherine could explain. Perhaps she just had to let her leave and oblivion would do its part.

"You know, 'babe' is actually perfect," she said thoughtfully, however, Jesse still observed her earnestly, without a flinch.

"Each moment with you is more than the moment before, you know?" Jesse couldn't pull away her eyes and to avoid her imminent kiss, Catherine pressed her lips against her hair, her cap, holding her tight.

"What am I doing? I don't want to hurt anyone, Jesse. I like you, I just don't want you to think we're together."

Jesse's face lit up. "Of course, what would your other girlfriends say to that?"

"Even you are more than I can handle," she said, grabbing her jacket collar.

"Oh, you're handling me just fine."

"This moment is all we'll ever have."

"That's all I care about." Jesse was unyielding, with an impression of airy nonchalance, and Catherine couldn't avert her eyes. Damn, Jesse.

Catherine nervously tucked her curly hair behind the ear, wishing she could gain control of her body again, wishing she could look away from those intense blue eyes. Yet, there was nothing else there.

"I don't doubt what I feel, and it's totally fine if you can't match that, Cath." There were no expectations and no questions asked. "Just have a good time. I don't care about having a title in your life, I want a purpose. I mean, I'd be lucky to have a title, I really liked *chick*." She grinned. "But I'm not after that. And I'm not that person. I don't need women waiting around, and I can't wait for the day you realize that. Oh, babe, I'm gonna rub it in, every waking moment of your life. As you can only expect."

Catherine held back a laugh, before finally burying her face against Jesse's jacket and chuckling. What an impossible woman. So they were having a good time. Once this ran its course, like everything else, she could just move on.

"Trust yourself," Jesse whispered, with so much character in her tone that it seemed almost like she was reciting a verse, which held Catherine as if by spell. Everything about this woman was effortless.

CHAPTER THIRTY

The parcel for New Hampshire was ready on Friday night, and Catherine gladly offered to take care of the shipment. She'd spent the entire week intent on avoiding Fletcher so she wouldn't have to lie about seeing Jesse. However, on Wednesday she had come up with an excuse and then spent the day on the river with Jesse. That was no longer circumventing the truth, it was lying, and her conscience initiated a torment every time Fletcher gazed at her, full of trust. God, she felt so guilty that she would have taken that package to Portsmouth on foot just so she didn't have to be in the same room with him.

After a lengthy negotiation with herself, Catherine decided to tell him—not now, but perhaps the following day, perhaps once it was over. She alone could not afford to analyze her actions and the feelings behind them. Though she was profoundly aware that nothing was meant to last, she still fancied Jesse more than she was supposed to. Damnation, she had turned into a liar and it felt like crap. It had never been her intention to hide anything, but she simply knew there was nothing to hide. Surely this relationship, like any other, would come to an end soon enough, and she wanted to spare herself a barrage of questions. She was afraid no one would understand anyway, so she decided her torrid little affair would stay secret for now.

"Did you know Jesse was here?" her grandfather asked after their Saturday lunch, unsuspecting, as they toasted the job well done.

"Yes, she swung by the shop, we talked," she murmured the last words and quickly took a sip of rum.

For two full minutes before we desecrated your shop. Dammit.

"Marj says her new album is set to release in early March. I'm already looking forward to that."

"Please don't tell me that's all you're going to listen to at the shop." She snickered with a sudden urge to hug his oblivious enthusiasm.

"Have you ever looked up her lyrics? When the music ends, you feel like you've personally met every single person from that song. Not everyone can do that." He shook his head, impressed. "I'm pleased you two are hanging out, but please, give her music a chance. The storytelling will stun you."

Although she would never confess, not even under torture, Catherine already knew all five albums, their chronological order, the number of songs, bonus tracks, and even someone named Mark Watkins, a record producer from New Orleans to whom Jesse was apparently very loyal ever since they first collaborated on "Just for a Night" in 2012. God, only Jesse could make country music sexy.

Fletcher was just about to continue his paean when the phone next to Catherine buzzed. She grabbed it, mortified that he would see Jesse's name pop up on the screen. Still, the call was to her French number and the name startled her. Ninon Allard, her costume designer friend.

Ninon was only a few years older than she was, but her dignified bearing, finesse, and sophisticated elegance made everyone believe she was a timeless diva in her own right. Ever since Catherine had met her eleven years ago, she'd looked the same. Her lush blond hair was pulled high in a messy bun at all times, and her red lipstick was impeccable day or night. She would always say, "My job is to expose the characters' souls with their outfits," and if one could reach any conclusions based on that, Ninon's soul was an extravagant, restless bunch of layers. She brought Catherine to collaborate on her last movie, and Catherine enjoyed every minute of it.

"Ninon? Is that really you?"

A few people were capable of bringing a smile to Catherine's face with each interaction, and Ninon was one of them. The sole sound of her harmless voice would chase away any apprehension or obsession.

"*Ma chérie!*" A familiar Southern French accent echoed in her ears. "Enough already. Come back home!"

"It's so good to hear you, Ninon."

The woman's soft, nasal "g" sound, pronounced syllables, and slow vowels were bringing familiarity that was setting Catherine at ease. She loved how Ninon pronounced her name. Leaning back in her chair as Fletcher went back into the house, she asked cheerfully, "How are you, Ninon? Are you in Paris?"

"Oh, darling, I've never been better. I've met the most fascinating man. He's a bit older, but he dances as if he were forty-five and not seventy-five. Did I mention that he's a baron and he owns a castle in Gascony?" Catherine listened, amused, as the woman continued, "We were at his yacht in Antibes. I got back to Paris yesterday, and who is the first person I run into? Chloe! Oh, I ripped her apart, I sure did. She told me you two had a chance to clear things up and that you were gracious. I don't doubt that, but I still wanted to hear it from you. How are you, sweetie? Did you honestly move on?"

She didn't know if that could be defined as moving on, but for a while now, Catherine hadn't been pondering everything she did wrong with Chloe. The mention of her name didn't bother her the least, when only a few months ago every recollection of Chloe would send her fuming. Catherine used to be so ashamed of herself that she evaded each attempt at conversation, never realizing she should cherish every single moment of that wonderful, liberating opportunity to finally be herself.

"I'm doing well. It was bound to happen sooner or later, Ninon, and I'm happy where I'm at now. I wish the best for Chloe."

"She was alone when I ran into her. Just so you know." Catherine felt she could hear Ninon smile.

Still, the information left Catherine coldly indifferent. She accepted long ago that it had nothing to do with her.

"If that's what she wants. I hope she finds someone."

"Wow, you really are gracious!" Boisterous gaiety rang in her friend's voice. "Does that mean you met someone? There can be no other reason for such generosity. You know I will find out. You better tell me."

Catherine laughed. She liked to think it had nothing to do with Jesse but rather her ultimate maturity level, yet she reluctantly had to admit that Jesse's acceptance of her messy self did play a role. Even before they had sex.

After each row with her father, her mother would rant, "Trying too hard will fuck you up every time, Catherine." She wished she remembered that during her relationship with Chloe. Every relationship surely required effort, work, compromise, and countless other nuisances, but she spent most of her days bending over backward as if it was the most normal thing to do—yet it never got easier.

With Jesse, she never had to pretend, there were no power games. Not only could she suggest anything and find support, but she also discovered it was so simple to listen and care for the woman in return. Honesty never seemed *too* hard with Jesse. On the contrary, it was exceptionally easy, even when the truth was ugly. She was the first one with whom she could speak about Chloe. Catherine could still recall sitting on those stairs and the words just flowing. She knew they could tell each other anything and find understanding.

"Hey, can't I be smart once?"

"Answering a question with a question! Definitely something going on there."

Catherine muffled her laughter and managed to compose her voice to reassure Ninon.

"If I ever lose my mind again and start dating, you will know every detail, I promise."

"For heaven's sake, how are you spending your days in that outpost?"

"I spend a lot of time outdoors, hiking, camping, enjoying the vast, green silence, helping with the garden. You would absolutely hate it here. But I promise, I don't wear flashy logos. And no fluorescent colors."

"Oh dear, you got me worried for a second!" Ninon cried out, and Catherine knew exactly how distant that life had to seem to the cosmopolitan woman. "That sounds like a welcome little break, but you've got too much talent to waste. When are you coming back?"

She knew the question would come, and she had to face it sooner or later. Surely, she would return to everything she had been building for years. Catherine just didn't know when that would be.

"I haven't thought about it."

"Well, it's time, Catherine. I thought there was someone holding you back there, but since there's not, it makes it even easier to pose my next question."

"Oh?" Catherine tilted her head with interest.

"Nicolas wants me to work with him on the movie he'll be shooting this spring, a period drama set in Louis XIV's Paris. It's a dream, Catherine. Oh! Long dresses, headpieces, austere men… it's a dream. Anyway, we chatted a bit and Nicolas mentioned he wanted you to join as well—to do all the choreography. When I talked to him two days ago, he said he'd call you next week. Please say yes when he calls, please."

Catherine had a blast collaborating with Nicolas and his crew on the first movie, yet she was still shocked to learn she could get a chance to repeat those intense emotions and the challenge of knowing millions of people would see your work. Never even realizing how much she missed it, the thrill brought an instant smile to her face. She had worked for years for moments like this. Should she throw away everything because her relationship with Chloe had failed? There was so much left to give, achieve, and feel. The first movie was a huge success, and this could have been the right moment to go back to Paris and reclaim her career. Jesse would probably be proud of her. Jesse? Where did that come from?

"I did not expect this," Catherine said.

"Yes, I had to call you to make sure you wouldn't turn him down."

If Nicolas called, there was only one right answer she could give him. This was her big chance to establish herself in something that she'd loved profoundly for the past twenty years.

"We'll shoot in Versailles, and we'll have so much fun together. He raved on and on about how much he dug your sense of humor and relentless work ethic. Imagine the violins and bourrée or whatever it was they danced back then. Oh, Catherine, just say yes when he rings! Do come back home already. It's time. You can't sit in that bubble forever."

The words echoed in Catherine's ears. Perhaps it was time to go back to reality. She understood she'd have to return eventually, but she refused to limit herself with a date. To be far from people, friends, acquaintances, the inquisitive old neighbor from the fifth floor—all that distance had worked for the past few months. Yet Catherine knew too much time had passed for anyone to care now. Hell, Chloe probably didn't care anymore. There were no more questions. Even she didn't mind thinking about it. She could go back to her apartment overlooking Jardin du Luxembourg, which her mother had been renting and which stood empty now. Go back to dance, her streets, her favorite little pâtisserie in Rue Montorgueil, late brunches on bright Sundays, the Seine breeze.

Her mind paused for a second, contemplating Jesse's sparkling expression just before she left. Was that what she would take into consideration when deciding about her life? Catherine sighed and rose to her feet, stroking the side of her neck. Jesse was there every single day, without big words and without expectations, and Catherine already knew she'd miss the friendship of that damn woman. Body as well, but okay, she didn't harbor any illusions that desire would go on for much longer as it was. She liked Jesse's presence, her humor, her silent support, her humility, and grace, and she found herself eagerly awaiting the sound of that sultry voice every day. Fuck, she should focus more on sex. That's all that really was. She wasn't supposed to sit here envisioning Jesse's reaction when she told her, nor how it would make her feel.

Catherine had no idea if she was prepared to return to her old life, her routines, the city's hustle and bustle, but she was sure about dance. There was no way she would ever give up on that. She couldn't. As she thought of this project and the ones to come, an unexpected wave of excitement swept over her.

"Thank you, Ninon. I can't wait to hug you. Now, please tell me where and when you met the baron. I'm dying to hear all the details."

CHAPTER THIRTY-ONE

Spokane, Vancouver, and Portland. Three more stops and she'd finally be able to knuckle down to work on her new album. In only a week, she would be ensconced somewhere between her farm and the studio, just creating. Jesse always found the creative process to be more fulfilling than anything that ensued after. Parties, interviews, even concerts seemed to be stealing her from what she loved the most. She had so many songs under her fingers, so many ideas, that everything else seemed to be a painful waste of time. Always with a feeling that she should be somewhere else, like each moment was a lost song that deserved mourning.

For so long, each person, each place Jesse encountered would end up being her invention. Nothing really lived. Nothing moved outside the walls of her imagination. Yet, that damn French woman proved to be a self-sufficient piece of art. Jesse didn't need to contrive anything, didn't need to add anything. She liked Catherine for what she was and for what she was not—with an ease that was astounding. What she made her feel was better than any song she'd ever written. Around her, there was no time for what-ifs and her imagination took a back seat. She could write a hundred songs about Catherine, but that would not be sane. Or anywhere near art. She wouldn't be caught dead writing sappy love songs.

The moment evoked memories of Sarah Audette, her big crush from ten years ago. Except, sadly, Sarah was only a product of her boredom. Corinne that came after Sarah was a product of her boredom too. When she wanted an emotion, she'd give it a name, dress it up, and let her imagination entertain her. So why was now different? God knew that damn French woman was far from perfect.

Yet, now there was someone whom she wanted to explore and enjoy, no dressing up. Would she even know how to? She knew how to write a love song, but she had no idea how to be with someone. For a moment, she closed her eyes and imagined having Catherine in her room. The way she'd mix and match her clothes, the way she'd cross her legs, the way she'd narrow her eyes, attempting to sound serious before smiling. How many more of those expressions and neurotic movements waited to be discovered?

If she could somehow talk Catherine into visiting her next week, she'd have everything she needed. The French woman and hokey songs. Damn. Jesse turned her gaze to the sky, grateful for the rain that was insistently tapping on her face as if trying to talk some sense into her. She loved the taste of it, soft and fresh, its touch on the windows, light and comforting, the look of clouds traveling, fast and restless, the leaves falling, wet and heavy. Sitting on the lakeshore, in the light drizzle, feeding the fish, she thought how the only person who would have appreciated the perfect boredom of this moment and who wouldn't have minded having her hair wet and her shoes muddy was the inspiration behind her doomed songs. So, she called.

* * *

Catherine tried so hard not to light up when she saw Jesse's name on the phone. It was not what a rational human being who was finally happy to be on her own would do.

"I finally found *Say Yes to Our Love*."

Oh, that seductive, raspy voice did wonders to her. *Merde.* Only then did her brain register Jesse's words. So she'd found the movie. *The* movie. It was as if Jesse could see right through her every secret. Catherine felt tightness building in her throat, but she regained enough composure to calmly ask, "Oh, and what did you think?"

"How could anyone say no to that?" Hearing Jesse's unsuspecting laughter, Catherine helplessly shook her head. Jesse just had to go and make her like her, with the perfect dimples and her wit and the gentle way she held her body. She attempted to compose herself as Jesse continued, "But no, it's a great movie. I didn't expect it to be so tragic."

"It's love, of course it's tragic. When you finally find someone decent, they die."

"Oh, am I dying?"

Catherine bit back a smile. What an unbearable woman. Jesse obviously had no intention of yielding.

"There's an end to every story. It's magical only if you get just the beginning."

"I understand that second part. People meet, fall in love, start living together, eventually marry, and we're taught it's the end of the story when in fact it's only the beginning. Love is a skill we learn. It requires work, and it's more than a passion we simply experience." Jesse paused briefly. "I just kept hoping Thérèse would somehow survive, but French people have to be so damn dark and fatalistic."

"We also have no morals, and you seem to be fond of that part."

"Oh, I don't nitpick parts to love, you know, I just love each and every one." Jesse's tone reverted to impish with effortless, natural disposition. "It forms an adorable, messy French whole, and I'm a lover."

Catherine shook her head. "I should introduce you to my French friends then."

"Do you think I'm finished with you?"

"You better not be."

"You know, that dance scene before Thérèse dies was utter beauty. It made me think."

"Oh. Nothing good ever came after 'it made me think.'"

"I don't want people watching me die," Jesse said.

"Lord, please stop watching European movies and bring Jesse back."

Jesse's smile made itself heard in her voice. "I was just going to ask you if there was anything else you worked on that I could watch."

Jesse refused to give up, so damned tenacious. Always so invested in all things Catherine that it only made her guilt sting more. Was she supposed to say now that she was contemplating moving back to France? How should she begin? Should she just spill it all? Why was she hesitant in the first place? Did she think she could actually hurt Jesse, or was she unsure she wanted to go back? Dammit. At times, she was convinced Jesse had the ability to read minds and that she had way too much fun with hers.

Catherine had considered telling Jesse about the movie for the past few days. When Nicolas called first thing on Monday, they'd had a pleasant chat. He briefly explained the shooting would start in early May and apologized because there would only be tedious baroque dances—and not many of them. Reiterating that he'd like to get a chance to work with Catherine again, he immediately forwarded the materials and gave her until Christmas to decide.

The sheer thought of playing with emotions in three dimensions excited her, but she did wonder if she simply wanted an excuse to go back to her old life in France—minus Chloe, of course. Catherine knew it was not a decision for Jesse to make and that the choice would ultimately be her own, however she still couldn't help but feel Jesse somehow became a factor in that thought process, and that was an uncomfortable reality. Why would she let a fling get in the way of pursuing her passion? Why would she let Jesse factor in at all, when she knew casual was the only option anyway? Was she out of her mind?

"There are three seasons of a variety show called *La Chance* on Canal+ and four music videos that will certainly not make you think," Catherine replied, ignoring the pressing thoughts.

"Wow, I didn't know I was dating a celebrity, Catherine. Okay, maybe not dating, but don't you think I won't find that. I also want to know the names of those videos."

Hearing her laugh on the other side, Catherine forgot why she was fighting so hard. That sound was so damn impossible to resist, and Catherine sensed that what Jesse felt for her was more than just physical attraction. Yet, Jesse had a career and a lifestyle that simply could not be trusted. Sometimes you just had to be more mature than your feelings.

"Does that mean I get to see you dance in one of your videos?" Catherine asked, turning the conversation in a different direction.

"I normally don't collaborate with my interests, but if anyone could make me try some new moves, it's you."

"We'd be sticking to dance only," Catherine said.

"Of course not."

Catherine grinned and then sighed helplessly. "I am a professional."

"Too bad I'm not," Jesse retorted, disarming her again with her airy laugh.

CHAPTER THIRTY-TWO

The week in the Pacific Northwest proved to be highly productive for Jesse. During the seven days between concerts, the band spent almost every minute rehearsing the songs from the new album. The elimination process proved to be easier than expected, and the twenty songs they were considering got narrowed down to twelve. There was the thirteenth song—or, more precisely, its twenty-five versions. If Jesse managed to find the missing piece, that would be track number one.

Yet, after several years of tormenting herself with a story that was still hard to process, Jesse could sense she was closer than ever, and that in itself was a reason for satisfaction. The team agreed on the narrative framework as well as the track order. The album was carved like a sculpture, and after those seven days in late October it seemed she could feel it in front of her. It turned out to be quite different from what she envisioned only six months ago, but then again, she was a very different person six months ago. The most vulnerable and personal of all her works, it burst out effortlessly. At times, she could hardly recognize the person behind those words. As if someone else's hand penned them, some other voice shaped them. All those thoughts were undoubtedly prompted by neurotic Catherine Des Lauriers, yet even Jesse was astonished by the speed with which Catherine's purity and passion inspired her to greater tenderness. Catherine offered her a sense of tranquil safety, and not only because everything else seemed like a tedious intrusion.

Jesse was not afraid of herself when she was with Catherine, and it made her throw verses on paper with astounding ease. The paper could reveal a monster, a demon, a coward, a child, and she'd remain undisturbed, carving deeper, her feelings louder than ever.

Every night, Jesse called. And every night, as she encountered that soft French accent, Catherine's cadences and timbre had a way of making her every monster heard and lulled to sleep. Talk about the very sound of contentment. It was so easy to envision Catherine's body next to hers, the warmth she'd feel in her arms, the mischief those arms would talk her into, their intensity and dexterity. Despite Catherine's resistance, the ties between them were so tangled that the sheer sound of that gentle voice could overcome the distances separating them.

Surely, she was too old for this—lying in the bed and staring at the ceiling, thinking about waking up next to someone. *Damn*. Jesse sat up and grabbed her guitar, determined to nail the twenty-sixth version of the song that had been haunting her for years, when her screen lit up.

"Do you know I still carry the impression of a wrench on my back from our first encounter last week?" That sweet, amused tone was bringing her home, and Jesse's body responded with an instinctive grin.

"I can't bring myself to regret that, Cath."

Catherine's response came back clear and resolute. "Your hands are under my shirt all the time."

"Now that's just not fair," Jesse protested.

"You should have thought about that before you depraved me, Jesse Morgan."

Jesse chuckled. In front of everyone else, she was who she was supposed to be, but with Catherine she was who she wanted to be. The truth was roaring around that woman, and yes, it was not safe, it was not convenient, and it was probably going to burn in the end, but next to Catherine, everything felt so right. How could she just stay a thousand miles away? Jesse had no idea where life would take them eventually, but now…now she wanted to enjoy her. And not hold anything back.

"I miss you, Catherine. Come visit me. We can drive down to Magic City," she said with her customary ease, then calmly added, "No expectations, of course, just us being around each other."

"Wow, Jesse, I always figured if you wanted a weekend of dirty sex with your new fling, you'd get a cheap roadside motel like everyone else."

"Oh, Catherine, I'm so charming in your head."

"I'd actually like to visit you and your farm." The firmness of Catherine's tone took Jesse by surprise. "I'll talk to Fletcher and let you know."

"You are finally going to tell Fletcher that you seduced me?"

"I did not seduce you!"

"Does that mean I seduced you?"

"Oh, fuck you, Jesse."

"Not fun without you."

Catherine exhaled loudly and Jesse could hear the smile in her voice. "It's not fair, Jesse. Just when I decided to be smart, there you are. You just had to make me like you, didn't you?"

"You're quite adorable."

"So when will I finally hear your new songs?" Catherine asked softly.

It took only a second before Jesse touched the guitar strings. All she wanted was to be alone with Catherine, and no one should write songs in that state of mind if they cared to maintain any artistic credibility.

Surely this woman would be the death of her.

CHAPTER THIRTY-THREE

"So, you were right."

Fletcher stared inquiringly, holding a spoon in front of his mouth. "About what?"

Catherine cast down her eyes and a slight blush flushed her face. "Jesse is like ten little puppies, one on top of the other. Simply adorable."

Fletcher gaped, pausing in her embarrassed gaze for a moment before he burst out laughing. He placed his spoon in the bowl and wiped his mouth, and when his stare met Catherine's again, he attempted to control his glee, to no avail. His exuberance filled the room, pulling Catherine in as well. To hell with everything—she deserved it. She knew Fletcher would understand.

"We've been talking a lot lately. We hung out as well when she was here last week. She's fun and I know all her songs," she confessed with a smile and glanced at him, relieved.

Fletcher was nodding his head, contented, as if his chicken pot pie had just started tasting a whole lot better.

"Well, Catherine, I could say a lot of things now, but I'm just happy that you're having fun." His bright eyes glimmered with encouragement, and the notion she was finally able to talk about Jesse pervaded her with a curious pleasure. Not that she had any idea how to define her connection with Jesse or how to control it, but his enthusiastic support made her want to reveal all the great things that he didn't know about Jesse. Like, how she'd find time every day to watch *La Chance* and ask insightful questions. Or how soft her lips were. Okay, definitely not that. *Fuck, Catherine.*

"Marjorie called it. She knew."

"Well, as you said, we're just having fun. She lives in Nashville, and I'll go back to France, so we respect each other's freedom and neither of us wants commitments. Nor promises."

"Uh-huh. Are you sure?"

"Yes, Pépé," she said as calmly as she could. To his curiosity she had to reply with decidedly firm conviction. Anything else would send her into an existential crisis over the complete and utter idiocy of her involvement with Jesse.

"I think you might have underestimated Jesse." Fletcher drew his eyebrows together and then broke into a wide smile again. "At least I got you to admit she's adorable. Because that she is."

Catherine grinned, as she could vividly picture Jesse joining in and nodding her head at that statement.

"I was wondering if you could handle the shop on your own for a few days if I went to Nashville?"

"Of course! My shop is my joy, not my job. I'm not greedy, I only take orders I can fulfill. You can stay with Jesse for as long as you want."

"I wouldn't stay long, of course. When I last talked to Mother, she mentioned coming over for Christmas, so I would definitely be back in time to see her."

"Knowing your mother, she'll say that and then show up for Easter. Stay in Tennessee for as long as you like."

Catherine walked around the table and slid next to him, instantly wrapping her arms around him. His bony shoulders responded affectionately, and Catherine decided it was time for another truth. She wriggled in her chair.

"There's something else as well. I was offered work on a movie that is set to be filmed next summer in France. As much as I like being here with you, it might be the right opportunity for me to return to my life in Paris. God knows I have to sooner or later, and this would be smart. Besides, I really do miss dance."

The old man glanced down, gripping her hand. After a few moments, his eyes flashed again.

"What about Jesse?"

Catherine grinned and gave him another tight squeeze.

"That's your first concern?"

"Of course. She makes you laugh, and that's one of my favorite sounds in the world. I'll miss you, but it would be easier if I knew you were happy."

"You should see me in the ballroom. Dance completes me. It's who I am." She nudged him playfully.

Sure, it would have been easier to resume her life in France if Jesse had not been sexy as sin. However, Jesse was a big star with a career of her own, and she'd probably forget all about Catherine by the next summer. No doubt the new album meant Jesse would have travel obligations of her own—promotional appearances on the late-night talk shows, endless interviews by the music media, maybe even another tour. It would be naïve to change her plans for Jesse.

"Pépé, thank you so much for taking me in and giving me a chance to restart. It means more than you'll ever know. *Je t'aime tellement.*"

"Oh, Catherine, save your goodbye. You won't be leaving just yet." He winked and clasped her hands again.

CHAPTER THIRTY-FOUR

When Catherine had envisioned what it would be like to fall asleep and wake up next to Jesse—and she had envisioned that far more often than she should have—she had never anticipated this.

She was lying in the dark of Jesse's room, stripped of the covers, with the cold slowly creeping up her naked body. Catherine couldn't grasp how Jesse was all cozied up right next to her while she was left inches away to fend for herself, engulfed in lonely shadows. As her eyes gradually adapted to the dark, she fixed them on the woman peacefully resting beside her. By God, she could swear that was a smile on her face.

Catherine rubbed her chin in thought. What if she just quickly pulled the covers back over herself? She tried to discern something, anything, that could help, but only concluded that Jesse looked too darn cute to disturb. She sighed and snuggled closer to Jesse, careful not to rouse her from sleep. The entire room was filled with Jesse's fragrance, but unfortunately that divine, fresh scent of long walks along the Mediterranean Sea did not appease her need for a comfy blanket. As she was bravely waiting for Jesse's peaceful, covered body to start sharing heat, it was becoming obvious it alone would not be enough.

Surely if she pulled only one corner of the covers, Jesse wouldn't notice. After all, she was shielded by miles of warm coziness. Attempting to gently wrap the covers around her back, Catherine found a remarkable resistance. She tugged again, but the damn thing remained stubborn—it did not move an inch and seemed completely stuck around that seductive body. Catherine paused on Jesse's peaceful face, now even clearer in the dark, before finally surrendering.

"How can you be so strong in your sleep? You look so delicate."

Ever since she'd arrived a few days ago, they almost hadn't left that room. When they finally attained their privacy, the raw, naked emotions seemed unstoppable. They weren't seeking reassuring words or profound analyses, and as a result Catherine could hardly feel her limbs. Everything with Jesse was so weightless, so intense, so short.

She must have dropped off somehow, because when Catherine was roused again, it was almost seven. Jesse's bedroom was surrounded by open space and high ceilings, and the light was quietly creeping through the shutters, gloriously painting the imposing walls. What a blissful way to wake up! Catherine turned around carefully, hoping to see the traces of sunlight on Jesse's tranquil, somnolent face, only to once more find herself alone in that big bed.

Every morning, regardless of when Catherine would wake up, Jesse was always gone. She'd find her downstairs, instantly abandoning playing with Lola or picking the strings, so she could shower Catherine with kisses. Although Catherine expected Jesse to go to the studio today, and she knew she'd have more time to explore the ranch, seven in the morning still seemed too early. When did that woman get up? If she hadn't been awakened by the coverless chill every single night, she wouldn't have suspected Jesse even slept next to her at all.

The sun peeked over the rolling hills and the house appeared unusually quiet, so Catherine decided to get up. Peering into the living room, she could still clearly recall their naked bodies intertwined in front of the stone fireplace. Catherine couldn't remember if that was yesterday or the day before, so she quickly proceeded to the kitchen and the deck with a certain sense of shame. However, there was no trace of Jesse. Not even Lola was there to run around her and turn over chairs.

Already filled with natural light beyond the entry hallway was a music room with a grand piano and at least ten other instruments that Catherine wouldn't dare try to identify. Complete with hardwood floors, rough-hewn ceiling beams, reclaimed wood plank paneling, and traditional ceiling moldings, the home was a farmhouse heaven, certainly not what she would expect from a music star. She walked outside and leaned against the railing. Sublime, gently rolling pastureland with barns in the distance was all she experienced from this vast ranch, mostly gazing through the window. Bathed in the morning sun, a pond was glimmering in the distance, while the perfect quiet of the morning was only briefly interrupted by the pure and sweet singing of robins. Woods and pastures that lay in front of her in the crisp morning air were almost beckoning her to explore them. Catherine decided to follow a narrow, grassy footpath meandering through the woods when she heard a faint neigh. Through the tall maples, she spotted two dark bay horses peacefully grazing in their paddock. Weathered wooden posts enclosed the area, extending into the woods on its northeast end. Catherine walked to the fence and leaned against a plank, but only one of the horses glanced at her with little interest before he continued grazing. He was dignified, with a white star gracing his noble face, and Catherine wished she could wrap her arms around his long, lustrous, stunning mane. It was neatly brushed out, tangle free and in perfect harmony with his glossy tail occasionally swinging freely. She couldn't keep her eyes off their beauty, but their paddock seemed so enormous she had no idea how one could ever get close to those two. After spending some time absorbing the view of the two charmers, she decided to take the trail down to the tall red barn looming in the distance. Catherine thought it would be exceptionally easy to get used to this life, before quickly berating herself.

When she approached the rugged, half-timbered structure she heard the sound of an engine running, and in a matter of moments Jesse appeared around the corner on her tractor, pulling up outside the barn and disappearing inside carrying hay. Of all the things, *this* was not what she expected when she got to Tennessee. Besides, no woman had any right to look so sexy in rubber boots, but apparently Jesse decided to ignore the rules.

Catherine snuck through the trees and peeked into the huge barn. Jesse was sitting next to one of the goats, gently rubbing her chest and feeding her green leaves. As much as Catherine resisted losing herself to the popular singer, she realized she was about to fall head over heels in love with this farmer. There she was, a talented, dedicated artist, still driving her tractor, riding horses, and walking through manure—unworried, far from any semblance of glamour. She enjoyed the rural life, and she was transforming from a farmer into a music star without any fuss, as if it were the most normal thing in the world. It was so Jesse. Never a redundant question, no drama, and watching her in her muddy boots, surrounded by hay, goats, and llamas, Catherine couldn't recall ever witnessing a more magical scene. She was about to fall hard for this woman.

A gentle nip at her ankle startled her, and she jumped forward, prompting Jesse to look up. *Oh, Lola.*

"What are you doing here?" Jesse's bewildered expression soon faded, replaced with a broad grin. "It's barely seven."

"As much as I'm fond of your bed, I figured there was a lot more to see around here," Catherine retorted and walked up to Jesse and the goat, the animal's head gloomily resting on Jesse's lap. "What's with the baby?"

"Pickles normally has a very strong personality, but this morning she was just lying down, keeping her distance. She usually gorges on grass and then gets scours. I got her to drink so she wouldn't get dehydrated, but we'll still keep an eye on her today." Jesse withdrew carefully, and the goat quickly jumped back on her feet, bringing a smile to the woman's face. "Pickles will be fine. Goats are delicate and sensitive, but Pickles here is a fighter. Do you want to meet the llamas?" Jesse asked, rising to her feet.

Finding herself in front of that alert gaze, Catherine could hardly resist bringing Jesse in for a kiss. She couldn't keep doing this to her. A kiss that intense was not just physical intimacy, and she knew she was starting to lose control of this situation. *Merde*.

"I'd love to," she replied and instinctively hugged Jesse as if it were the most natural reaction in the world. Okay, now it was too late to remove that damn arm. Catherine gave Jesse an inquisitive stare instead. "Do you always get up this early?"

"I do." Jesse's blue eyes beamed back at her. "I'm not going to have animals if I can't spend time with them."

"So, I have no chance of waking up next to you?" Catherine teased, recalling that content expression peeking out from under all the blankets only a few hours ago.

"If you wake up at six, you do." Jesse's unsuspecting eyes lit up, and her lips curved a gleaming smile. "Is that what you want, Catherine? To wake up next to me?"

Catherine expected Jesse's playful manner would make her flinch, feel embarrassed, or at least cast down her eyes, but today she refused to fight those feelings.

"It would be a lovely sight."

Jesse set her lips to hers, and as she savored their taste, their softness, Catherine had no intention of resisting the pleasure invading her body. Wrapping her arms around Jesse's neck, she gathered her closer. Yes, this would not end well.

Outside, the sun shone bright in the clear blue sky and the llamas frolicked about in the pond, dipping in and looking at them coyly with their huge, beguiling eyes, their adorable ears perked up as if listening. Catherine felt an instant need to cuddle each and every one. The goats were lounging around them, seemingly disinterested. Unlike the wooden fences she noticed around the ranch, this area had woven mesh fences in the distance, still giving the animals plenty of room to roam.

"Meet the ladies." Jesse gestured to the animals who instantly welcomed the two women by locking their curious eyes with theirs. "Llamas are very smart, calm, and cool, but each has a very distinct character, as I'm sure you'll notice soon enough."

Jesse drew near to the biggest one in the herd, who stared at them transfixed, but when Jesse started rubbing her neck, the llama quickly responded by nuzzling up against her. The llama's joy when Jesse hugged her almost matched Catherine's when she felt those same arms wrap around her body. Not blinking, not breathing, with the stupid smile spread across her face—yes, that was exactly how she looked.

"This is Pixie. She is shy and curious, and if she could, she would cuddle twenty-four hours a day. She weighs three hundred and fifty pounds but is really like a baby. Once you start rubbing her neck, she will step on you to get you to stay, so watch out." Catherine walked up to the llama and, feeling her warmth and affability, she quickly enclosed her arms around her neck. Catherine capitulated to the gentle touch as Pixie sank deeper into her embrace.

"If you let her, she'll stay like that all day." Jesse's expression softened and she motioned to the llama that was observing them from a safe distance. "Over there is Duchess. She watches everything from afar but will get jealous if she doesn't get your attention. You'll notice she's acting up to make an impression. Unless you have a camera ready, it will be difficult to win her over. However, if she spots someone recording, she'll be the first in line. Aspen over here is somewhat of a therapist. She'll stare at you with her empathetic gaze that makes you want to tell her all your deepest, darkest secrets. She will expect a carrot in return, however. Rocky here is eight months old and he loves playing chase."

"Who takes care of them when you're touring?"

"Rachel is looking after them when I'm away, but whenever I'm here, I can't wait to hang out with them." Jesse petted Rocky, whose ears instantly pricked up, which made Catherine chuckle. "They are loving companions. And speaking of loving companions, care to join me in the studio today?"

Jesse's curious glance brought Catherine back to reality. As much as Catherine was prepared to enjoy the bucolic farm life with Jesse, unrestrained and isolated, the idea they could be seen together still perturbed her. To get acquainted with Jesse's friends would make everything more difficult when the parting time came. No, their clock was ticking. She was endeavoring to memorize the details, the animals, the quiet of this ranch, and Jesse, quietly standing in front of her with her hands shoved into the pockets of an old gray hoodie and a look of silent understanding in her tender gaze. Catherine couldn't imagine a day being more complete than this one.

She shrugged. "I'd rather stay here, if that's okay."

Jesse nodded her head perceptively, without insisting too much. "Of course, don't worry."

Considerate and patient, Jesse understood as if she had always been there. Yet, in a few months, they'd become strangers. Catherine had made a name for herself in France, and everywhere else she'd have to start over. To sacrifice her dreams for someone she'd just met would be wrong. Her career waited in Paris. All the time and effort she had invested, everything she'd accomplished so far, would mean little here. As much as she liked the farm life, she was not someone who could idly sit around all day waiting for Jesse to come home. Catherine needed her independence.

"I should only warn you that Rachel will swing by sometime today. She'll just drop off my dry-cleaning."

"That's cool," Catherine replied, and her lips instinctively descended on Jesse's, her hands quickly sliding under the woman's shirt. It would suck later, but no point in wasting time now. God help her.

CHAPTER THIRTY-FIVE

Catherine had no intention of idling about waiting for Rachel to pop up. If she wasn't smart enough to evade emotional attachment and affection for Jesse, she could at least avoid having their worlds intertwine more than necessary. Getting to know Jesse's friends, becoming part of her world, growing closer to her would only complicate matters between them. No, to have everyone stare and pry would be an atrocious affliction, but more than anything, Catherine dreaded the questions and everything she would have to admit to herself. As if she wasn't in too deep already.

After Jesse left for the studio, Catherine briefly lay in the hammock, delighting in the pristine fall day. Bright yellow leaves were turning to vibrant amber, which she left in Colorado back in September. Only a few days ago a snowstorm bid her farewell in Maple Springs, so the delicate glow of fall she encountered in Tennessee was a welcome change, one that she wanted to embrace uninterrupted for a few moments. She liked this ranch, the llamas, the goats and the horses, the peace and charm of natural surroundings, Jesse's life. This was definitely not how Catherine pictured the life of a star, particularly not Jesse. Nothing in the entire house was made for appearance. It was a home, warm and unpretentious, much like Jesse herself. Maintaining this ranch was undoubtedly a lot of work, which she enjoyed alone. Catherine would never forget the first time she set her eyes on Jesse, but the woman turned out to be so much more than the adorable face she saw in the shop that day. If only she could be so oblivious again as to stereotype the singer and convince herself that she wouldn't care.

Catherine's thoughts were interrupted by a playful puppy that was attempting to reach the swinging hammock with her front paws, so Catherine leaned down and scooped her up in her arms.

"Do you want to show me the ranch, Lola?" she asked, playing with the dog's long, floppy ears. Lola tilted her head in surprise and then leaned her pudgy belly against her shoulder.

It seemed like everything on this ranch was intent on stealing her heart. Catherine stroked her silky soft, foldable ears and her chubby belly for a few minutes before deciding it was time to go explore her surroundings.

Ever since she'd arrived three days ago, Catherine couldn't part from Jesse's alluring body. However, the more time they spent making love, the harder it was to convince herself it was just sex. The looks they shared now were deeper, more intense. At times, they would find each other just staring without a word, in almost silent appreciation of what the other one felt. Catherine felt comfortable with Jesse's body, she felt comfortable with herself, with her own desires and needs next to Jesse. Their sex was more than anything a revelation of trust. Trust that any darkness, any vulnerability, any emotion would be safe in those arms. Those moments were so full of oblivion, yet they would make them so aware of each other that Catherine knew well she would be around Jesse even if only to listen to her speak.

They had talked every single day for months before touching one another, and Catherine never wanted that to end. Oh, what was wrong with her? She tried to shake off the whirling thoughts.

They had managed to escape promises so far, and Catherine's career decisions were clearly her own. However, the fact that she still had to tell Jesse about the movie offer suddenly started to loom uncomfortably. As much as she appeared strong and ready to tease, Jesse's defense from the world was withdrawing into herself, and the last thing Catherine wanted was to ever hurt her in any way. Why couldn't Jesse simply be an arrogant womanizer? It would make the whole damn ordeal easier to bear.

Catherine had caught only a glimpse of the quaint little town Jesse called home on their drive from the airport. The rolling hills, fire pits, and antique shops created an instant bond, but the rural view before her could quell any apprehension. The puppy rushed up and down the hills, enthusiastically jumping through the fences and only occasionally stopping as if to acknowledge the sheer beauty of this scenery, the idyllic pastures, the sun reflecting off the ponds, the distant bleats, the fall foliage of the surrounding forests. What made that explosion of colors so memorable each year was its temporal nature. Perhaps that was also what made her bond with Jesse special—the notion it would end.

Catherine quietly followed the orange-tinged trail through the woods when a herd of black-and-white cows appeared in front of her. *Merde!* She quickly turned in search of the red barn roof, but between the tall red oaks and the wallpaper of cows, it was nowhere to be found. Yes, she was pretty sure Jesse didn't have any cows. The cows kept staring blankly at her as Lola insisted they should continue forward. All Catherine needed for her life to be complete was a trespassing charge.

"Lola, wait!" Not heeding her words, the dog kept pulling on the leash in a desperate attempt to dig her way under the fence to a tantalizing shrub of red berries. "I swear, if I end up trespassing on some celebrity's orchard…Lola, get over here."

In her defense, Jesse's farm also had numerous pastures with wooden fencing, so anyone could have made that mistake. It all looked the same. Catherine turned back while Lola sank her paws into the ground, refusing to relinquish her berry treasure and letting out a loud bark as a final sign of resistance.

"Please, Lola, don't bark now. God, of course, she couldn't have gotten a Chihuahua." As if she heard Catherine's grumbles, the dog finally stopped and innocently locked her guilty eyes with Catherine's.

"Okay, I'm sorry, I'm sorry, you're cute," she admitted and squatted down to pet the dog. Lola quickly nuzzled up against her as Catherine started turning around. "We need to get out of here now, otherwise you risk never again tearing up another cardboard box in your life."

They took the same way back, or at least Catherine thought so, because the walk back seemed to last for ages. Her eyes kept scanning the surroundings for the red barn, so when after twenty agonizing minutes of roaming she finally spotted a red rooftop, Catherine let out a laugh of relief. The red roof didn't guarantee she wasn't on someone else's property nor that the barn was actually Jesse's, but it was her only chance. If that meant barging in on someone in the middle of their lunch, so be it. As she was nearing the barn, her confidence grew. Catherine started recognizing the clearings and the treetops, so when she finally caught sight of the fuzzy llamas lounging around their pond, she heaved a sigh of relief and gratefully stroked the underside of Lola's snout.

Duchess was the first one to spot her. Like she was getting ready for a fashion show, she instantly adjusted her strut and ostentatiously turned her attention to the barn. She curved her swan neck, and Catherine gladly offered her the admiration she was seeking. Noticing Pickles was not among the goats frolicking in the hay, Catherine went over to the barn to check on her. As soon as she approached the barn, she heard faint steps moving along the stalls. She instinctively peeked inside and found herself staring into the eyes of Jesse's assistant. *Oh, merde.* She had barely recovered from the trespassing.

"Hi, I'm Rachel, Jesse's assistant," the young woman exclaimed brightly, extending her hand before Catherine had a chance to react.

She was every bit beautiful as she appeared in the photos, long blond hair flowing over her shoulders and bright blue piercing eyes. Standing this close to her, Rachel reminded her of Jesse. Damn, why did everything remind her of Jesse?

"I'm Catherine, Jesse's friend," she managed to utter, shaking her hand.

"Hon, I've seen Jesse's 'friends.' They don't stick around long enough to have breakfast. She's crazy about you, Catherine."

Her words made Catherine squirm with embarrassment. "Thank you."

"I didn't mean to make you feel uncomfortable, it's just that I've known Jesse for almost eight years, and I've never seen her as besotted with someone as she is now." When she noticed Catherine blushing, she laughed and added, "Okay, I keep doing it. I wanted to check on Pickles before I leave. Looks like the baby is doing just fine."

"That's a relief." Catherine relaxed a little. "Jesse says you're taking care of the animals when she's away. How did you learn all that?"

"My daddy has a farm down in Perry County. We had a thousand acres, and I grew up surrounded by goats, horses, cows, sheep. That's how I met Jesse. When she got Dallas, she needed someone to keep an eye on him when she was touring. I was eighteen and looking for a part-time job. Before I knew it, I was a full-time celebrity assistant." She chuckled, patting Catherine's arm. "Not that Jesse's demanding, on the contrary. I often ask her how she became famous in the first place. I reckon she's the most low-maintenance person I've ever met, but I'm sure you already know that." She winked, and her Southern drawl paired with her friendly chattiness easily lowered Catherine's defenses. "Are you here to check on Pickles as well?"

"Well, that was my intention before Lola took me on an hour-long detour. I'm pretty sure I trespassed on one of the neighboring farms." She motioned her head to the east.

"Oh, that's Jessica and Justin Timberlake's farm over there."

Petrified, Catherine could only blink.

"I'm just messin' with ya, hon." Rachel burst into infectious laughter, and her sunny disposition made her an endearing character. "That's Old Marv's farm. He and his wife, Tammy, are

Franklin natives. He was a two-time NFL Defensive Player of the Year back in the seventies. Tammy's kitchen is open twenty-four hours a day. You should have stopped for her cinnamon rolls. Lawdamercy, that woman can bake. Mmm. I swanny, the whole farm smells like cinnamon. Jesse loves them. They even gave her Pickles, so this little girl has a bunch of siblings over there. Sometimes we go to visit, don't we, Pickles?" The goat rubbed her neck against Rachel, letting out a steady bleat.

People should really stop duping her like this.

"You'll find everyone here as welcoming as all get-out," Rachel went on breezily, petting the goat. "I know Jesse would never allow you to lack anything, but should you ever be in need, please let me know. We are all one big family here," she drawled and looked at her in encouragement. "I'm so glad I ran into you, Catherine. Jesse said you'd probably freak out if you saw me, but this went well, right?"

"Nooo, she said that?" Catherine tried to sound astonished, as if to protect Rachel's naïveté, but sudden curiosity possessed her. Rachel was chatty and Jesse trusted her. Endeavoring to evade questions, Catherine forgot she could ask them. She longed to know all about Jesse, and in front of her stood a loquacious well of knowledge. Oh, she shouldn't, yet she knew she was frail before her curiosity. Moreover, she wanted to prove to Jesse that she was capable of having an adult, mature reaction. She was most definitely not freaking out. No, no.

"Come on." Catherine started walking toward the house. "Let's grab coffee, I'd love to hear more about you."

CHAPTER THIRTY-SIX

Eight hours. Eight hours of vain efforts to hit that song the right way, only to find disappointment every single time. Something was still missing, like a hole gaped in every single word, and the thought that she would have to wait for another album to drop that song made her frown. Jesse didn't want Catherine to see her brooding and she certainly didn't want her to dig into the reasons for this pensive mood, so when Catherine briefly left the bedroom, Jesse seized the opportunity to turn her face toward the wall.

What exactly was she trying to protect her from? Catherine had come to Tennessee to spend some time with her and was left alone all day while Jesse pursued the same notes she had been chasing for years now. Guilt settled on her like a ton of bricks. Every self-deception, every misstep she had ever made was clear when she looked into those fierce, dark eyes. So, that's what had been wrong with all her past relationships. She'd been trying to feel when in fact feeling was effortless.

The instinctive merging with this woman was so enthralling, and the sensations discovered were so raw yet so captivating, that she could only surrender with gratitude. She wasn't going to force a single thing. Thinking wistfully of the morning spent with Catherine in the barn and a thousand questions that woman would ask, she heaved a weary sigh. Not only did Jesse want to do better, but she also couldn't think of anything more interesting or exciting than spending tomorrow with Catherine. She was resolved not to spend it in bed, however tempting that might be. Maybe she could fix the fence and feed the animals before Catherine woke up, and then after breakfast they could take a nice, slow drive down the Natchez Trace and get away from the world. Just the two of them. The thought assuaged her enough to close her eyes again. As she was drifting off, with only a few more senses left, Jesse heard Catherine behind her back, sneaking into bed. A wiggle was soon followed by unexpected low moaning.

"Oh, Jesse, oh, Jesse." Catherine emitted a suppressed cry of delight, followed by lustful moans and giggling. "Oh yes, God, you're sexy."

Jesse instantly broke into a smile and opened her eyes wide to the semidarkness of the room, intrigued by Catherine's little performance. Obviously completely alert by now, she wanted nothing more than to see what Catherine was doing and jump on her, but she just lay with suspended breath, amused, dismissing the idea to turn around. She refused to stop the show Catherine was putting on in any way. The woman was breathing heavily and moaning all alone, occasionally calling her name as if Jesse was the one pleasing her, obviously taking pleasure in knowing Jesse was as far from sleep as ever.

"Oh yes, don't stop." She was letting out moans of lust, which Jesse infallibly found arousing. Catherine certainly knew how to get a woman's attention, and Jesse struggled to resist a clear pulsating sensation developing between her thighs. The perfect stillness of her body only enraged the storm of sensations seizing her. In that deceiving darkness, Jesse could feel aching shivers down her spine as if touched by Catherine's heavy breaths. Each moan, each move left her lying in awe, gasping for air. Without a breath or a thought other than what imagination commanded her, she could almost feel her fingers gently pressing Catherine's waist and deftly moving lower, amidst her sighs and wriggling, the air pervaded with the smell of their wetness.

Catherine somehow found exactly what she needed today.

Yearning for that body, Jesse could no longer hold back. In an instant, she rolled around and found herself on top of Catherine, her hands sliding lower. She didn't measure up to the eyes staring at her.

"Where were we?" Jesse finally caught her breath as their gaze locked in an unyielding passion.

"I was just about to make love to Jessie J when you showed up." Catherine smiled softly.

"You lucky lady."

"She's good."

"I could have fallen asleep and missed all this."

"Yeah, like you did all the times before," Catherine teased and then surrendered to the tender touch.

CHAPTER THIRTY-SEVEN

As soon as she opened her eyes, Catherine realized her covers were gone. Again. That damn bandit. Feeling the cold creeping up her naked body, she slowly rolled onto her other side, expecting to find a warm, happy bundle to hate, but Jesse was already gone. Despondent, Catherine fell back into the cold of the bed. Who in their sane mind got up at six every morning? More importantly, how did she manage to be so sexy with so little sleep?

The fierce rays of sunlight shone onto her face, so Catherine lazily stretched and reached for the clothes that were still lying scattered across the floor and bed. She couldn't wait to see what Jesse was doing at this ungodly hour. When she went downstairs, she was surprised to learn it was well past eight. As expected, Jesse was nowhere to be found. However, waiting at the table was a feast featuring croissants, beignets, fresh strawberries and pancakes with maple syrup, hash browns, grits, eggs, a fruit smoothie, and a pot of coffee with a note: "Fixing the paddock fence, be back soon." Catherine decided it was appropriate to let this moment melt her completely.

This French-American breakfast had been arranged with a lot of care and looked delicious, so even though Catherine badly wanted to watch Jesse fix the fence, she never considered ignoring the effort Jesse had already invested. No, it had to be honored. With great relish, she finished the pancakes and drank up the smoothie, making a firm promise to herself to get up at six tomorrow so she could share this moment with Jesse. She left a few croissants and eggs for later in case Jesse was hungry and walked out into a sunny November day. The thought of seeing Jesse feeding the animals, taking care of the horses, or fixing the fence infused her with unusual warmth. What an odd infatuation of a mostly reasonable woman, Catherine thought, yet she could hardly wait to have Jesse close. She found her just as she was attaching the upper horizontal board to the post while Dallas and Fargo grazed impassively in the distance. Catherine walked over to the fence and stared at Jesse from behind as she was attaching the board, feeling contentment she had never experienced before.

In a few months she'd return to Paris to work on the movie and leave all this behind, and Jesse's scent, her mornings, her kisses would belong to someone else. Yet Catherine could hardly bring herself to regret this feeling or imagine a day when she'd forget it. This was something that was only hers, only theirs, and once they parted, this perfect moment would keep them bound forever. It could be enough. It had to be.

Her eyes settled on Jesse's sculpted forearms below her rolled-up sleeves, and she quickly muttered a desperate curse. Jesse looked so strong, so cool, so self-reliant bent over that board, yet somehow she appeared more vulnerable than ever.

Who would take care of her in the years to come? Was she going to be happy? Would they meet by chance in thirty years, and would it even matter then?

They both needed their careers to keep them grounded, to give them voice, to inspire stories they could share with each other. As much as Jesse was talented, Catherine could not imagine country music being overly admired in France, and her own independence was far too important to her. There was no way she was going to turn down this or any other similar job. She couldn't make a relationship work when she and Chloe lived in the same apartment, so she didn't harbor any illusions it would work out on different continents. So, yes, eventually they would part, and she'd better cherish this moment of fastening the board to the paddock post with everything she got.

Jesse would not remember this by next November, she thought just as the woman turned. Her impish blue eyes instantly brought a smile to Catherine's face, and she realized it was time to tell her about the movie.

Oh, if only this time of tranquility and seclusion could have lasted longer. Catherine tilted her head.

"How are you so sexy at everything you do?"

"Well, Catherine Des Lauriers, you certainly know how to romance a lady."

Catherine leaned her forehead against Jesse's, marveling at the slight blushing caressing her cheeks. Could she possibly fall any harder for this woman?

"Dallas here loves chewing on wood, so I had to change the board before it fell apart."

The horse seemed more intrigued by the windfall of apples around the fence.

"He's so handsome it's hard to hold it against him."

"He sure is. He was raised to be a track champion, just like his parents. However, when Dallas ruptured his tendon right before the Kentucky Derby, his owner was so disappointed he couldn't bear to look at him again. He'd see only a lame horse and the millions he lost. I got him when he was two months into his recovery, and he certainly never disappointed me."

Hearing Jesse speak about Dallas with so much warmth, Catherine felt an instinctive need to hug her. Jesse let out a throaty chuckle.

"Do you want to make a little trip?"

"Oh? What time are they expecting you in the studio?" Catherine helped her lay a half-chewed board on the trailer, and as a token of appreciation Jesse pressed her against the tractor.

"I'm not going today." For a second, her gaze shifted to the forest behind Catherine's shoulders before settling on her dark eyes again. "We need a break after yesterday, and I thought the two of us could drive down the Natchez Trace," she added airily, still making Catherine wonder if there was something she was not saying. Yet, her eyes were firm, her smile disarming, and the silence didn't make her waver, so Catherine quietly nodded.

"Come on," Jesse urged her, motioning to the tractor. "Sit next to me. Once we drop this off, we can go home."

During their ride back, Jesse was raving about the trace they were about to visit, and Catherine couldn't remember ever knowing anyone who would so fervently rave about everything from the rushing waterfalls at sunset to the intricacies of fixing barn roofs. Nothing was ever too big or too small for Jesse. There was no drama and no heavy expectations, and Catherine had to admit that with Jesse's playful disposition the world no longer seemed an inexorable, revolving misery. She liked the person she was becoming around Jesse, intuitive and unburdened.

"Do you have any plans for after Thanksgiving?" Jesse asked casually just as they entered the house. Perhaps now was the perfect time to tell her, but Catherine wanted to spend one more moment in gentle oblivion.

"Not right away. My mother was supposed to visit for Thanksgiving, but now she's saying she can't make it before Christmas, which means she'll probably come in February."

"Does that mean you could perhaps stay a bit longer?"

"You know I will eventually have to leave." Her eyes captured Jesse's. "I don't want you to get used to it, Jesse."

"I know." Jesse nodded as her blue eyes searched for a trace of hesitation in Catherine's countenance. "I promise I'll never get used to it."

Jesse finally smiled and wrapped her arms around Catherine's waist. Their kiss was tender, Jesse's lips lingering on Catherine's for one blissful moment. "Where does one find another babe like you? How did I even find you?" She chuckled. "I love having you here. Besides, you mentioned wanting to travel more. We could go to Atlanta, find a place to dance, visit a cabaret in New Orleans, a show in New York."

Catherine beamed and pulled her closer.

"When I first told my mother that I thought I liked girls," Catherine said, "her first instinct, first reaction, first thought was to go to a cabaret and persuade them to take me because she felt I needed to get more comfortable with naked female bodies and expressing myself around them. Yet, I fell for the only woman who was actually dressed, our instructor. We stayed together for two years."

"Can't help but feel I should somehow be grateful for that." Jesse frowned and fixed her gaze on Catherine. "But I'm thinking we can skip the visit to the cabaret, then. I never really cared for those instructors."

Catherine grinned and settled her head on Jesse's forehead.

"We can always dance, even here. My body is my form of expression."

"Aren't I lucky? And, you love sleeping naked."

"Not quite. You have a penchant for stealing blankets in the middle of the night."

"What? No way."

Catherine nodded firmly, which prompted Jesse to grimace.

"Well, as you can see, I'm used to sleeping alone."

"Oh, Jesse, you're so full of shit."

Soft lips brushed Catherine's cheek and a thrill instantly bolted through her veins.

"I'm sorry for stealing your covers," Jesse said. "Your body is a gift I don't take for granted."

"Then come. Dance with me, stranger. Like this is our first and last encounter."

Catherine gathered her into her arms, and Jesse's body listened to her velvety whispers, followed her with easy trust. As they swayed, Catherine knew she wanted to let those hands take complete control of her body. She never wanted to let go.

In a matter of moments they were in a kiss and on a table, chasing away the thoughts weakening them. The trace could wait a few more hours.

CHAPTER THIRTY-EIGHT

The slow drive down the winding greenway took them through rural towns, rolling hills, small cafés, picnic areas, and a quaint postcard mural. They stopped for hot biscuits and country ham at a local inn and strolled through lush, colorful, and peaceful trails before going back to the roadway lined with autumn hardwoods for more awe-inspiring scenery. A deserted Wednesday in November with no cell reception and no crowds made the tender silence around them only deepen their bond.

One day like this with Catherine was enough to make up for months being away. Stealing occasional glances at the woman, Jesse knew she could take this as slowly as needed. She'd wait years for this. They didn't need to speak about the future for the present to be good. Yet, at times, Jesse would find herself wandering into distant years ahead, and she wished she could touch Catherine's cheek like now, harmlessly, in some dark hour of the night, hear her talk, still able to astound her. Get to know all the little vanities and the unbearable gloominess that would unmistakably reveal a nostalgia for all the moments, all the sorrows, all the experiences she already missed. She traveled through memories waiting to be created, eager to live immoderately in the hour they were given, oblivious to all the affliction awaiting, of the losses to come, and she still found a way to miss her. Just like this, sitting next to her, absorbed in the reverent thrill of the nature surrounding them.

How had she even reached this point? She could have spent an entire day watching Catherine pensively eat cookies beside a streamlet. Surely she had more substance than that. Yet, Jesse wanted that woman now more than she ever wanted anything. God, who knew shortbread could be so sexy?

* * *

When the scenic route took them to Alabama, they pulled up near the river to share their lunch. The sunlight was escaping through the tall trees and it was a pleasantly warm day, so they sat at the back of the car, next to each other, staring into the surrounding wilderness. Catherine quickly finished her sandwich, crackers, cheese, and even fruit, while Jesse continued to plod along. Wasn't she the slowest eater in the universe, always taking her sweet time to enjoy every bite? Catherine could barely keep her eyes off the woman, as the intimate silence sent a feeling of serenity across her senses. How could she have this gift reveal itself to her without it asking anything in return? What could she do for Jesse?

"What kept you so long in the studio yesterday?" she asked innocently, curious to see Jesse put down her sandwich.

"There's a song I've been writing for the past five years," she replied slowly before cracking a smile. "I wanted it on this album, but it's just not there yet." She shrugged thoughtfully.

"What are you afraid of?"

Jesse cast down her eyes in silence, and Catherine paused, surprised. Was this the first time she saw Jesse hesitate in the middle of something? Catherine longed to know, yet the last thing she wanted was to hurt Jesse in any way by pushing her.

After a moment or two of observing Jesse, she calmly added, "It's always fear holding us back. Never fear who you truly are. Give yourself more and you'll be fine."

Jesse grinned. "Is that coming from you, Catherine Des Lauriers?"

"Honesty is the ultimate tyranny of art. Eventually, it will draw out what you refuse to concede."

With quiet assurance, Jesse gazed at Catherine. "Being around you helps me be myself," she acknowledged as though without any fear, and before Catherine had a chance to react, Jesse continued, her eyes fixed absently on the river, "There were four of us. My youngest sister, Taylor, was eight when I moved away. She was imaginative, chubby, with an unbearable inclination to deprive our wardrobes of clothes that were a few sizes too large and then inevitably ruin them with peanut butter. Then she turned into a very artsy teenager and wanted to be a singer. She always seemed like a happy kid—you'd never hear her complain about anything. Except maybe my musical choices. Kept annoying me, saying she wished I could be as cool as Miley Cyrus, little imp. She was just a typical seventeen-year-old when five years ago, she killed herself. The last thing she told me was a very carefree, 'I'll talk to you tomorrow.' Just like any other day. She didn't leave a note, and I often close my eyes and try to imagine what she saw as she was dying. To understand... We were so angry at her, but my parents...I don't think they ever reached the stage where they would forgive her or accept what happened. We all had a hard time coming to terms with the loss and guilt, but they simply decided to never talk about her. They removed her photos, rearranged her room, they can't even bring themselves to say her name. They refer to Owen, my brother, as their youngest. Like Taylor betrayed them, like Taylor broke some silent promise. As if she abandoned them without a word and deserves to be punished, as if every memory of her should be wiped out. I want them to finally forgive her, but I can barely get them to talk about her. They just shrug. Let's pretend everything's great. The favorite pastime of happy families." Jesse spoke effortlessly, focused, displaying courage and strength that made Catherine love her even more. "This song was supposed to be about her. I want them to listen and I want them to love her. I don't want to drag out their pain, but I want us to have her again. We need to be able to talk about her. Even in loss. I want us to forgive her, but I don't know… Something always ends up missing, and I start doubting myself only to realize I don't want to deepen their anguish."

"Your family may need to hear it so that you can finally forgive yourselves, not Taylor."

"I don't want it to be about us. I want it to be about her and others thinking about ending it all. They deserve that, and I feel like I owe it to Taylor, but I don't want to hurt my parents. However I look at it, it's just wrong."

"So, give Taylor voice one last time," Catherine said, and Jesse settled her curious eyes on her as she spoke. "Write it from her perspective. Make that her song and let her say goodbye. You say she wanted to be a singer? So let her say goodbye in a song. Maybe your parents just need to hear those words." As Jesse stayed silent, Catherine instinctively gathered her in her arms and Jesse silently rested her head on her shoulder. "You are strong enough to deliver that message to your family, I know you are."

"That's actually lovely, thank you."

Suddenly, this seemed so much more complex than a simple fling. But then again, Catherine had always been well versed in the simple art of making things complicated. The album's release party was set for the first day of March, and by then, Catherine knew, she'd be long gone.

CHAPTER THIRTY-NINE

When they returned home, it was past seven already, so Jesse immediately hurried to the barn to make sure the animals had enough hay. Watching that pretty face on a tractor will never stop being funny, Catherine thought as her eyes followed Jesse hurrying to the barn. The kinder and the gentler Jesse was, the more complicated everything seemed. Jesse made her believe she, too, could be easygoing and significant, and she wanted to live in that world—relaxed, simple, warm, far from everyone. Sure, she didn't need this now when she was finally at peace with herself, now when she knew she was about to go back to France. Yet she wanted to fully feel each of the few moments they had left together. Even if it meant agonizing torment later, which it undoubtedly would.

Half an hour passed and Jesse had still not come back. A peculiar unease seized Catherine, so she decided to walk over to make sure Jesse was fine after their little chat. Sure, she seemed content and cheerful, but Catherine knew well that Jesse's smile could hide anything. Catherine found her petting the goats and humming a melody, then running to scribble something down in a notepad she kept on the desk right next to the tack room before returning to the goats again. Watching Jesse in a rush of inspiration brought an amused grin to Catherine's face, and it infused her with overwhelming warmth. How had she gotten this lucky? This woman could take her every apprehension, every insecurity, and pulverize them without saying a word. Her deep blue gaze lost in time made her even more beautiful, if that was somehow possible. Once she had ascertained that Jesse was simply absorbed in music, Catherine quietly withdrew.

* * *

Upon her return, Jesse found Catherine beside the piano closely examining the awards displayed on the shelf, with Lola sniffing around her. With a sharp sense of guilt, she hurried off to shower, but when she came back, she found Catherine relaxed and serene, sitting at the piano and observing her.

"What do I need to do to get this hat trophy?"

"Have a major heartbreak, stop believing in human kindness, embrace disappointments."

"I can do that."

"What if," Jesse said, "I don't let you?"

She watched Catherine flash a captivating smile and pat the piano bench next to her. Jesse was the best version of herself beside that woman, and she didn't know if Catherine would ever comprehend that. Lighthearted, she sat next to her.

"While you were in the studio yesterday, I was practicing this." Catherine resolutely threw her hands on the keys and, to Jesse's astonishment, started playing her song. The very song Jesse was performing when she first spotted her in the festival crowd. The moment forced itself upon her recollection—consternation on Catherine's face, her intense dark gaze, the wild beating of her own heart.

It seemed like a lifetime ago, yet the thought was still the same—*Who is this woman?*

Catherine cleared her voice and, never pulling her eyes away from Jesse, solemnly declared, "From Jesse to her mysterious ex-lover. *Floating down the river of my childhood, with the whole world lying next to me.*" She started singing with a bright tone, leaving Jesse speechless. She probably should have been blushing, but instead she could only admire the scene unfolding before her.

"You're honoring my ex better than me." Jesse laughed, impressed, while Catherine was entertaining herself, singing wholeheartedly.

"Lay, lay naked with me."

Jesse thought she never really wanted anything until now.

Would Catherine trust her if she told her how she wrote that song? Her truth was often so simple it was hard to believe. She saw two people lying on the boat deck and pictured their conversation. Imagination was the closest she ever got to love. Until now. She never cared this much for anyone, including herself.

When Catherine finished her performance, she found Jesse's half-lidded eyes fixed on hers in silent adoration.

"I never listen to my music, but that was worth every second. Is there anything you're not good at, Catherine Des Lauriers?"

"Trusting myself around country singers."

Jesse grinned and took her mouth in a long, gentle kiss. "Aren't I lucky that I'm the only one you know?" she murmured.

"I know Dolly Parton."

"Oh, come on, French. I was so close," she whimpered, rolling her eyes to the ceiling in quiet exasperation.

"How come you don't listen to your music? I mean, it's not *that* bad," Catherine asked softly.

"Thank you, babe," Jesse replied, hoping to annoy her, but Catherine had already grown to love the nauseating name. "I need to keep the emotions fresh for my shows. When did you learn to play the piano?"

"When we lived in Madagascar, my father insisted I take piano lessons. Of course, my faithful Farai would accompany me regularly. My piano teacher could not for the life of him understand why my mother always took me to those classes dressed the same. With a red bandana around her neck and glasses she couldn't see through."

Jesse laughed, looking at her curiously. "So what did you play in Madagascar?"

Without a word, Catherine again placed her hands on the piano, glanced at Jesse, and started playing.

"Seriously, Catherine? How old are you?" Jesse's eyes danced around her face, endeavoring to hide the admiration for her left-hand dexterity.

"Shut up, Jesse. It's hardly Beethoven." She took a deep breath and fearlessly shouted, "Deep in my heart there's a fire, a burning heart."

Her gaze settled on Jesse, who couldn't look away from those eyes, the poise, and the passion in her tone, so Catherine had to nudge her with an intent stare.

"Well, come on! You could help me with the singing part, you know?" She flashed one of those bright smiles that would erase Jesse's entire existence. Every thought except that she wanted to love every inch of that body for every moment of her life. Listening to her was utter surrender.

"I'm living in my, living in my dreams."

Her powerful voice in the sappy eighties hit reverberated throughout Jesse's heart, so she joined in. As if that was what it took for her gaze to reveal reverence, visibly impressed, Catherine nodded. "You've got talent," she admitted, mesmerized.

"Now you tell me that." Jesse laughed and joined in, playing by ear.

Seeing how much Catherine believed in her earlier that day, Jesse started doubting the notion that artists were not allowed to be happy. What she was feeling next to this woman was damn close to that.

* * *

Catherine was unable to fall asleep, and it wasn't for the missing blanket, though Jesse was already wrapped up in that soft warmth. Draped over the foot of the bed was another one, thoughtfully left there for Catherine. However, that night she was not interested in comfort. It wasn't owing to the feminine, sensual scent of the woman lying beside her either, though one needed to be a damn saint to fall asleep next to it. For the first time in her life, she wasn't what everyone expected her to be. She didn't have to be anything, and it was liberating. Jesse was dedicated to her every little whim, accepting of her every insecurity, and Catherine could not just ignore the strong bond formed between them.

Yet as she tossed and turned, tormented, she struggled to come up with a scenario where Jesse and she wouldn't end up hating each other. She couldn't tell if Jesse would understand her need for autonomy, but Catherine knew that as much as they needed to be good together, they needed to be good on their own as well. Why would a music star with an army of followers ever agree to that? Also, did Catherine even have it in her to trust again? Jesse's attentive and courteous nature had a way of warming her heart, but it wouldn't be right to have any expectations from someone living across the ocean. Even if they were capable of having perfect days together like today.

"I desperately need you to be an obnoxious ass," Catherine whispered as she tenderly brushed the blond strands of hair away from Jesse's sleeping face, as if she were seeking an answer on that placid countenance.

"I guess you'll have to fall in love with me, Catherine."

Jesse's murmur startled her, and Catherine unexpectedly found herself in front of that irresistible roguish grin and the slumberous gaze.

"Fuck you, Jesse! I thought you were asleep." She held her stare and finally smiled as Jesse pulled her in for a kiss.

"No shame there, Catherine, I'm perfectly adorable."

"And devious," Catherine protested between those ardent, deep kisses and strong arms bringing her even closer. To say she genuinely cared about Jesse would be quite inadequate.

"I think you forgot something." Jesse pulled away for a moment and frowned, leaving Catherine to stare at her, stupefied.

"What?"

"To take this off." Jesse's hands deftly slid under her shirt and slipped it over her head. "I love waking up to the sight of your naked body. Look at this." Her fingers were softly tracing the curves of Catherine's breasts and the contours of her ribs. "This is much better, Catherine. Per-fect. Also, I want these panties." She readily pulled them off and buried her face in them. "Actually, I wanna wear them tomorrow, carry you on me all day." As she took a deep breath, inhaling their scent, she seemed utterly pleased. "Now, good night," Jesse said and playfully rolled over onto her other side, her face still pressed deep into Catherine's panties. Catherine laughed helplessly and quickly snuggled next to Jesse, planting a kiss on her neck.

Oh yeah, this is gonna suck so bad.

CHAPTER FORTY

When she woke up the next morning, Catherine found herself tucked under a fuzzy blanket. She presumed Jesse had already left for the studio, so she stretched and grabbed her phone. It was eight, later than she expected, and she rolled out of bed and into the shower. Downstairs she encountered an impatient Lola who couldn't wait to accompany her to the barn. It was a wonderful, sunny morning, and Catherine hung out with the llamas and the goats before she walked around the pond and into the forest. Wary of fences and determined not to wander off this time, she inhaled the scent of trees and the silence, realizing she could get used to this with exceptional ease.

Except she couldn't. As much as she liked this ranch and the harmony she achieved with Jesse, Catherine knew she couldn't give up on herself. Not only did she need her career, she also needed the love and self-esteem that dance would inspire. She wanted Jesse to admire her the way she admired Jesse.

Nicolas had sent her the materials a few days ago, and her mind was already brimming with ideas. While Jesse was in the studio, Catherine sat at the computer, noting down the movements, listening to the musical sequences, envisioning the audience, the room, the costumes, and exploring the rhythm. Her mind was constantly trying out various combinations and patterns, and Catherine couldn't wait to see the end result. She wished this thrill was something she could have shared with Jesse instead of something that would ultimately divide them.

Calm and unwavering in her desires, Jesse managed to wrap Catherine in the feeling of comfort and trust, which was not easy at all. Yet no matter how close they got, Catherine was still going back to Paris. Her home, her language, her streets and, above all, her dance and her independence were waiting there.

Jesse's future was in Nashville. As much as Catherine grew to appreciate her talent and charming good looks, she couldn't envision her music having much success in Europe.

When she got back, Catherine sat at the computer and continued to read the materials, trying to focus on the flow of the sections she'd be choreographing. She called Fletcher only to hear that her mother was still not coming and that she could stay in Tennessee till New Year's if she pleased. Considering she was in too deep already, Catherine couldn't imagine what would happen should Jesse ask her to stay longer.

Eventually, Catherine got engrossed in the shapes and transitions, and her body had started to follow the music when a pair of blue eyes peeked through the door. It wasn't even noon yet, so Catherine instantly retreated, bewildered, and shoved her hands into her pockets in a coy gesture.

"What are you doing here so early?" Catherine stammered, embarrassed.

"Now I understand why you didn't see the message I sent." Jesse grinned and, holding her gaze, mischievously added, "Could we just pretend I didn't come back, and you continue dancing? You're kinda stunning."

As if she'd been caught in something forbidden, Catherine shrugged with a tense grin, then attempted to change the subject. "How was the studio today?"

"Amazing, we absolutely nailed it, and we're almost done," Jesse replied, beaming. "Even Taylor's song," she murmured and took Catherine by the waist, looking at her with such gratitude that Catherine feared her rib cage would crumble down and that tears would well up in her eyes.

God, that woman would make her forget everything she ever promised to herself. Deep longing was ravaging Catherine's senses, and all she wanted was to hold Jesse tightly and protect her from the world, hide them from the future.

"Thank you, Catherine."

Jesse enfolded her softly in her arms, running her fingers through her hair. Catherine had been trying hard not to feel anything for so long, and all it took was that familiar gesture to crush all her defenses and leave her heart open.

"I was so unfair to you, Jesse, and I'm sorry."

"I'm aware country music is not for everyone, don't worry."

"No, not that, you were so patient with me, and you're a wonderful human being. Everything they were saying about you in Maple Springs was true."

"Oh. So you haven't changed your mind about my music?"

And God, she could always make her smile.

Since their first encounter, they had no foundation whatsoever for falling in love. A chance meeting in a pottery store. It should have ended at the same moment it started. Yet, it didn't, because for some reason Jesse kept coming back.

As Jesse wrapped her arms around Catherine's waist, her every tender look made the silence more unbearable. Catherine allowed Jesse to focus on her music and her album, and now she was running out of excuses. It was time to talk about goodbye.

Jesse pulled her against her body and her gentle mouth brushed across hers. "I won't tell anyone how much you enjoy country."

"I will miss it, you know."

"You don't have to, you know."

Catherine chuckled, breathing in her fresh, alluring scent. Although she longed to kiss Jesse back, her body refused to move.

"Okay, what if I promise I'm going to keep listening to your work back in Paris?"

"Why Paris if you can listen to it live?"

"I was offered a job in Paris. The same director I worked with last year wants to collaborate on his new movie this spring. I haven't confirmed yet, and I didn't want to bother you with it until you finished your album, but anyway, it's time to go back to dance, back to my career. In Paris."

* * *

Jesse stared at Catherine for a brief moment, hoping she didn't look too flabbergasted. Even though she felt every single bone was imploding beneath her skin, she strived to offer a supportive face.

So this is why people drink.

"We dance in the States too." She attempted a weak grin.

Catherine embraced her tenderly, remaining in silence.

This could be it, then.

"You're remarkably talented, Catherine, and you deserve that chance. I'm so proud of you." Jesse hoped her set smile valiantly hid her feelings. So maybe she wanted to die, maybe she wanted to disappear at the bottom of the ocean, as a lifetime of misery flashed before her eyes. It could all end so soon, but it wasn't like she didn't know that possibility existed. She had agreed to all this. Borrowed time was all she ever had. For as much as she hated her miserable life right now, Jesse was pleased for Catherine. She cared for the woman, and she wanted to see her happy. Even if it didn't include her. Catherine deserved the chance. Why would Jesse's career in Nashville be more important than Catherine's in Paris? There was no other way to frame it. Catherine's dreams deserved to be supported, even if it meant Jesse would lose what had become her reason to smile.

"I don't want to think about it yet," Catherine muttered, kissing her hair and playfully thumping her on the chest. "I'm so mad at you."

Jesse flinched, grimacing in pain. "What did I do now?"

"You made me fall for you, you asshole. Why would you do that?"

"You helped me feed Chuck."

She gave a half-smile and every atom of her being started rebelling. These warm, lasting hugs, Catherine's skillful fingers tangled in her hair, her fresh sea scent—all of it couldn't be reduced to a distant memory one day.

"I'm still here," Catherine whispered. "Let's go to Memphis together," she added cheerfully, and Jesse recognized it as an attempt to cut off the surging darkness, unable to keep her eyes off Jesse's.

"Listen, Catherine. I don't care if you move to the South Pole. This doesn't have to be our ending." Jesse fixed her gaze on her, dismissing every thought of surrender. Catherine was setting her at ease to the point where she felt perfectly safe letting her guard down. She was in love with this woman, and even if they were never to see each other again, she needed her to know that. "Going to sleep last night, for the first time I understood what peace and contentedness felt like. I'd wait years for that feeling again."

"You are so stubborn."

"You, Des Lauriers, give the worst compliments."

A smile broke across Catherine's face, and Jesse could feel Catherine's lips brushing against hers as she spoke so close to them.

"I can't picture my life without you, Catherine, and I can't think about other women."

"You'll get there in time."

"I might." She frowned teasingly. "But I don't care to."

"Jesse, you have so much to offer, and you deserve more. What would our future together look like?"

"I had it all figured out long ago." Jesse instantly raised her arms, still firmly pressed against Catherine's body, and flashed a cheeky grin. "You don't believe things are meant to last. Therefore, we'd take it as slow as possible, so you start trusting me. In five years or so, we'd go on our first real date, like the ones you tell your friends about." Her tone was impeccably solemn, befitting of a proclamation. "You'd stand there in a floral dress, nervous, not knowing if I wanna kiss you, and of course I'd pretend I was cool to hide that I was really feeling weak in the knees. Then if things go well from there, we may proceed toward awkward displays of affection like fixing each other's hair or collars, or even occasionally posting each other's photos on social media. But we can still debate that. By year eight, we'd be so irretrievably infatuated with each other that we'd be getting dressed with the lights on. Ten years in and we'd have our first argument followed by you saying, 'I love you,' and me giving you a drawer in my house. Fifteen years is when I ask you to marry me for the first time, and you politely say no but add you appreciate my interest because you're a nice person. I totally think you're the one, so I ask again, three more times over the course of the next two years. Now, that fourth time is when I'm positive it's going to happen. I have a number-one hit, I'm on the cover of *US Weekly*, I take you to Virginia, Magic City, Vegas, and when I pop the question on a beach at sunset—"

"I thought we were in Vegas."

"They have beaches there. Captured by the magic of the moment, you briefly consider it, but say no again. We end up never getting married but nevertheless have fun together."

"Come on, you have to ask the fifth time. Everybody knows that."

"I have my pride, Catherine." She gave her a light kiss, and her lips shut out everything outside the present moment again. "And yes, we'll go to Memphis."

CHAPTER FORTY-ONE

The weeks that ensued were the continuation of an intense, impulsive wonder that started back in August. They spent every possible moment together as if they were studying an unknown civilization that would be lost in a matter of seconds—devouring every impulse, absorbing every progression as something to build their uncertain future upon. Thanksgiving came and went imperceptibly, and so did Christmas and New Year's, and neither dared to mention the peril looming over them. They went to Atlanta and New York, fixed the barn roof, hung out on the ranch. Never discussing their farewell, like they both silently decided to experience those last days together to see exactly how profound bliss could be.

Catherine knew it was impossible to be near that woman and make sensible decisions. Paris might not be far enough. Whenever she got close to Jesse's soft skin, she could feel the power of her own body. There was no holding back, as if a world would explode inside and create grounds and skies to be eagerly explored. It was becoming real, and Catherine was sensing that she had to put miles between them quickly in an attempt to feel safe again, safe from feeling.

Upon her return to Maple Springs, their phone conversations kept them close as they had in earlier days. Though every single morning she woke up with the firmest intention to send Jesse to obscure oblivion, Catherine could still sense Jesse's instincts, her affection on her skin. Every time Jesse's name appeared on her screen she would feel her body moving to the rhythm of those sweet words like some abominable teenager crushing on an illusion. *Good luck forgetting, Catherine.*

She stared through the window for a minute or two, quietly observing wind gusts blowing snow across the yard, hiding Maple Springs and revealing her bare, hollow future. Dejected, she flung herself onto the bed, arms spread out. She always did have a special talent for a good fiasco, didn't she? To forsake that touch, the gentle way Jesse's fingers closed around her chin and pulled her in a deep kiss, the ensuing feeling that every kiss in her life was waiting for that one, that was a high price to pay for her career. Yet, to expect Jesse would settle for someone across the ocean who'd never be around was absurd. It wouldn't be fair anyway. *Damn. That's what you get for messing with country singers.*

Striving to focus on her future without Jesse, Catherine grabbed her phone and found a dear name. It was high time she applied herself to this movie.

"Darling Catherine! You better not be calling to tell me you turned Nicolas down."

Catherine could vividly picture the sulky pout, the reproachful gaze of that dignified woman, and she realized just how much she needed her familiar voice, her merry laugh, her rolling Rs.

"Hi, Ninon. No, you just have to give me the scoop on you and the baron. I'm dying to know. How are you?"

"Oh!" Catherine could hear her puffing on a cigarette. "I'm fine, I'm just having an existential crisis."

"What happened?"

"The baron is in love with me."

"That's not the most atrocious thing in the world." Catherine smiled.

"Isn't it? What if things work out?"

"Isn't that the point?"

"One day you meet someone who doesn't fit your life at all and yet nothing in the world feels more natural than having them close. Arnaud is collecting porcelain dolls, birdwatching, and deflecting attention. Can you imagine *that* with me? Yet he understands me like no one ever has. We have entire conversations in a single glance."

Okay, perhaps that was not what Catherine needed. Could she at least hear Ninon out without comparing a seventy-five-year-old baron she'd never met to Jesse? Damn her feeble heart. She was a better friend than this.

"You know," Ninon went on, "no matter how many times we face loss, each time it becomes slightly worse, and you start resenting yourself a little more, and one thing you learn, one thing you master, is that things are not built to last. But what if we were wrong? What if we only need to be bolder? It would mean we wasted so many years of our life on ignorance. I, Ninon Allard, was an ignorant fool. Things sometimes do work out. It is possible to be happy." Ninon's tone was overcome with indignation, her majestic composure lost. Catherine was used to seeing this grand woman catching herself being unguarded before anyone else even had a chance to come close. She was brushing the feelings off like annoying particles of dust threatening her divine, impeccable appearance. Faux pas, she called them in disgust.

Ninon huffed and continued, "Darling Catherine, you dare to look behind those dreadful porcelain dolls and you discover a treasure. Arnaud says that we should let love inconvenience us, let life inconvenience us, because we are so used to manipulating everything to fit our needs. Maybe what we need is an inconvenience. Enjoy people for who they are, not what they need to be. Enjoy yourself. We don't need molds to be beautiful."

"Then don't overthink it," Catherine said. "Don't live anyone's expectations. There is nothing the two of you need to do except what you feel at that moment."

"You see why I love choreographers—you are forever surrendered to your passions, your instincts, so aware of your frailty, so naked in your feelings. On the other hand, I am using extravagant fabrics to hide their absence."

"If you fear something, it's very much present."

"It is now. Damn that man! Oh, darling, I don't want to annoy you, and don't you think you will avoid that answer. When are you coming back to Paris?"

"You could never annoy me, Ninon, and I can't wait to meet Arnaud once I'm back. He sounds like a perfect gentleman."

"You're coming back?" she shouted.

The thought of returning to Paris provoked excitement for the first time, and Catherine had to admit the emotions of this woman were absolutely contagious.

"I would never miss watching you re-create the era of power dressing and communicate Louis's absolute rule with your brilliance. I can only imagine the world you'll create. Fashion as we know it was invented back then, and you'll get to bring that to life. If I can contribute with a few movements to accentuate the colorful, voluminous, and extravagant soul of the art pieces you'll create, I'll consider it a success."

"Oh, darling, I miss you so much, my faithful partner in glamour and luxury. Will you let me have a cape in one of these gliding movements that stop the time?"

"Is that what you want?" Catherine chuckled at Ninon's art of flattery. "I've started reviewing the materials, and I'll send them your way today so you can plan. We'll have a lot of bodies and a lot of movements."

"Darling Catherine, do tell me we'll have legs galore. You know there is nothing I love more than tight silk breeches hugging the studs' legs."

Ninon's fervor was hard to resist, and Catherine couldn't help but laugh. What she needed was a distraction, a confirmation that they'd be fine. Working with that crew again would be a delightful pleasure. Yes, she would enjoy every minute of it. Except when she remembered that while they were getting the tight breeches to fit the legs of their skilled dancers, Jesse's legs would most likely be wrapped around some skinny, tanned body in a room full of lust. Ouch, indeed.

"Oh, we'll expose those lines all right. I'm anticipating a lot of silk flowing around those muscular, virile bodies."

"We not only get to impress the world but also satisfy our vanity, two things I love the most." Ninon's animated, defiant laugh was ringing out in a luscious legato. "Have you ever met Charles who will be in charge of lights? He's an absolute magician, darling. He worked on *La Frontière* last year," Ninon continued, and Catherine could feel her voice tearing her away from Jesse and nearer to an inevitable reality.

CHAPTER FORTY-TWO

A fierce snowstorm was slowly moving out of Maple Springs, leaving behind an unbreakable stillness and a magical landscape shrouded in white. The fresh, fluffy snow absorbed the few sounds the mountains were producing, letting the silence reign, so Catherine startled when she heard the squeaky gate open and close, prompting her to glance at the clock. It was barely past six, still too early for Fletcher to come back from the shop. Faint steps coming from the outside seemed lighter and slower than Fletcher's, so Catherine headed for the door with an inquisitive expression. Her eyes blinked and her mouth gaped as she saw her mother wrapped in a long, black coat and a brimless cloche, standing on the porch and shaking a light dusting of snow off her coat.

"Mother! What are you doing here?" she stammered in shock.

"I told you I'd come! Several times. Did you forget, oh dear Catherine?" Her mother carelessly waved off her question and hugged her.

Hearing her laugh, Catherine knew there was no point in discussing reason or the concept of time with her mother. She had always been an irrational entity whose whimsy and impulses had to be accounted for well in advance. Planning left no room for excitement, and Pearl Fitzgerald wouldn't have it.

Moving past Catherine, who was still gobsmacked, the woman entered the warm house filled with the smell of cinnamon apple pie Fletcher made earlier that day. She carelessly tossed the hat aside and fixed her blond bob.

"No Christmas tree, Catherine? Why do you always have to be such a grinch?" she said, somewhat disappointed, and then pulled Catherine into another hug, prompting her to laugh. One could hardly discern if Pearl Fitzgerald didn't know it was February or she simply mocked her own flakiness, but even with her mother's strange sense of humor and fickle temperament, Catherine had to admit that she missed her. "Oh, you look lovely, dear." Her dark eyes bore into Catherine as she cupped her face. "No signs of a crushed heart, no signs of shattered hopes and dreams whatsoever. Good girl," she added before turning around. "Where is my father?"

"He is closing the shop today," Catherine replied, then quickly added, "I'll call him now."

As pleased as she was to see her mother, Catherine knew it was only a matter of seconds before Pearl launched a barrage of uncomfortable questions and unsolicited advice. Catherine could only hope that Fletcher would be home soon because no one should have to deal with that enhanced interrogation alone.

"Wait, leave it be." Her mother clasped her arm and sat her down. "The two of us have a chance to chat now."

Merde. She was not going to escape this.

"I can't wait to meet this girlfriend of his," Pearl whispered, patting her on the knee. "What is she like?"

"Marj is a lovely lady. Vivacious, gregarious, affectionate. They complement each other well."

"Are they sleeping together?"

"Mother of God!" Catherine's eyes widened. "Please be kind to Fletcher, Mom. You know he is very private. Don't make him feel uncomfortable, please."

"Why would that be uncomfortable? Nonsense! It's a perfectly sensible question." With an impatient hand gesture Pearl dismissed Catherine's concerns as silly, probably wondering where she'd gone wrong in raising her only daughter. "I hope they do. Sex is a wonderful thing. It makes you connected like nothing else. I'd like to know he's content in that department as well."

Poor Fletcher. With Marjorie's loquacity and her mother's directness, he'd better go into hiding for the next few weeks.

Pearl was still fixing her scrutinizing gaze on her, so Catherine finally huffed, helplessly shaking her head. "Fine, they look connected. Oh God, Mother. Please don't grill them. Ask me anything you want to know, I implore you."

As if she had waited for that statement her entire life, her mother smiled. "Okay. What about you?"

Oh shit, she hadn't thought this through. Her mess of a love life was about to be on full display in front of her blunt mother. She should have guessed. "I'm fine. Would you like a drink or something to eat?"

Unsurprisingly, Pearl ignored her question. "Is that why you ran away to this godforsaken corner of the universe almost a year ago?"

So suddenly she knew what month it was. Catherine scoffed. "That was ten months ago, I'm doing better now."

"Why are you fidgeting, then? Why are you looking down?" Pearl's intense stare didn't waver until Catherine raised her eyes. "More importantly, why haven't you returned to France?"

Catherine long ago learned that it was impossible to lie to this woman. Even though Pearl lived in her own little world, she possessed acuity like few others. Catherine already knew the subtle way her mother would let her entrap herself.

"I'm planning to, probably in a month or so. I'll work with Nicolas this summer. He's making a period drama set in the court of Louis XIV," she replied.

"That's wonderful, dear. I hope the movie won't be as depressing as the last one. I'm just saying." She threw her hands up in the air. "What is it with the human fascination with sad endings? Are we that sadistic, or does it just make our lives look better?"

"Perhaps they are just realistic. Sad endings help us feel normal."

"Aha! So knowing that the rest of the world is equally fucked-up and disillusioned gives us the right to pity ourselves? I knew it. It's Chloe, oh my little Kiki." Pearl enfolded Catherine gently in her arms again, patting her back as if she expected her daughter to finally cough up the burdensome truth.

"Mom, you just flew for ten hours. Wouldn't you rather have something to eat or drink? You must be exhausted."

"Nonsense. Let me hear everything. I know Chloe was here, because I was the one who gave her the address. I didn't raise you to run away from problems." She gave her a stern, admonishing look. "Are you two getting back together?"

"Hell no!"

"So once you return to Paris, you're not going back to your apartment in Montmartre?"

"Of course not. I need a fresh start. I'm over what she did, and I have no interest in revisiting that issue ever again."

"Thank goodness. I liked that girl, but she's an even bigger mess than you. I'll have our apartment in Jardin du Luxembourg ready for you. Oh, isn't that going to be wonderful? You are coming back home!"

Her observing eye didn't miss Catherine's less-than-enthusiastic reaction. "Catherine?"

Jesus! Catherine could swear that woman had the ability not to blink for ten hours when she directed that piercing gaze right through you, intent on finding out everything you couldn't even explain to yourself.

"What is it, then?" she asked, her flinty stare insisting. "Are you afraid you'll run into Chloe with someone else? Is that why you're still here?"

"No, Mom, I'm over it. I already ran into Chloe with someone else. We weren't a good match, that's all."

"Well," her mother said with a crooked grin. "You know who I always liked? Elise Toussaint!"

Catherine's bewildered laugh echoed across the room.

"I know she still lives in Paris. She might be single." Pearl folded her hands as if in prayer. "Heavens, the body of that woman! Oh, my dear Catherine."

"I don't know and I don't care to know, Mother," Catherine replied in one breath, shaking her head. Elise was a nude model at the academy her mother attended, and Catherine could not remember why she ever thought it would be a good idea to go on a date with a woman whose naked body her mother stared at for ten hours a day. It must have been a testament to the persuasiveness Pearl Fitzgerald possessed. "It was one date, ten years ago. You are the only one who remembers that there even was a date."

"I'm just saying. You could use someone uninhibited."

Catherine doubted any woman could compare to Jesse in that department. She had a spark that would light the world around her. It felt dirty just to watch her sing.

"Mom, I'm fine. And I'm most definitely not a prude. Don't you worry about me."

"If you are truly over this whole story with Chloe, what's keeping you here?"

Of course she wouldn't let go of that. With her mother's eyes fixated on her, Catherine couldn't come up with a better answer than the truth.

"I met someone."

"Here?"

"I know, I couldn't believe it myself."

"A local girl? What's her name?"

"Mother, you left this town thirty-five years ago. Her name is not relevant." Pearl tilted her head, unimpressed, patiently waiting to get her answer. "God, her name is Jesse. Jesse Morgan."

"Morgan? Is she related to Dave Morgan?" Pearl surveyed her face inquisitively.

"Yes, I believe that's her dad."

"Well, my, my, Catherine." She smirked. "Dave Morgan was every little girl's crush. Tall, blond, deep blue eyes, gentleman's manners. He was ten years my senior, and I don't know a single girl or a teenager in a thirty-mile radius who didn't have the hots for him. Your dear mother included. Now his daughter has inherited that fatal charm. Those are good genes. My, my." Biting her lower lip, Pearl fixed her dreamy gaze through the window.

Good God, could it be any worse? Catherine agonized, hoping her mother would go back to inquiring about Fletcher.

"So, when do I get to meet her?"

"You don't." As soon as she uttered those words, her mother let out a loud scoff. "She doesn't live here. She was visiting from Nashville."

"I want to know everything."

"You shouldn't worry, Mother. I'm going back to Paris anyway."

"Why would that be a problem? Tell me everything." Seeing Catherine remain firm, Pearl calmly added, "Should I ask Dave Morgan? I wouldn't mind spending some time with that hunk of a man. I bet he's suave as ever. He seemed like one of those men who would age well. High cheekbones, thick hair, big strong shoulders. Mmm. A real specimen of human perfection."

Mother of God. Catherine buried her face in her hands. "Mom," she protested in despair.

"I would ask him. And just so you know, I would stand up for you. What is that daughter of his thinking? Seducing someone so vulnerable. He'll be hearing from me. They should be careful with that irresistible charm and unrivaled beauty. It's his fault as well!"

"Jesse didn't do anything wrong. She's wonderful. That's the problem." Catherine never doubted her mother would talk to every living soul in that town if that was what it took to find out what she wanted to know. "My life is in Paris and hers is here. That's all."

"Catherine, dear, do start from the beginning."

It would be so easy to recount every little detail of their first encounter, the way Jesse stared while Catherine struggled to find a single English word, Jesse's soft shirt outlining her perfect breasts, the shivers her raspy voice provoked, the intense attraction binding them—but Catherine had no interest in talking about Jesse for hours. No. She had to forget. Determined not to let her mind wander, she cleared her voice.

"I liked her. I was unusually attracted to her, so I thought, we'd just have fun. But whenever I was around her, I ended up having too much fun."

"And she?"

"She's one of those eternal optimists who believes we can find a solution. Yet, I know I'll go back to France and she has a very successful career in Nashville. I'm old enough to know that this transatlantic love affair would soon become a burden, and I don't want us to hate or resent each other. This way it will always be a fun memory."

"Big deal. You've been watching too many movies, Catherine. Fun memories are illusions. Overall, memories are nothing more than charming traitors. You know what's fun? The present. As long as your present is fun, find a way to keep it like that. There are no guarantees in life. So, what does she do?"

Catherine sneered at herself.

"She's a songwriter, a country singer, actually."

Pearl appeared to be in her nonblinking phase again. "Is she any good?"

"I'd say she's exceptional."

"Oh, dear. Does that mean she knows Blake Shelton?"

Catherine let out a helpless laugh. "I thought you'd be worried about all her fans and women throwing themselves at her, about my shattered dreams and crushed little heart."

"Why would her popularity worry anyone? Catherine, dear, if one wants to cheat, they will find an opportunity. Especially today with all the dating apps, Tinders, Instagrams, social networks. Anyone can do it. But not everyone wants to do it. If anything, living in the spotlight would make cheating harder for her. You can't punish one woman for the mistakes of another. Enough with that nonsense. Give that girl a chance. I'm sure she will make her own mistakes."

"We'll be living on different continents."

"Oh, Catherine, when did you become so unimaginative? Does Fletcher keep any alcohol here? Your reasoning frustrates me."

Catherine grinned and went over to the cabinet to pour her mother a cognac.

"So what is Dave Morgan doing these days?" Pearl asked. "Does he still live here?"

"He's married and he's got grandchildren, Mom."

"Catherine, even I understand your father-in-law is off-limits."

Catherine shook her head and smiled. What an impossible woman! She gave Pearl a drink, and just as she was about to ask about the exhibition her mother had been preparing for the past six months, Fletcher appeared at the door. Shocked, he stopped in his tracks.

As much as she was grateful for being saved, Catherine felt sorry for Fletcher. She gave him a sympathetic look and started counting down till the bombardment began. Three, two, one.

"Pearl!"

"Papa! You seem reinvigorated. Is that because of the late-night action with your new girlfriend? I want to know everything!"

CHAPTER FORTY-THREE

With snow slanting down and wind gusting, Jesse was patiently driving to Maple Springs, wishing the minutes could go faster. It had been almost three weeks since she last saw the unbearable French woman, and she'd come to the realization that twenty days were more than enough. They hadn't spoken as much last week, but Catherine's mother was visiting, and Jesse had two weeks left till the album release, so she wasn't too worried. It was a perfectly mature thing to do, taking care of business, so they could enjoy their time freely once they were together.

Still, three weeks without Catherine's touch seemed unreasonably long, so refusing to overthink, Jesse decided to take a plane and get her kiss. She was craving the rush of those lips, Catherine's low sighs of pleasure, the way she talked about mundane matters like car insurance with her hand deep in Jesse's panties.

The drive from Denver to Maple Springs took her forever, and even though she knew the roads of her hometown by heart, it was snowing so fiercely that she couldn't see a couple of feet in front of her. When she finally reached the corner where Fletcher's house stood, she felt both relief and agitation. As she stepped out of the car, her eyeballs almost froze and the wind seemed intent on tearing the skin off her, which was all considered perfectly acceptable when you're dumb and in love. As she forced her way through two feet of snow, the short walk across the yard suddenly looked a mile long. About to pull her beanie down over her eyes, she spotted Catherine beside the window. Jesse's lips instinctively formed a smile and her senses were quick to remember every single caress of those secure hands, the way her body moved. She could feel Catherine so close, as if they were in the same skin, and Jesse thought her body would disintegrate from the thrill. A few more seconds and she'd get her kiss.

* * *

Catherine was staring in shock, having a hard time believing her eyes. She quickly left the windowsill and opened the front door.

"What are you doing here?" She gasped.

"This." Jesse flashed a devilish grin and her lips descended upon Catherine's, pulling her into the warm oblivion of their embrace.

"You're crazy."

"I've missed your terms of endearment."

Jesse's frozen nose paired with the perfectly shaped snowflakes caught on her eyelashes started to thaw Catherine's heart. Determined not to surrender to the utter beauty of that moment and the woman in front of her, Catherine fidgeted and turned her gaze to the house.

"Do you want to go for a ride?" she asked.

Jesse replied with a perplexed smile. "It's a whiteout. You can barely see the road. Where would we go?"

Catherine shifted from one foot to the other and shoved her hands into her pockets. Wearing a light silk blouse and inhaling the insistent snow dust, she could feel every pang of the cold. Of course she wasn't sure about any of this. Jesse's big blue eyes were peering at her so innocently that Catherine doubted she even possessed the ability to speak.

The snow kept insisting with swift snowflakes passing between them.

"Somewhere we could be alone," Catherine finally answered.

Jesse gaped at her with naïvely puzzled eyes.

"I was looking forward to meeting your mom first." When Catherine's stare remained flinty, Jesse quickly added, "Not that I don't want to be alone with you. It's just that she seems so elusive. It would be fun to meet her."

Now was obviously not convenient, but Catherine had to defy every damn instinct that screamed in her ear. Listening to her own dumb heart for her entire life had caused her nothing but misery. The time had arrived to be reasonable—as difficult as that might have been.

"Jesse, I don't want to entwine our lives any more than necessary."

"I see."

Bitter cold seemed to have turned Catherine's jaw immobile and her face impassive. Yet she could feel every fiber of her being burning, and the heat under her skin threatening to erupt, to claim Jesse in a senseless kiss. The line between loving this woman and leaving her for good was exceptionally thin. She hoped Jesse couldn't see that.

"So you were just going to leave?"

"I would have stopped by," Catherine finally replied, attempting to claim her reason back. "We just don't need to make this harder than it needs to be, Jesse. What's the point? I'll be gone in a few weeks, and halfway around the world is a lot more distance than Tennessee to Colorado."

"It doesn't have to be that way. I don't care where you live. We can make this work." Catherine stood motionless as if her body joined the bitter cold. Jesse continued, her gaze unrelenting, "It doesn't have to end. I could spend one part of the year in Paris, and you could come here when possible. We can make it work."

A despondent, wistful expression overcame Catherine's features as she watched the snow swirl around Jesse's maroon jacket, and her sad eyes peering from under her beanie. The country star was persistent, that was for sure.

"What will become of the llamas, then?"

"Catherine."

She couldn't ask Jesse to leave her family, friends, llamas, everything she loved for their uncertain time together. The price should never be that high. Sooner or later, they would break up anyway. That was how they would start resenting each other. That was how the hate would creep up. One day, Jesse would be grateful for this.

"Catherine. I'll always remember the first time I saw you. I thought, 'Isn't this the most beautiful woman you've ever seen?' You were so gracious, refined, passionate, an absolute goddess, and I stood there, an idiot. No one's ever made me feel that way. All I could think about was, 'How do I see this woman again?' I just knew that I was fucked."

Catherine grinned recalling that moment—her dusty, muddy appearance, her desperate arms hugging the column—and she looked up into Jesse's sincere eyes.

"It's time, Jesse. I don't belong to your world, and mine is five thousand miles away. I don't want to keep you from living every emotion you want."

"Every emotion I have is related to you. Now, that's anger." She grasped Catherine's gelid forearms. "Catherine, I'm going to love you wherever you are. I don't need to look at you every single day to know how I feel. I love you and I don't expect that to change anything. Just know that your insecurities will not make me love you less."

The eerie winter silence lingered around them and all they could hear were the swaying tree branches and the snowflakes breaking the stillness of the air.

"You're a shiny jewelry window, Jesse." She gently caressed her face, a gesture she knew Jesse absolutely adored.

"Okay, now we're getting somewhere." Jesse smiled contentedly.

"You're a dream someone holds on to, too good to be true, and ultimately, not real. Nothing really lasts."

"Catherine, there are many aspects of my life that are fake, but if there is anything real in it, it's you."

"You did more for me than you'll ever know, and I'll never forget that. We shouldn't let the ending ruin what we had."

"Don't say that." Jesse shook her head, then seemed to be searching for a glimmer of hope in Catherine's eyes. It was an unspoken request that Catherine could not bring herself to fulfill.

"I can handle falling in love with you, Jesse, just not crossing that line to love. I'm sorry," she said, aware she was a wretched moron who'd crossed that line long ago. She only hoped she wasn't too far off.

"I don't know how to forget you, French." Jesse's voice started to fade.

"You will." She attempted to appear serene. "My mother is the only person still remembering Elise Toussaint, a woman who posed for her and took me out on one date ages ago."

"You see?" Jesse said and forced a smile. "That's why I need to meet her. So she can talk about me in twenty years."

She wasn't brave enough for this shit. Catherine couldn't recall ever uttering more difficult words, but she knew they were for the greater good. They had better be.

"I'm not that sure. I'm sorry, Jesse."

Jesse nodded and remained silent for a few moments, as if she needed to gather the courage to deal with what she was about to say.

"When I love someone as much as I love you, Cath, I just want them to be happy. I want you to wake up every single morning, look at the person next to you, and think, 'Wow, she's the best thing that has ever happened to me.' So I'd never agree to be anything less than what you deserve, anything less than the best thing that has ever happened to you. If that's someone else, I'll wish you luck and curse your poor taste." Jesse's tone was soft, but firm. "If I can't be the best thing that has ever happened to you, I don't want to be anything." She paused and a bright, recognizable smile flashed across her face. "Good luck, Catherine. I'll leave before you freeze."

Jesse leaned forward and briefly brushed her lips across Catherine's, but before Catherine had a chance to react, Jesse pulled away and left.

Catherine's heart rebelled, wanting to shout after Jesse. Yet, as the figure of her love receded into the distance, Catherine knew the words wouldn't come out. Instead, Jesse just silently walked out of her life.

CHAPTER FORTY-FOUR

Jesse sat in her car, not feeling the biting cold. With snow pounding the windshield, she absently stared at the hollow whiteness for a few minutes—or a few hours. Grasping the steering wheel, she was unable to force herself to start the engine. Actually, she refused to move. Moving would mean leaving Catherine behind forever, and she still couldn't deal with that, so she sat, avoiding movement, the future, the consequences, and the pain that awaited. If she just stayed in this moment, perhaps she could rewind it back to a few minutes earlier, when life seemed like the greatest gift ever, when everything seemed possible, when the two of them seemed real. If only she could go back to the moment when she was pulling up, eager, because she was about to finally get the hottest kiss in the world, when she could still delude herself that they would find a way to stay together.

Was this how it all ended? Was she supposed to go on with her life now like Catherine had never been there? No, Jesse couldn't bring herself to acknowledge the goddamn finality of it all, so she decided to sit motionless as the snow shrouded her from reality. She didn't even know how to go back to the life she had before she met Catherine.

There were so many words still suffocating her, everything she'd never get to tell her, never get to share with that damn woman, a million little things she loved about her. The way Catherine could stare into her eyes for ages, how Catherine's hand would always find its way between her thighs, even when they were around other people. Yet somehow Cath would become timid when she needed to ask store clerks for help locating something or bother strangers for directions. The quirky "I know you, but I don't know them" distinction was a logic that apparently made perfect sense to Catherine, and Jesse found it endearing even though she didn't fully understand it.

It wasn't fair. Catherine was being completely unfair, and she clearly was suffering from a lack of imagination. Of course they could figure out the distance, they just needed to make a plan. Jesse shook her head, yet she had no one but herself to blame. She should have known better. She should have seen it coming, that this was too perfect to be true. No one could be that fucking happy and survive. It should have been obvious.

Still upset with herself, she rested her forehead against the steering wheel and tried to release the burden with a deep sigh. She'd better quit that nonsense. Being in love, what the hell was she thinking? How stupid to think she could have more.

She had an accomplished career, wonderful friends, a life that was full. Before she met Catherine, she was perfectly fine. Jesse never felt her life lacked anything, and she certainly never realized she was this fragile. Her head was a goddamn rollercoaster of thoughts, ranging from *She may just need more time, more space, more reassurance* to *There's got to be more to this.* Yet a flash of painful clarity crept through all of them. Of course it was over.

Had she met Catherine before Chloe did, it might have been different. If she could have gone back to summer days some fifteen or twenty years ago—what would their encounter have looked like back then? Surely, Catherine would have found something to brood over, but Jesse couldn't imagine resisting that woman under any circumstances. Catherine would have found a way to get under her skin. The intelligent way her eyes would smile, her comfort in silences, a variety of emotions carving the lovely lines of her face—any of these would have knocked down her defenses. She could see them talking about dreams for hours, camping in isolated places, and traveling the world. It could have been so simple. If only they had met at the very beginning. If only she could be that person who made her happy.

Forget the yearning, the scars, and the suffering. She wanted reciprocated love, Catherine's love. And her art agreed. To start that car would feel like stepping into the abyss, so Jesse stuck with this illusion of control and remained immobile. Yet this was it. She knew Catherine would not run out after her, and she couldn't even trick herself into believing that was possible. No, this was it.

Catherine was trying to tell her, but no, she had to be so damn obstinate. An idiot. She stared at the house, lost in the blizzard, and imagined that this was probably how being buried alive felt. So close to everything she'd never have.

Realizing that she'd never get to be near Catherine again, it felt like hell. Never again getting that "Wow, there you are!" thrill upon seeing her. How did people ever recover from this shit? She didn't even dare think about how tomorrow would feel.

One day Catherine would become a nice song, and that would be all that was left of them.

CHAPTER FORTY-FIVE

It had been almost two weeks since she'd last talked to Jesse. Ever since she left her standing silently in the midst of that blizzard, Jesse didn't call, didn't text, didn't insist. She respected Catherine's decision. Yet, not hearing from her the first day, the second day, and the third day proved far more excruciating than Catherine could have ever expected. She found herself mindlessly looking forward to the ringing of the phone, only to promptly become downcast. It was never Jesse. Reading about her in the papers or on social media meant nothing anymore. Jesse was saving her emotions for people who were close to her, and Catherine had to accept that she no longer belonged there. The only insight to Jesse's intimacy from now on would be her songs. Even though Jesse turned feelings into words with remarkable bravery, Catherine realized she would miss knowing the stories behind those verses. God, her mind would come up with so many wrong scenarios. Just what her life needed. To believe they could be friends after everything was as idiotic as it was naïve. Catherine would still live on a different continent, and she didn't want to be just Jesse's friend, now, did she?

Her big plan—no hurt, no anger, no resentment—good luck with that. Somehow, she felt even sulkier than last spring.

She poured herself a glass of wine and then pushed it away. This was not irritability, she had to confess, it was sheer sorrow. Why did she have to miss Jesse all the time? If only someone could give her a date when it would all stop, when she'd be able to claim her life back. When she would stop yearning for her. Her imminent return to France presented the only valid hope. She would dedicate her thoughts to something she loved, get a sense of accomplishment. She would no longer wonder how Jesse felt, where she was, whose blankets she was stealing.

"Dear daughter, you look like someone who's been stupid."

Startled out of her contemplation, Catherine quickly turned her head to find her mother leaning over the counter with a cup of tea.

"It's more of a permanent condition now, I'm afraid."

Her mother tried to encourage her with a smile before bringing in the chair and sitting next to her.

"Oh, this could take a while. What did you do wrong? On with your list! It better be a damn list, otherwise you have no excuse for this face."

"I wasn't fair to Jesse, and I wasn't completely honest with her," she said carefully, staring into her glass. "I wanted to protect us both from disappointment and be smart. I don't want to hurt her."

Pearl exhaled loudly and then fixed her golden-blond waves and wispy bangs, as if the stress of those deep sighs ruined her perfectly styled bob.

"Don't you see it?" Pearl said once she was finally pleased with her hair.

"See what?"

"That it still sucks. You're convinced you came up with this grand plan to protect yourself from disappointment, and yet you've been sitting here for the past two weeks absolutely miserable. You think you'll go to France and magically forget? Perhaps you will, but what are you going to do when you fall for someone again?"

"I don't want us to hate each other one day."

"Really? That's your argument? You don't even hate Chloe. You simply realized you two weren't a good match. That's what people do. You move on. If you don't want to trust Jesse's feelings, trust her actions. What's the worst thing she's done so far?"

"Nothing. She's kindness personified, but we've known each other for only six months."

"Six months? Your father would find a way to annoy me every six seconds. Catherine, I understand that when you invest so much in so little, like you did with Chloe, you can only feel hollow. But you can't punish Jesse for your past."

"I only wanted to be mature."

"Well, then you should know that you don't control the world, but you control your reactions. Yes, it may end in disaster, but you're a big girl. You dealt with that before, and you can handle it again. Jesse doesn't deserve this. Even if it goes on for a couple of years, it's better to be happy for those two years than bitter and distrustful for the rest of your life. That's not a pretty look. Catherine, that's the only wisdom of life. Take what you can now and don't worry about the future. It's promised to no one."

Catherine cast down her eyes, pondering if she was only making one miscalculation after the other. There was nothing she wanted more than Jesse, her country music and all. The thought that she had hurt her was too much to bear.

"Are you in love with this woman?"

"Yes. She has that damn effect on people."

"Then consider yourself lucky and don't waste a perfectly good feeling on fear. You're an artist, for God's sake, you should be honest with your feelings. Besides, Jesse sounds like a little angel." Pearl waved her away with an ease that was as amusing as it was persuasive.

Laughing, Catherine buried her face in her hands. As much as she loved choreographing, she never worked seven days a week. Would stealing a few days every other week really be that impossible? If they organized their schedules and projects well, it could buy them even more time. A lot of time. Her mother was right. Fuck fear. Shit had happened in the past, and she dealt with it. When difficulties popped up again, she'd deal with them too. If Maple Springs had taught her anything, it was that ultimately she'd find a way and everything would be okay. Tomorrow was her perfect chance to make things right.

"Oh, God help us. Mom, have you ever been to Nashville?"

"No, are we going?"

"Yes."

"What's in Nashville?"

"Jesse, Mom. Her album release party is tomorrow."

Pearl let out a shriek of exhilaration and darted from her chair. "Oh, Catherine! Do I pack light and fashionable, or clever and glamorous? I'll go for clever and glamorous. You learn through your mistakes. Imagine running into Blake Shelton fresh off his divorce."

"Oh, heavens!"

"And he calls me out for dinner. You've got to be prepared."

"He just got married, Mom."

"Exactly. Marriage is when things go wrong."

Bringing her mother along could only end in disaster, a goddamn disaster, but she needed to make that statement. She had to prove she could be all in, intertwining their worlds and trusting Jesse. She knew talkative Rachel would help, and Catherine only hoped she could keep a secret for a day.

"Are you completely sure about this?" Pearl inspected her face. "I don't want you to go there if you'll change your mind in a month."

"There is nothing in the world I want more. I don't know why I thought pushing her away would make things better in the first place. I won't change my mind," she replied firmly, surprising herself.

"You better not break her heart."

"I won't."

"Good. Should I pack my purple pillbox hat? What if Jesse's there with a date?"

"Mother, you've just established that Jesse is a little angel. You are really not helping."

"It's a possibility you should be prepared for."

Just the thought of seeing that smile again sent a flutter of joy and a rush of passion traveling through her nerves to the very last fiber of her heart. Hell, she'd take twenty years of pain for that one flash. Ignoring her feelings wouldn't keep her free of pain, or the possibility of pain. She finally knew that cutting it off at the pass was a silly idea and would never work. She couldn't do that to Jesse—there were no excuses. She wouldn't be a damn coward any longer. It was time to find out if Jesse had really meant it when she said that Catherine's insecurities wouldn't ever affect how much she loved her.

"Well, then I'll make a fool of myself, won't I?" She nodded energetically. "I love Jesse and I want her to know how special she is to me. She can do whatever she decides then."

Her mother was right. She'd be damned if she ever again worried about tomorrow. She'd grab the moment she was given and let the future take care of itself.

CHAPTER FORTY-SIX

Two weeks were not much, unless you were trying to forget someone, Jesse learned. It had been exactly fourteen days since they last talked, and the abyss Jesse was staring into seemed deeper with each passing day. So this was what Catherine tried so hard to avoid. Smart woman. Had she known it would hurt this much, she never would have taken that damn banana bread to Catherine. She would have stayed in her car and savored every last crumb.

Yet, she had to suffer through this party, which dragged slowly, with people who were having fun and needed her to be equally jazzed. Any other time she'd enjoy these occasions, but now...now she didn't feel like she deserved to be celebrated. All the exhilaration of the people around her only accentuated her own misery. She was not in the mood to talk, and she was not in the mood to fake joy. Now and then she would catch a pleading look from Annie, standing in the corner and reminding her that other people's livelihoods depended on her laughing through her misery, so Jesse would eventually go back to what she had done her entire life—hiding loneliness with smiles. Except this time, it was different. She knew exactly what she was missing, and all the parties and all the music of the world couldn't silence her growing desolation.

The worst part was that she knew going home tonight would not end it. She'd have to come back tomorrow and the day after and the day after, for more pretending, interviews, photos, songs about Catherine. No wonder Catherine had been irritable when they met. The woman knew what hell on Earth feelings were. If only Jesse had some Maple Springs she could run to, away from everyone. Or at least from herself.

The evening was just getting started, and Jesse already felt like she had spent all the words she had. She was eagerly anticipating the moment when she'd go back to the darkness of her room, even if it only meant staring at the ceiling. Soon after, hopefully, she could embrace the illusion that all this was just a bad dream. That somehow the morning would be different. Those few moments before she'd fully wake up were the only happy moments she had in the last two weeks. In those few tender, clear moments of reality, Catherine was always there, chiding her for her impatience and wrapping her long arms around her, resolving all her apprehensions, all the hurt, convincing her they'd never been real. Finally! Jesse could feel the soft brush of those elusive lips as she'd pin her against the wall, inching closer to her mouth. Yet instead of the lips she'd go for the ear as retribution for the cruel punishment Catherine had subjected her to.

Thank God things are normal, Jesse would think, relieved she woke up from that nightmare. Still warm from sleep and encouraged by Catherine's kisses, she would open her eyes only to watch Catherine's contours gradually disappear, leaving nothing but the cold ceiling of her room. No Catherine, no music, no bad dreams, just the still silence of her own room and a ghostly space to her left where only a few seconds ago Catherine had held her tightly and their kisses intensified to the point she felt brave enough to open her eyes to reality. Oh, those mornings were a dreadful enemy. The notion that she would have to go through a whole day of absently talking to people who cared about her was almost as brutal as the grief of having to wait that same eternity to wake up again and have those few moments of intact happiness right before opening her eyes.

She hated the damn pillow, the walls reminding her of Catherine, and the TV where Jamie and Larson had it all. When she would catch herself leading imaginary conversations with Catherine first thing in the morning, she would know then and there just how awful the day ahead would be. Surviving the next moment became the only realistic goal she could have.

Jesse scanned the room already filled with agents, producers, radio and TV hosts, familiar faces, friends. All these people showed up here to see a fraud, a liar. She couldn't possibly teach them anything, so what was the purpose of all this celebration? She was but a madwoman who would jerk awake five times in the middle of the night just to obsessively check her phone, knowing she would find it silent. Across the room, she encountered Logan's sympathetic glance as if he could sense her surging feeling of annoyance. Compared to her now, Jesse realized just how gracious Catherine was to answer all her questions when they met, and how she must have hated every single one. Just uttering a single word now would mean falling into an eternal hell of hollow conversations, so she grinned back at Logan, aware that one smile now meant fewer questions later. She had to do it for Annie and the guys, even though all those pleasantries seemed like a waste of time to her. God, she was turning into Catherine.

Yet, of all the wrong things she had ever done, one positively stood out mocking her. Jesse would have to sing a song she wrote to Catherine, a song she chose as her first single, probably a hundred times in the next month or so. Now, wasn't she a Little Miss Brainy? She scoffed at herself, looking forward to the moment she'd finally get home, far from all the talking silhouettes, for some sleep and those few moments right after. The only time she could be happy.

She gave a long sigh, preparing her face for questions, but just as she was about to walk over to Annie, she sensed a curious stare behind her back. Jesse stopped on instinct. It was her album release party. Of course people would be staring. Yet the strange sensation of someone watching was so intense Jesse felt she had to turn around.

The moment she turned, her eyes met a familiar expressive gaze. There stood Catherine. Really? Had her delusions taken the next step?

No, that was definitely Catherine. Not even her imagination would put together *this* outfit. Her tailored, elegant white suit looked bold, but a single-button blazer with seemingly nothing underneath was jaw-dropping. Everything else in that room faded in a second, vanished in the thin air of beautiful insignificance, everything but those dark eyes staring at her and a smile so contrite it melted her inside. Jesse's grin was instinctive, her heart pounding so fast she was sure Catherine could hear it. Could she really be this lucky?

There she was, that irritable French woman, surrounded by photographers, journalists, producers, strangers, in the world that didn't belong to her, and as always, overly self-conscious, nervously tucking her soft curls behind an ear but bravely holding Jesse's gaze. Jesse couldn't even fathom the terror Catherine must have been feeling, dread from being observed, from exposing her vulnerable self to this huge crowd, from becoming a part of Jesse's world and the risk of having her heart shattered in front of everyone.

Yet Catherine maintained a grace that took Jesse's breath away. Hell, Jesse's whole body came alive just from that sharp, thoughtful look. Catherine was absolutely stunning, and Jesse couldn't stop her mind from wondering if there was anything under that seductive white blazer, revealing so much and not nearly enough. Her fingertips could still recall the absolute bliss that skin could provoke. Damn French woman. She always knew how to leave Jesse speechless. Jesse loved her more than anything else in the world, and she knew exactly how trying this was for Catherine. The woman didn't have to say a word for Jesse to feel like the luckiest idiot in the world.

Catherine took two hesitant steps toward Jesse.

"My mom is giving interviews, and I'm pretty sure she's talking about you. Or Blake Shelton."

"I'll be sure to thank her. Does she even know what I look like?"

"She has no idea whatsoever."

Afraid Catherine might overthink her actions, Jesse took another step and hugged her hard. Her body craved her so badly she wasn't sure she would be able to ease back. She was breathing in Catherine's scent of pure ocean air, the warmth of her breasts, the subtle touch of her fingers gliding across her ribs—and it was never enough.

"I'm sorry, I'm sorry," Catherine whispered against her neck.

"I can't believe you brought your mom here, you fool." Jesse could not stop laughing, yet she could clearly hear the sound of her heart melting. This woman had complete control over her.

Catherine's initial expression of nervousness and trepidation was swiftly replaced by one of wonder.

"You're incredible, Jesse, and it's not just in the mornings, you know. Every time I see you, I think, wow, she's the best thing that has ever happened to me. You've been so patient with me, you're practically a saint. Now I want to make you happy." Catherine said it all in one breath, followed by Jesse's amused gaze. She then paused. "Let's not allow our love or relationship to be defined by the mistakes we'll certainly make in the future. Let's make the most of this moment and let's just enjoy each other."

"Okay. Except, we won't make mistakes."

"Well, even if we do—"

"We won't," Jesse assured her with an irresistible smile and then gently placed her hands on Catherine's face as she finally claimed her lips in a long, intense kiss.

Catherine's body surrendered, apparently not minding in the least the camera flashes going off. Instead, she whispered only for her ears, "So, Jesse, do you have ten days for Paris in June?"

"Do you have any idea of what you're getting yourself into?" Jesse replied softly. "I might ask you to take me for a sunset cruise along the Seine, or wander hand in hand from charming cafés to sultry bars, or even stop at Pont des Arts to steal a kiss and be one of those deplorable couples who dance around streetlamps at dusk."

"Then we shouldn't forget the lovers' picnic in a quaint little park or tacky photos at the top of the Eiffel Tower."

"Uh-huh, absolutely. It's just that I cannot for the life of me stop wondering if you're wearing anything underneath that blazer." Jesse's absent gaze followed the edges of her collar, and Catherine chuckled.

"Now, that's more like my chick." Catherine gently enclosed and lifted Jesse's chin, finally meeting her stare. "Of course I'm not. I'd never do that to you," she replied gently.

Jesse shut her eyes against those words.

"Are you real?" she whimpered. "Catherine, you are so beautiful, you can't keep doing this to me."

"Catherine?" They were both startled by a smooth, silky voice. "Is this your gorgeous girlfriend? Jesse, you're stunning, just like your father."

Jesse pulled away, and her bewildered, fast-moving eyes looked alternately between Pearl and Catherine.

"Hi, nice to meet you. I didn't realize you knew my father."

"Oh, Jesse!" Pearl blushed and looked up coyly. "Who doesn't? That one's hard to forget."

"Heavens, Mother!" Catherine gazed pleadingly at Jesse. "Nothing happened, don't worry."

"I'm sure Jesse is aware of her good genes." Pearl shot a reproachful stare at Catherine and then turned to face Jesse again. "Lovely party, dear. Have you already forgiven my silly daughter? She's quick to doubt, bless her, but she's a good girl."

Catherine looked silently at Jesse, embarrassed, never interrupting her mother and allowing the two women to get to know each other. She stoically endured her mother's stream of consciousness, and Jesse thought she had never seen anything more gracious than Catherine's quiet suffering. Her dark eyes, her flowing hair, her lips compressed in absolute despair as she listened to her mother's stories... Jesse loved every subtlety of this woman's face, and she couldn't wait for the hour when she would gather her naked in her arms. She was absolutely gorgeous and yet so much more than that. To expose oneself to this world required a lot of courage, but Catherine also brought her unpredictable mother along as an act of atonement, a testament of trust, and it took Jesse only a few minutes next to Pearl Fitzgerald to understand exactly how big a risk that was for someone as private as Catherine. As much as she admired Catherine's candor, her mother's seemed to be on another level, with no restraints whatsoever.

In spite of Jesse's assertions of their infrangible bond, Pearl concluded that her daughter could use some marketing to make up for her past decisions.

"I raised her to be independent, Jesse. She's not needy," she went on, paying no heed to squirming Catherine. "While you're touring, she won't call you all the time—oh no, she can give you the space you need."

Jesse had a hard time stifling her laughter, but she let Pearl talk some more, enjoying the sight of Catherine blushing. God, she would tease her about this the first chance she got.

"Jesse, have you ever tried her Baked Alaska? It's absolutely divine. I'll admit, Catherine is not the world's greatest cook, but she can always serve a fine dessert."

And she can serve a fine dessert? Jesse beamed at Catherine. This was getting better and better.

Catherine recognized her amused expression and shook her head helplessly until both cracked up.

"I would always tell her, be adventurous, be daring, Catherine! It's in her blood. Oh, Jesse, I can't wait to get to know you better." Pearl loosened up a bit when she beheld their tender hand-holding. Maybe Catherine didn't need PR after all.

"I'm so happy the two of you are here," Jesse replied with a smile. "I'd love to hear more about you, Ms. Fitzgerald. Catherine mentioned you'd be having a solo exhibition in Marseille."

"Please, Jesse, Catherine made me listen to all your albums on our way here, it's safe to say you are no longer a stranger. You can call me Pearl. You have a wonderful, sensitive soul." She gently stroked Jesse's shoulder and then added excitedly, "My exhibition is in May and you're invited, of course. Similar to what you described in that song, *ways of the world, waaays of the world*," she sang, unworried, "it aims to display the experience of inner peace amidst constant chaos."

"Oh, how interesting." Jesse chuckled. "Thank you, Pearl, I can't wait."

"Oh God." Catherine grinned up into Jesse's carefree, mischievous eyes. "I think I need a drink. Mother, do you want me to bring you a drink?"

"No, no, I was about to get one. The two of you stay here. I'll be back with a bottle of champagne. We need to toast that this visit of yours hasn't turned into a disaster. At least not yet." She winked and glided away, her ringing laughter following behind her.

"Oh my God. My life needs this woman." Jesse chortled, watching her disappear into the crowd. "I love that hat—I didn't get a chance to tell her."

"Oh, she'll be back, don't worry."

Jesse again paused lovingly in Catherine's eyes.

"Thank you. I honestly didn't know a person could be this happy until I saw you standing there tonight."

"Wait until I serve a fine dessert." An easy smile lit up Jesse's face, and Catherine continued in a more serious tone, "I know this is not the place, and we're going to celebrate your talent tonight. But before they interrupt us, I just want you to know that I'm sorry. It was hell, and I don't ever want to hurt you again."

"I think that means that you kinda love me."

"Oh, come on."

Jesse nodded contentedly. "I must be something special if a girl like you *kinda* loves me."

"Stop!" Catherine playfully thumped her chest as they both laughed.

"Why?"

"I don't want to love you more than I already do."

"Trust me, Catherine, you can never love me too much." Jesse smirked and their bodies responded with another firm embrace.

"Also," Catherine said and finally moved to meet her eyes. "'Perfectly Matched'? Your first single? I'm pretty sure that song is about me."

"Indeed." Jesse nodded. "It debuted at number seven on the Billboard Hot 100."

"But it's my song and it's beautiful. Why am I only at number seven?"

"Don't worry." Jesse caressed her cheek. "For me, you will always be at number six."

Catherine's face brightened up as she enfolded Jesse in her arms again. "That's all that matters, thank you."

"Oh, Catherine, look at us experiencing inner peace amidst constant chaos."

"God, you're impossible." Catherine burst into joyous laughter, and the quiet contentment was exactly how Jesse felt with Catherine's head on her shoulder. Reporters, camera flashes, distant murmuring, nothing really mattered. Jesse knew she could figure anything out with this woman. Somehow, they'd figure it out together, but before they did, she was definitely getting another kiss.

EPILOGUE

Winning a Grammy was every musician's dream, but getting it before your flawless archrival did was not something a person could ever let go of, was it?

"Can you believe I got a Grammy before J.Lo did?" Jesse flashed a smug smile and looked at Catherine delightedly. One thing she'd learned in the last year and a half was that it was not easy to win against J.Lo, so she cherished those proud moments, even if they were short-lived.

"I'm certain I saw her tearing up during your performance," Catherine replied quickly with genuine enthusiasm.

"You were looking at J.Lo during my performance?"

Catherine instantly squirmed. "Only because she was in my field of vision while I watched your performance attentively. She sat so close," she said earnestly, clearly aware she needed to come up with a credible explanation.

"Uh-huh. Isn't that lady perfect?" Jesse muttered. *Damn that woman!* Jesse's album won a Grammy for Best Country Album, and her performance of "Last Love," the song she wrote for Taylor, was one of the most memorable moments of the evening, generating a torrent of positive headlines and reviews, and leaving the audience in tears. Too bad one of them had to be goddamn perfect J.Lo.

"'Raw, powerful, and inspiring,'" Catherine read from her phone, her voice imbued with pride. "'Jesse Morgan gave a showstopping rendition of her single 'Last Love,' a heartbreaking song about loss, forgiveness, and family. Performed with exceptional courage, the hit tore down those in attendance.' Oh, Jesse!" Catherine exclaimed and kissed her fervently, and Jesse decided it was impossible to scowl after all.

Damn that kiss. One was never enough, she thought as her arms slid around Catherine's waist and pulled her closer.

Her gorgeous nemesis aside, the last year had brought more happiness than Jesse ever knew existed. The two weeks they spent in Paris while Catherine worked on the movie were filled with unbridled decadence and indulgence, up until Jesse had to go back to the States to promote her most successful album so far. In its first week, the album had over 25 million streams and had earned almost 700,000 equivalent album units before the end of the year.

Jesse returned to France in late July to witness Ninon's luxurious wedding in a castle on Côte d'Azur. She instantly hit it off with the benevolent baron, who sparked her interest in birdwatching. Still a better option than porcelain dolls, so Catherine considered herself lucky. Jesse and the baron spent the hours leading up to the wedding in search of a rare Little Bustard in a stony plain of La Crau, exchanging philosophical wisdom and driving Ninon crazy.

Even before they visited Paris, Catherine and Jesse understood that their future could only be together, regardless of their address. As they were trying to grasp how those addresses would look on different continents, at the wedding reception Catherine ran into her former teacher Gino De Wit, who was thrilled to hear Catherine was in the States. While they were reminiscing about the time they managed to set up a show in under three weeks, Gino revealed he was working on a small

Broadway production with a tight deadline and offered to let her co-choreograph *Orlando* with him. Even though the musical played in one of the smaller Broadway houses, seating just under six hundred people, it opened in November not only to critical acclaim but also became the first musical of the season to recoup its production costs in less than four months. It continued to fill all the seats, week after week, promising to become the highest-grossing musical in the history of that theater. Particular credit went to an incredibly talented young star, Robert Chaillet, a Frenchman who found an instant understanding with Catherine. There were some early talks about Tonys and a national tour launching in over thirty cities in the following year, as well as a rave write-up in *Entertainment Weekly*'s best stage shows of the year edition, praising "the elegant and exhilarating choreography." Even Marjorie and Fletcher, who now lived together, came to New York to see the show.

Never before had Jesse gotten the chance to observe Catherine at work, and if she hadn't been hopelessly in love already, seeing her dance, create stories, and play with her instincts in motion would have done it for sure. Catherine knew how to bring the stage to life, and she was aware of her imagination in ways Jesse never knew could be a turn-on.

Most importantly, the two never doubted they would find a way to be together. They shared their time between a house in Brooklyn they leased when the first rehearsals started, any city Jesse was performing in, and mostly their farm in Nashville. Thanks to Catherine's powers of persuasion, and much to Lola's chagrin, they added three bunnies to the family.

Taking the phone from her hand, Jesse wrestled Catherine down onto the bed, her expression showing hunger and amusement.

"Guess who called me today?"

Catherine welcomed Jesse's body by wrapping her arms under her shirt.

"Who?" she asked.

"Maple Springs Town Council. Considering I was in Europe last summer, they wanted to make sure I'd be available this year."

"Nooo!"

"Oh yes, Catherine, it is happening. The Festival is back."

"The pandemonium, vendors, hot dogs, the whole package?"

"You included."

"But you just won a Grammy!"

"It's family." Jesse shrugged. "You better get used to those festivals every year, Catherine. This is just the beginning."

As Jesse's lips descended on hers, she heard Catherine's soft voice in between their kisses.

"God...bless...that...freaking...festival!"

More Titles from Bella Books

Printed in the USA
CPSIA information can be obtained
at www.ICGtesting.com
JSHW021019290124
R13292400001B/R132924PG55392JSX00001B/1

9 781642 475135